ALL STAR

ALL STAR

MCKENZIE BURNS

To the football girlies.
And to the Green Bay Packers. Go, Pack, go.

FANTASY WORKS BY MCKENZIE BURNS

From the Shadows

Through the Flames

Legacy of the Night

Rise of the Dragon

ROMANCE WORKS BY MCKENZIE BURNS

Starstruck

Star-Crossed

Love on Tour

WORKS WITH APPEARANCES BY MCKENZIE BURNS

Magic & Moons: A Fantasy Anthology

Chaos & Curses: A Collection of Unfortunate Tales

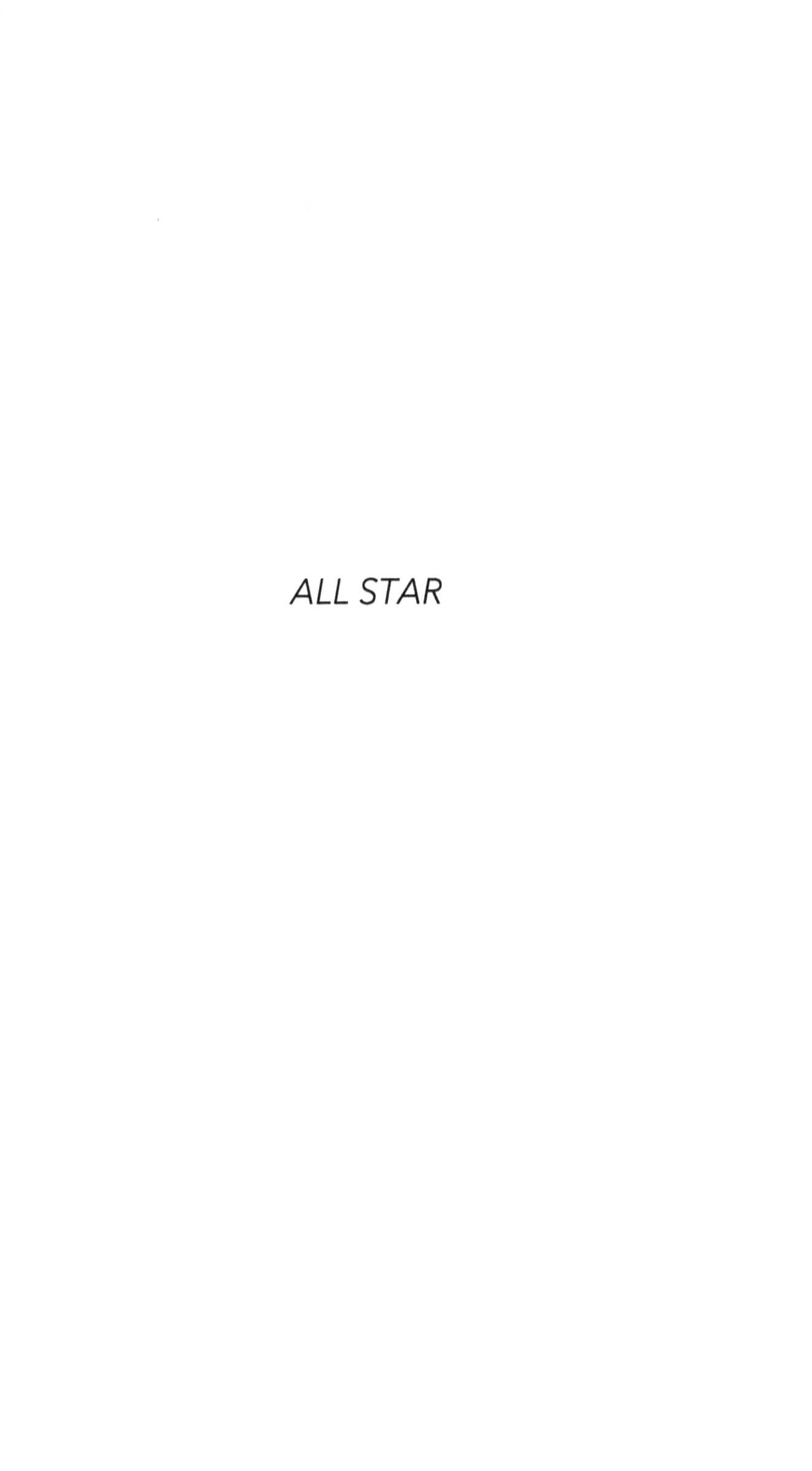

ALL STAR

SIX YEARS EARLIER

THE GRUMBLE OF the truck's engine was heard before I saw the old, rusting hunk of metal coming up the gravel path. Good thing it was red. At least that helped disguise the wear and tear a bit.

But looks didn't matter to Ryan. All he cared about was getting from Point A to Point B, and in Timberland Creek, those two points weren't usually too far from one another. Old Red did the trick, even if she wasn't the prettiest ride.

I waited in my spot leaning against the hood of my own aged—but significantly less beaten up—sedan, arms crossed over my chest. The questionable noises coming from Old Red ceased as soon as Ryan cut the engine, but I couldn't help my grin when the driver-side door creaked as it opened.

"Still haven't oiled that thing?" I called out.

Ryan narrowed his eyes at me as he hopped out of the truck, but he was smiling. "You're the one related to the mechanic." He slammed the door shut and winced in a brief moment of panic we'd experienced before. It was never a guarantee the door would stay on. "Can't you ask him to lend me a hand?"

"You have his number, too, you know."

"He'll listen to his princess before he listens to the kid who's barged into his house and stolen his food for the last ten years."

I lifted a challenging brow. "Ten?"

"Fifteen, maybe."

"It's a good thing you've got football, because your math isn't checking out, man."

"Okay, twenty years—max."

I rolled my eyes. "Get him a nice ticket hook up for a few games next season and he might be persuaded to help."

"Nothing a game at Camp Randall can't fix."

I chuckled, but knew it would take a lot less than a decent seat at a Big 10 college football game to persuade Dad to help Ryan out. He was basically another son to my old man—not that our family was in any shortage of those as it was. After three boys, I'm pretty sure my mom had been desperate for me to come along.

Ryan stuffed his hands in the pockets of his faded jeans. He'd probably been wearing the exact pair for half as long as he'd been raiding my family's pantry for snacks. The same could be said about my clothes. High-fashion wasn't exactly a worry around here.

He nodded off to the side, in the direction where the path we'd both driven up continued but became a little too off-road for our beat-up cars to handle. "Wanna get going?"

I nodded, not needing to say anything further. This was our routine. Drive to the edge of town, park under the big ash tree, then walk further up the way to the abandoned barn neither of us could figure out the ownership of. We'd discovered it when we were ten, on a bike ride gone a little too adventurous. At first, it had been the best secret fort two kids could ever ask for. But over time, it became Our Spot. The one place in town where we were almost one-hundred-percent certain no one would find us. Where we could talk to one another without fear someone would overhear what we came to confess.

Secrets were sacred in a small town like ours. Especially as it became more and more clear that Ryan had some sort of future ahead of him in football.

Me? I didn't have much going on. But Ryan? I'd noticed his invites to Our Spot increasing more and more as we progressed through college.

"So, what's up?" I asked as soon as we'd settled in the grass outside the barn, both of us using the least-dilapidated wall as a backrest.

Ryan's head tilted back until it hit the wall, too. His blue-eyed gaze was on the sky as he said, "I don't know what I'm doing, Harper."

"Well, yeah. No shit, Sherlock."

I laughed as his foot lifted and his heel landed on my shin, not hard enough to actually cause any pain. A perk of growing up with brothers? Your best friend—who also happened to be a guy—knew you could handle a little rough-housing.

"I'm serious," he said with his own smile. When it faded, I knew he meant what he'd said.

"Okay," I said, nodding. "Spill."

Ryan sighed and ran a hand back through his blonde locks. They were a little longer than usual, the same way they always got during the football season, with a little wave developing.

"I only have one more year. I've been playing football since I was six, and now it's all almost over." His head tilted to the side, his eyes landing on me with a stare that made me swallow a sudden lump in my throat. "It's like you said: I'm not a smart guy. I'll have my communications degree, but what am I gonna do with that?"

"First of all, you know I was giving you shit about not being smart," I replied, poking him in the side of the head with my index finger. "A dumbass wouldn't have gotten into UW-Madison."

"I got in on a football scholarship."

"And do you wanna place bets on how many of your teammates will or are damn near close to flunking out? All they want is an agent to notice them, while you're passing your classes *and* getting some attention."

It was all the sportscasters talked about whenever college

game day rolled around—how any team in the NFL would be stupid not to draft Ryan Caldwell. And how mind-blowing it was that he hadn't found any representation yet.

But I didn't say any of that. He'd probably heard it plenty before. Instead, I was focused on another issue.

For as long as I'd known Ryan, he'd never failed to respond to one of my questions, hypothetical or not. So, when his eyes drifted back to the sky, I knew something was up.

"You're scaring me," I said, my voice a little softer, my brow furrowed. "What're you thinking about?"

Another few nervous beats of my heart pounded in my chest before Ryan finally sighed again.

"An agent reached out to me," he whispered.

"When?"

"At the end of the season." He flinched when I reeled back and punched his shoulder.

"Hey!" he exclaimed, rubbing the spot I'd hit. "What was that for?"

"For not telling me for two months!"

"It was a couple months, Harps, not a couple years. Geez."

I crossed my arms over my chest. "As your best friend, I demand to know everything immediately. Especially when it's as amazing as an agent reaching out to you. Ry!"

The last punch must have traumatized him because Ryan recoiled when I reached toward him again. This time, I grabbed him by the shoulders and shook him—as best I could, anyway. He was the perfect build for his tight end position: six-four and over two-hundred pounds of pure muscle. It made it pretty difficult for me, at five-five and one-forty to compete, physically.

"This is huge!" I continued, beaming. "So, you don't really *have* to be done, do you? You can keep playing."

"Sure, but do you know the odds of me actually making it in the NFL?" he asked. "There's, like, a one-and-a-half percent chance of me making it on a team."

"Maybe you're better at math than I thought."

He shook his head. "I Googled it. Because for a second, I actually considered it, but now?"

He trailed off. I watched his jaw tighten, the worry creases form in his forehead, then reached for his hand, covering it with my own.

"My parents were so proud when I got into Madison, you know?" he continued, that tiny touch I offered apparently enough to give him the courage to say more. "I'm the first person in my family to go to a big university—and graduate."

"That's still the plan, even with the agent?"

"Well, yeah. I just told you the statistics. I need something to fall back on if the football thing doesn't work."

Okay, maybe he *hadn't* been paying attention to the hundreds of people that talked him up in the sports world. This pessimism wasn't coming from a man whose athletic talents were consistently complimented. This sounded like legitimate self-doubt.

"And if it does?" I asked.

"What do you mean?"

I shrugged. "I mean if you don't fall into the ninety-eight-and-a-half percent of guys who enter the draft but don't make it."

Ryan huffed a laugh. "You're making it sound like you actually think I have a chance."

"I do," I confirmed. "What kind of best friend would I be if I didn't?"

"A shit one."

"Exactly. And I *refuse* to be that."

I'd been that for a lot of people, especially as they up and left Timberland Creek, headed out of town for bigger and better things. Not Ryan, though. Never Ryan. No matter what happened, I imagined nothing would ever come between us.

I squeezed his hand, still under mine. "What are you leaning towards?"

"I'm going to graduate," he said, so matter-of-factly that I didn't doubt for a moment he would follow through. "But…"

"But football," I finished.

"But football," he repeated.

Silence fell again, interrupted only by the soft spring breeze rustling the tall grass around us, the occasional bird chittering as it flew past. If we listened really carefully, we could hear a rare car driving past on the main road, the tires kicking up the gravel.

"I say go for it," I finally said. Ryan's head turned in my direction so quickly, I was shocked it didn't roll right off his neck. I only shrugged in response. "Football is what you love. I say give it a shot. You'll have your degree if it doesn't work out, and you can figure out what to do next from there. But you'll never know what could happen with the draft if you don't put yourself out there and try."

Ryan's hand turned, and suddenly his palm was on mine, his long fingers wrapped around my dainty-but-callused ones.

"Promise you'll be there?" he asked in a whisper. He stared into my brown eyes with an intensity we'd never shared before. My stomach tightened. "I don't know if I can handle it without you, Harps."

"When have I ever not been there for you?" I retorted.

A small smile curled the corners of Ryan's mouth. It was crazy that he'd even felt the need to ask something like that. In all the years I'd known him, we'd never abandoned each other. We'd suffered through it all together: childhood, the rough teenage years, the back and forth of college visits, and now we'd finally reached the beyond. The points in our lives we'd only dreamed about way back when we'd first met.

It would have been impossible not to support Ryan through that, too.

"You really are the best, Harps," he whispered. "I don't know what I'd do without you."

I smiled. "Good thing you'll never have to find out."

CHAPTER ONE

PEOPLE MIGHT ARGUE that fall in Timberland Creek was one of the most wonderful times of the year. Fire-hued trees along winding roads. Pumpkins and mums outside every storefront. Apple picking. The infamous haunted lighthouse tours. Football on every TV at every restaurant, pub, or the likes.

I was not one of those people—namely because of the last item on that list.

I took another sip of my beer as a collective groan went up around the bar. Why I'd let my oldest brother, Derek, convince me to join him and his wife, Sarah, for an afternoon out at Ziggy's, I'd never know. Actually, I did. Wanting to hang out with Derek, who rarely came back to visit aside from holidays and milestone birthdays, won out over the misery I knew I'd be put through during this particular game.

"That was the most idiotic play call I've ever seen," Derek

complained. "Third and long and we decide to run it up the middle?"

I didn't say anything, even though I was thinking the same thing. Our wide receivers would have been our saving grace, given the Lone Star Stallions' defense had been having trouble catching up with us for down-field play. It had been flag after flag for pass interference all game. One long shot from our future Hall of Fame quarterback and we'd have all but guaranteed ourselves a first down.

And, boy, did I want that first down given the current score. A little over one quarter left, and it didn't look like we had much of a chance to catch up.

Granted, it was only pre-season. The outcome of this game wouldn't matter in a couple of weeks when the real season started, but still. Seeing your team lose was never fun.

"They look like they've never played a game before," Derek continued to gripe.

"Would you stop?" Sarah chastised, hitting him on the arm with the back of her hand. "It's not all bad, is it?" She turned to me wearing a kind smile, and I knew exactly what question was coming next. "You must be happy your friend is winning, right, Harper?"

"Mhm," I replied before taking another, bigger sip of my beer. I set it down then called out, "Rosie, mind if I get another?"

The owner and one of the current bartenders for the crowded game day gave me a thumbs up before she jostled around with her other staff to continue fulfilling orders in the packed bar. Ziggy's was like this every Sunday, but today was something else. Today, Wisconsin's team was facing off against the team of Timberland Creek's golden boy, Ryan Caldwell.

Pre-season or not, around these parts, it might as well have been the Super Bowl currently airing on the TV.

"He's playing pretty well," Derek commented. "That touchdown catch was key in getting the early lead."

I nodded again. I could go on forever about what Ryan had or hadn't done in the game so far to contribute to the Stallions' success. For years, I'd helped him go over his stats, watch film, analyze play after play after play that made him the second-round draft pick he'd become.

Those days were gone. As were the ones of watching his games. I'd given up on those around the same time Ryan had stopped talking to me—had stopped coming home to Timberland Creek altogether, actually, trading us for the life of fame and fortune that came with a successful career in the National Football League.

"Think he'll get another Pro Bowl selection?" Derek asked.

"Probably." It was the safe answer, seeing as Ryan had made it the last three years of his five-season career.

"It's so crazy you two know an actual football player," Sarah gushed. "It's like something out of a movie."

"It's more Harps than me," Derek said. "Those two were attached at the hip for years." His brow furrowed as he seemed to consider what he'd just said. "You get the chance to see each other much with his schedule?"

"Not really." Rosie placed my new drink in front of me, and I downed what remained of my last one.

"Makes sense. Bet he's all over the place." Derek snapped his fingers, face lighting up. "Did you see that new commercial he's in? For that insurance company, I think. Or was it the aftershave?"

"It's both," I said, hating that I knew the answer. What choice did I have, though? If I was going to watch football, I was going to run the risk of seeing one of the plethora of commercials Ryan had done over the last few years.

Not that the commercials were a surprise to anyone. Ryan was a looker. Always had been, even in those rougher puberty-ridden years with acne and braces. His training regimen had kept him in shape through college and into the pros. And after he got his first shampoo commercial, he'd kept his blonde hair long—not in a messy, he-should-cut-it-but-won't way. More of a tangle-your-fingers-in-it-during-great-sex kind of way.

Not that I'd ever thought of it like that. It was just what I heard from the hundreds of female tourists that came through town, wanting to see where *the* Ryan Caldwell grew up.

"Damn. Can't believe that's the same kid who used to pee in the inflatable pool," Derek said, earning another love tap from his wife. "I mean, c'mon—look at him."

We followed Derek's gesture, and look at him we did along with the rest of the patrons of the bar. Plenty were still tourists—fall was, despite my distaste, actually a pretty big deal around here—but a good half were locals, too. And it was those locals who watched the TV screens with the same heightened interest as they did for our home-state team as the Stallions' quarterback scrambled, vying for an open man downfield.

Derek lifted out of his chair. Even I couldn't stop myself from unabashedly staring as he pulled back and launched the ball in a perfect spiral downfield, only for it to land perfectly in Ryan's arms.

Ziggy's erupted, most of the people in the room so used to cheering for Ryan on the high school field that it was just natural to do so on a professional level, too. I was the odd man out, opting to instead clutch my drink with both hands to keep them from balling into fists.

It was a bad choice. An awful choice, actually, because as soon as the linebacker slammed head-on into Ryan, I jumped and the drink tipped over.

The flags went flying on the screen, and everyone in the bar had gone quiet; even the non-locals knew what Ryan meant to this place.

"Holy shit," Derek mumbled. At his side, Sarah's hand was over her mouth. I loved her, but the woman didn't know a damn thing about football, which went to show how bad the scene on the TV was.

I'd lifted myself out of my stool, using the bar around the bottom as a support. My eyes hadn't left the screen where—dammit, if they cut to the sidelines one more time, I was gonna scream.

"I know it's our guy, but he needs to be ejected," Derek said. "That was clearly targeting."

I didn't disagree, but I couldn't speak. Not as the cameras were finally back on where Ryan lay on the field, surrounded by medical professionals.

"Did I see Whitfield land on Caldwell's leg after that one?" a man a few seats down at the bar asked.

"If he doesn't have a concussion after that, I'll be shocked," another added.

"Shit, here comes the cart," yet another said.

Sure enough, the screen was now showing the open-backed medical cart, ready to transport Ryan to the locker room. That or the hospital.

The idea of the latter made whatever drinks I'd already consumed churn in my stomach.

"That's a rough loss for the Stallions," the announcer said through the speaker system at Ziggy's. "Ryan Caldwell is a leader on this team, both in the literal sense and when it comes to scoring. It will be interesting to see how they can adapt without him here."

"Yeah, Mike," the other announcer agreed. "It's no secret that Caldwell is one of the best tight ends in the league right now, and losing someone with his level of accuracy and versatility is going to be hard to overcome."

Ryan was barely moving in the back of the cart as it drove off the field, applause from the fans in the stands coming in loud and clear through the broadcast.

"We'll have a better report later," Mike the Sportscaster said. "But it wouldn't shock me if that was a season-ending moment for the promising young Ryan Caldwell."

"Hate to agree with you, Mike," his partner added. "And I hate to say… I mean—man. That's the kind of stuff you see end *careers*, not just seasons. Head injuries are no joke, and that was one heck of a blow. Whitfield is going to have to pay a hefty fine for that one, no doubt about it."

"Yeah, he'd better fucking have to pay a fine," Derek shouted, slamming his palm on the bar top. "Suspend him, too, while you're at it!"

The others watching nearby mumbled their agreement, but I couldn't focus on it. I was still stuck on those two major words from the commentators: end careers.

CHAPTER TWO

"ALRIGHT, TIME TO settle down, folks."

Mayor Turner hit the gavel on the podium like a judge commanding order in a courthouse. It might have been seen as more threatening if most of the people hadn't known her A) since they were children or B) as the kindergarten teacher at Timberland Creek Elementary. How she'd transitioned from that to politics was beyond me, but Cathy Turner treated the town the same way she'd treated her students: with the utmost love, care, and support. If anyone was going to make sure this town continued to run successfully, it was her.

Plus, her husband, Phil, was the only accountant within a twenty-mile radius, so she didn't need to worry about the financials with him around to help.

A hush fell around the room as more and more of the gathered crowd tuned in to the gavel's slap.

I leaned closer to Hemi and whispered, "Do we really need

to be here?"

"Yes," she replied, playfully hitting my knee. "Coffee shops are a large part of the community, so what would it say if we hadn't shown up?"

"That we were busy?"

"Hush." She hit my knee again, and I chuckled. "You young kids need to learn what it's like to give back to your community."

"I do give back," I argued. "Do you want to know how many of these people wouldn't survive their days without the caffeine I give them?"

Hemi, more than used to my sarcasm after three years of working together, shook her head, grinning. I leaned back in my chair, knowing her lack of response was as much from not wanting to put up with my usual bullshit as it was a sign to actually be quiet and listen.

Mayor Turner smiled from her place on stage, her hands on the podium. There couldn't have been more than ten of us in the basement of the town hall building. Until a few years ago, I hadn't even known this place existed. But once Hemi started deeming me her right-hand woman, my visits had become more frequent.

"Thank you all for coming here," Mayor Turner began. "I know there are plenty of other things you'd like to be doing with your Thursday evenings—especially this time of year—so your attendance is very much appreciated."

A few guys cheered at the subtle mention of football season, and Marty Nelson called out, "You're lucky the Packers aren't on, Cath!"

That earned a few more laughs, including one from the mayor.

"Oh, I would never," she assured everyone with a wave of her hands. "I feel like that would lead to an immediate impeachment." Mayor Turner waited for the polite chuckles to fade before she went on saying, "Okay, but in all seriousness, I'm sure you all know what this is about. We're reaching the point of the year where we need to finalize plans for the annual Fall Festival."

My eyes slid sideways to stare at Hemi who remained unmoving and focused in her seat.

Traitor. Wasn't it bad enough I had to spend the majority of my days this time of year making endless pumpkin spice lattes?

"The Timberland Creek Fall Festival, for many of us here, is seen as the end of the busy season. A time where we close our doors in preparation for the next time tourists join us in town." Mayor Turner's face shifted from hopeful to something a bit more somber. "But this season, it might be the last time some of our friends are able to open."

I'd never known what people meant when they said tension was palpable until that moment. Not a single person in the room moved, aside from our shifting eyes as we all tried to find who was reacting more intensely to Mayor Turner's claim.

It was no secret this town's economy relied primarily on busy season, but it was very rare that more than one of us shut down in a single year. Thankfully, most of the time, closures happened as the result of the owner retiring. In recent years, though, we'd all seen it. The decline in tourism. It was impossible to miss when we'd all been dealing with the months of overcrowded sidewalks our whole lives.

It wasn't a reflection of the townspeople. The whole population of small business owners in Timberland Creek were beyond dedicated to their shops and restaurants. It made for some kick-ass quality, and everyone knew it. I didn't know a single place around here that was rated below four stars online.

No—it had everything to do with the economy in general. Less people were taking vacations, and if they were, it wasn't to po-dunk Wisconsin. Why put your money here when you could go to places like Dubai or Bora Bora?

Except places like Dubai and Bora Bora wouldn't see the same impact our town would if people ever stopped going, and now people in this very same room as me were at risk of losing everything they'd worked towards.

"You're all welcome to disclose yourselves as you see fit," Mayor Turner continued. "But for the rest of us in the room, we know all about the time, hard-work, and dedication it takes to keep a business afloat. So, that being said, I wanted to propose a plan to enhance our Fall Festival. Include a fundraiser or two to raise money and help our community members get through to the next tourist season."

Muttered agreements filled the room, and I nodded along. Duh, this was the plan. If Mayor Turner hadn't suggested it herself, someone else in the room surely would have.

"Is everyone in favor of starting this meeting brainstorming?" Mayor Turned scanned the room. "Think of some easy-to-implement ideas? I know we only have a little over a month until the Fest takes place."

A hand that led to a colorful-bead-bracelet-adorned wrist lifted into the air immediately, and Mayor Turner pointed at its owner.

"I was planning on being at the gallery's tent most of the day," Mary Nelson said from a few rows up. "I'd be happy to stay longer and do some quick commissions? They wouldn't be too extravagant since I'd want to get through a lot of them, but it might be something."

"Custom pieces are huge right now," added her husband, Marty. "And we can ask Quinny if she'd be interested in participating. Auction off a discounted weekend at one of her rental properties?"

Mayor Turner nodded along. "Those are wonderful ideas," she said. "We can always count on the Nelson family around here. Anyone else?"

It took a minute, but then another hand went up.

"Yes, Tori?"

My eyes drifted to the other side of the room where Tori Albrecht sat up a little straighter in her chair. "I know he's not here, but I'm sure Jackson would be willing to have a special signing at the Turning Pages booth. I could also text my other friend—J.M. Wright. She writes fantasy, too, so that could be a big draw for the fall. All that witchy stuff." I couldn't completely see her face from where I was sitting, but I knew Tori came up with another idea when she perked up.

"And—this one is a big maybe, everyone," Tori prefaced, twisting at her waist to see as many people in the room as possible. "But Jordi happens to be dating to Alfie Fletcher."

"Wait, *that's* your friend Jordi?" another one of the younger members of town, Elise, asked in her Scandinavian accent. "Why didn't you say anything?"

Tori shrugged. "I didn't want to sound like a name-dropping asshole until I was sure enough of you liked me around here."

"Tori, language," Mayor Turner scolded politely. "Who's Alfie Fletcher?"

"And Jordi is the same person as the author you mentioned?" Hemi asked.

Tori nodded at Hemi and said, "Yes, J.M. Wright is her pen name." Then to Mayor Turner, she clarified, "He's an actor. British. Hot. Played a vampire for about ten years on TV. Great guy, actually."

"You know him well?"

"Well enough," Tori said. "Spent a lot of time hanging out with him a few years back, and I've seen them a few times when Jackson and I've gone back to Chicago to visit my family."

"You think he'd be willing to participate in the Fall Festival?" Elise asked with more interest than I'd ever seen from anyone at a town hall meeting. Usually these things were snore fests— hence my original disinterest in being here—but Tori had just potentially turned it into the most exciting event the town had seen in months.

"I can definitely check," she said. "They might be busy, but those two owe me after they skipped my wedding for the BAFTAs."

"Aren't those the same thing as the Oscars?" Rosie Donahue asked. "But British?"

"You were at my wedding," Tori retorted. "I'd say it was much better than some stuffy awards show."

I chuckled to myself. Tori wasn't wrong, though. She and Jackson had thrown quite the party. Would have been cool as hell to have an actor there along with everyone else.

"Why don't you reach out to your friends, Tori, and we'll see what they say?" Mayor Turner suggested. "That would be quite the draw it sounds like, if you can manage to persuade them to come."

"Oh, I'll persuade them. Don't worry."

"I don't doubt that." Mayor Turner was smiling as she shook her head at one of our town's newest additions, then returned her attention to the rest of the room. "Okay, does anyone else have any ideas for—"

She stopped when the push-bar door opened at the back of the room. Every head turned to see who was arriving late to the meeting—and in such an obnoxious way, at that.

I don't know why I was shocked to see who it was, but the clatter was a little more understandable once I did.

"Careful, careful," Dave Caldwell mumbled as he extended

his arm, holding the door open for his son who attempted to squeeze through the frame with his crutches. To the rest of us, Dave added, "Sorry, folks. Had a bit of trouble getting down the stairs."

Ryan cussed under his breath as his crutch caught on the center support beam in the double doors. He dragged it through aggressively, each consecutive hit resounding like a tin drum throughout the space until he found success.

"That brings up a good point, Dave," Mayor Turner said to the room. "Accessibility in older buildings."

"Oh, don't go spending town money on reconstruction projects just yet," Mr. Caldwell replied. Ryan was still grumbling, his face set in a look of something between embarrassment and utter disinterest. "Ry will be back and better than ever in no time."

"Well, there are other members of our community who might benefit, too," Mayor Turner said with a tightness in her jaw that told me she was trying *really* hard to remain diplomatic.

If there was one person in this town that was going to talk up anything and everything Ryan Caldwell did, it was his dad. Dave Caldwell had books of stats from every game Ryan had played. Literal video tapes from pee-wee leagues filled with footage of his son trying to catch a pass when he was no more than three feet tall. Binders full of information on every college and university football program that had scouted Ryan in high school.

Where I'd been there for moral support and realistic, no-shit advice, Dave Caldwell had other plans. It was likely due to his borderline obsessive nature with his son's football career that Ryan landed where he was today. Worked out, I guess, even if I'd always thought it was a tad weird.

"I haven't seen Dave Caldwell at one of these things in years," Hemi mumbled out the side of her mouth to me. "Not since Gina shut down the boutique."

"I'll give you three guesses why now is the time he decided to show up," I whispered back. "First two guesses don't count."

"Flaunt the famous son?"

"Exactly," I confirmed, my eyes following the father-son pair as they made their way through the rows of chairs, trying to find one that was easily accessible for Ryan.

"Maybe if they'd shown up on time, they wouldn't need to cause such a display," Hemi continued.

I huffed a laugh. "Please. Dave Caldwell not make a scene? Not in his nature."

Hemi chuckled at that as the man in question tapped Tori on the shoulder and asked her to move.

If looks could kill...

But she must have deemed the argument not worth it—or was just more mature than Dave and realized a town hall meeting wasn't the place to cause of ruckus—and scooted a seat closer to Rosie.

Dave helped Ryan lower into one of the same metal folding chairs the rest of us were in, then flipped the one in front of him around. Ryan lifted his injured leg onto it, giving me the best view of the black brace that went from his ankle to his thigh since he'd come into the room.

A torn MCL is what I'd heard it ended up being, along with a concussion. Whitfield, just as Derek wished for, had been suspended for four games for targeting. Ryan, on the other hand, was due to be out for the majority of the season during recovery—maybe more with all the league's new rules about head injuries.

I'd caught a sports talk show one morning before I headed down to Sunrise Brews for my shift. He'd apparently gotten a brain scan done. They didn't show the pictures of that—instead viewers had gotten clear shots of his post-op leg, which was lovely to see while scarfing down some eggs and toast—but from the sounds of it… Ryan was lucky, that was for sure. And that was probably putting it mildly.

The scrape of the chairs and the muttering between the father and son were the only sounds in the room. My eyes drifted back to Mayor Turner. She was chewing the inside of her cheek. I tilted my head down, trying to hide my smile. Not even my sweet kindergarten teacher could hide her annoyance, no matter how hard she was clearly trying.

Dave settled into a chair behind his son and folded his hands on his lap. I couldn't stop my eyes from rolling at his polite smile—as if he hadn't just disrupted the entire meeting.

Mayor Turner raised a brow.

Dave gave her a thumbs up.

"Alright then," Mayor Turner continued. Ryan crossed his arms over his chest and slouched in his chair. "So… where were we again?"

"The fundraiser," Rosie called out.

"Ah, yes. Thank you. I'll open it up to the room again to see if we have any more ideas for—"

"Ryan can sign some stuff."

Once again, all eyes shifted to Dave Caldwell, none of them appearing at all interested in his new interruption.

I almost felt bad for Ryan. Almost. His dad was making it pretty hard for the town to rally around him at the moment. Cheering for the hometown hero was a lot easier through a TV screen, when he wasn't blatantly being waved in front of us as someone of importance.

The hometown hero in question was currently paying more attention to blowing his hair out of his face, arms still crossed over his chest, than the actual conversation. It made me wonder if he was just as used to his dad's antics or if he truly didn't give a crap about the conversation at hand. Something told me it was the latter. After years of well-paid TV spots and highly publicized Make-A-Wish events, doing the right thing for the town in which he was raised seemed below the level of stardom Ryan had reached.

Mayor Turner's eyes flitted between the Caldwell men as she asked, "Does… Ryan *want* to sign things?"

Clearly, she'd noticed the same disinterest as me. It would have been nearly impossible not to.

"Well, he'll have to talk to his people before he agrees to any public appearances—"

"You've got to be fucking kidding me," I muttered under my breath. Hemi tapped my thigh with the back of her hand.

"—but charity never hurt anyone's image."

The level of oblivious Dave had reached to not notice every occupant in the room turn to whoever was sitting next to them and give the classic *what-the-fuck* face was pretty impressive. Even Hemi couldn't refrain from sliding her eyes over to me, probably regretting her subtle reprimanding of my comment from a few seconds before.

"Besides," Dave continued, "little boys love signed stuff. They'll be crying to their parents to get a freaking napkin signed if it means—"

"And girls."

I was fairly certain I'd never spoken at a town hall meeting before, so it was just as much of a shock to myself as it was everyone else when I uttered those two simple words. They'd slipped out almost from instinct. Growing up in a world where—god forbid—women took an interest in sports had forced me to learn how to stick up for myself.

And fight against the assholes who still held the totally outdated sexist mindset of women in sports—or at the very least taking an interest in watching them.

No one in this town would have been surprised to hear me voice my stance on the matter. It was more that I'd voiced anything at all that had them turning in their seats to look at me.

Even Ryan.

Given the brief widening of his eyes then following furrow in his brow, I wasn't sure he realized I'd been in the room. He probably assumed I'd up and left the town like my siblings. Couldn't say I blamed him, since that's all I'd ever talked about since I was a kid—the day I'd finally be able to jet-set around the country in some big-time gig I landed after graduation.

Nope. Not me. He was staring unabashedly at the only Bennett—aside from my parents—to not make it out.

And if not for my desire to win the stare-down with his dad, I would have turned away from the unwanted attention. Ryan's eyes burned into me, and it took every ounce of will-power in my body to not sneak a peek at him. But doing that would give Dave the W.

Dave didn't seem any more willing to stand down than I was, though, going as far as to narrow his eyes at me.

"Harper," he said, voice flat. "Didn't expect to see you here."

"Surprise," I replied, showing just as much enthusiasm.

I'd seen Ryan's parents around town from time to time. At the grocery store, at a restaurant, in Sunrise. Little casual run-ins. His mom would usually acknowledge me, but her husband… it was almost impressive how well he gave a cold shoulder.

Still, all the time away did nothing to ease Dave's clear distaste at seeing me.

I quirked a brow at him. "Well?"

Even at my distance, I could see Dave's jaw tense.

Oh, yeah. He definitely did *not* like my surprise appearance at this meeting.

"Well, sure. Girls will want autographs, too. I mean—hell!" Dave huffed a laugh. "Have you seen this kid?" He ruffled his son's hair, and Ryan's face twisted. At least it finally got him to stop staring. "We could charge extra for the ladies to get a picture with him."

"Not what I meant," I replied with a stiff smile.

Dave's mouth hung open with the tease of some sort of smartass remark, but I never got to hear it before Mayor Turner cut in. "Perhaps it might be a good idea for Harper to help?"

My eyebrows shot into my hairline. "Excuse me?"

The same sentiment was echoed from both the Caldwell men across the room.

"Not that I think you're incapable of thinking of plenty of… riveting ideas, Dave," Mayor Turner said, her eyes darting between both parties in question. "But it's clear that Harper sees a different side of this whole situation?"

"The non-misogynistic one?" I asked.

A twinge of pink colored Mayor Turner's ears as she said, "Well, I don't know if I would have said it that way, but—" Poor Cathy. This was probably the most drama she'd seen since one of her students smuggled a raccoon into the school when I was a sophomore in high school.

"We don't need any help," Dave interrupted. "Ryan has a whole team of people at his disposal. No offense, but Harper would slow things down."

Offense taken.

"Who's to say Ryan's team will approve this anyway?" I shrugged, then leaned forward in my seat, resting my forearms on my knees. "I mean, Tori's already probably got the biggest draw. I don't think we need more than one celebrity at this little celebration. Attendee safety and all—"

"Whoa, whoa, whoa." Dave held up a hand, his attention now straying to Tori who wore a smug smile. "Another celebrity?"

"Yup," Tori confirmed, popping the P. "You aren't the only one in this town with connections, buddy."

This was one of the many reasons I loved Tori. She hadn't thought of inviting Alfie or her friend more than fifteen minutes ago—let alone actually ask if they'd come to small-town Wisconsin to help at a local festival—but she saw what I was doing. And if anyone was going to help me take down a sexist asshole, it was her.

If her connections said no… well, we'd deal with that can of worms later. For now, there was nothing like watching Dave Caldwell deflate at the possibility of his son *not* being the biggest star in the room.

I watched Dave come to terms with that, his throat bobbing as he swallowed the reality. His mental cogs were clearly turning. I'd thrown in a trick play he hadn't been expecting in his attempt to flaunt his offspring.

But he ended up not needing to say anything at all. His son

beat him to it.

"I'll do it."

"*What?*"

It had been years since I'd heard Ryan talk—post-game interviews I'd caught against my will, not included. Just those three words… they had my heart clenching. There'd once been a time where Ryan's voice was all I'd heard. At school. During drop-ins at my family's house. In hours-long phone calls. At parties. Bonfires. Everywhere.

I'd almost forgotten what it sounded like—the deep and somewhat raspy tone—without the cheering fans and other chaos following a football game to dilute it. I'd always used to joke with him that if he didn't make it in football, he should try to be a folk singer with a voice like that, except that he couldn't sing on-tune for shit.

My single-syllable protestation appeared to have surprised him just as much.

What did he *mean* he'd do it? I'd meant to rile Dave up, not convince Ryan to actually go along with this. That was the *last* thing I'd wanted.

Oh, for the love of god—don't tell me his precious little ego couldn't handle not being the only big name in town. Like father, like son, I supposed. It was a completely cringe-worthy reason, but not so far-fetched, all things considered.

I mean, what other reason would he have for agreeing? Doing something kind for the town he'd abandoned?

I almost snorted at the thought.

"Let's do it," Ryan repeated, staring up at his father with an intensity that dared him to try to argue the decision. That same stare found me a moment later. "And, come to think of it, maybe it *is* best that you help out, Harper."

The tightness in my chest transitioned into a terrible sinking feeling.

"Don't you have to check with those people your dad mentioned?" I tried.

"We will," Ryan said with a shrug. "But if it's left up to Dad, we'd miss that whole demographic you just brought up. You'd teach us a lot. And you'd potentially help us double our reach."

"Ryan—" Dave tried to interrupt, but his son held up a hand. Even Mr. Caldwell knew when to stop. The room full of other locals probably helped tamper the tantrum that would have likely occurred otherwise.

"I'll need to help at Sunrise—"

"Hemdeep, would you be able to sacrifice Harper for the day of the festival?" Mayor Turner asked. Her teacher voice was turned on. The same one she'd used on us as kids when she was ready to settle the many pointless arguments five-year-olds managed to get into.

My silent pleas must not have gone through because Hemi shrugged. "Yeah, probably."

"Then there we go," Mayor Turner said with a strained smile. "Harper and Ryan, maybe you can get together at some point and plan your booth and float?"

Shit. I'd forgotten about the parade float. Every business

represented at the festival would have a part in the parade to kick off the day—a way to introduce the festival goers to them and entice them to stop by their booth.

They could be as extravagant or as simple as the business wanted, but something told me Ryan's would be the former, without question.

"I—sure…" I reluctantly agreed, mostly because I was tired of the conversation and the attention it was bringing.

"Wonderful!" Mayor Turner slammed the gavel down on her podium again. "Well, I'd say that's plenty on that topic for the evening. If anyone else has any ideas, feel free to bring them forward to me in private, but let's move onto the matter of deer crossing signs. It seems that lately we've had a problem with…"

Not that I cared about the amount of traffic signs in the town to begin with, but there was no chance I was listening to the new conversation. A cold sweat had overcome my body in the horribly hot room. Had the heat kicked on since we'd arrived? The sudden temperature change made me antsy. Eager to leave as soon as possible. And even though I knew everyone else had moved on, I couldn't help the feeling that they were all still watching me.

No. It wasn't everyone. Just the one person whose attention I wanted least.

Ryan held apparently no shame when it came to his staring because he was back at, even worse than before. Except this time, I had no problem staring back.

Who was I kidding? That was a lie. My heart rate picked up

with every second our eyes remained locked, and I wanted so desperately to look away. Because with each increasingly heavy breath, I couldn't help but ask myself the same question.

Why?

Why did I get myself into this?

Why did he leave?

Why did he think he could show up here again?

Why did I still care?

Thankfully, he allowed my winning streak against the Caldwell men that evening to live.

Ryan broke our stare first.

CHAPTER THREE

ONE PERK ABOUT becoming right-hand woman to the owner of a coffee shop was getting first dibs on the rent of the apartment upstairs. Hemi got the cabin out back, so technically I was still getting the lesser deal, but hey—affordable housing in a town where housing was limited to begin with was a blessing.

Especially when it meant I could finally say *adios* to my parents and my childhood bedroom after twenty-five years.

I woke to the fresh smell of ground coffee beans the same way I did every day. Whether I worked or not, Hemi was at the shop bright and early preparing for the day, which meant no need for an alarm clock.

Peeling back the blackout curtain behind my bed, I peeked outside the window. The sidewalks weren't too crowded yet, but they would be soon. As the only coffee shop in town, tourists flocked to it. There was no Starbucks or Dunkin' around these parts—unless you wanted to drive forty minutes to the closest major town. Seeing as it was much easier to simply walk up the street from their rental homes or condos, Hemi reaped the benefits of the nation-wide caffeine addiction epidemic.

One look at my phone told me it was six-forty-eight. Sunrise opened at seven.

With my hair in a messy bun—the grease had finally won—and donning a white, long-sleeve bodysuit and a pair of worn overalls, I bounded down the back stairwell and into the "employee only" portion of Sunrise with two minutes to spare.

Still, it didn't stop Hemi from saying, "You're late," like she did every morning.

I chuckled as she blindly handed me my steaming hot to-go cup of coffee, sans lid. Freshly prepared with a splash of cream. The steam wafting up from it hit my nose and let me know she'd used my favorite flavored beans. Nothing beat cinnamon this time of year.

"If I was late, wouldn't this be cold?" I teased.

Hemi shook her head while she continued the last-minute prep for the day, but as I went to retrieve my apron from the hook beside her workstation, I found her smiling.

Call me crazy, but the day I'd started working at Sunrise Brews would probably go down as one of the best days of my life. Over the years, I'd worked in every restaurant, boutique, and mom-and-pop shop that came and went in Timberland Creek. None would compare to Sunrise, and that was largely due to the woman in charge.

Hemdeep Batra, despite our twenty-year age gap—though it was only ten if you asked her—had become one of my best friends. She'd guided me. Taught me how to run a business. The secrets of the trade. And even if I hadn't followed the paths of my brothers, moving out of town and pursing a job in my field of study, I was happy.

Some of us just didn't leave Timberland Creek, no matter how many times my siblings offered their commentary about how I should spread my wings. They called it brotherly love. I called it a pain in my ass.

It wasn't like I'd never wanted to leave—or that I'd never tried. The option just… wasn't in my cards, I guess.

Besides, who would be around to help Hemi? My mom? My dad?

Knowing I could be the one they depended on was enough for now.

"You feeling better after yesterday?" Hemi asked when I fell into step beside her. She'd finished most of the pre-opening duties, but I'd worked here long enough to immediately notice what was left.

"I was fine yesterday." I turned to her, my brow furrowed. "Why? Did I sound sick or something?"

"That's not what I was talking about."

"Oh."

She was talking about the meeting, then.

I didn't give her the satisfaction of offering any other

commentary, though, continuing to stack mugs that would be used for customers who stuck around the café to enjoy their morning brew.

"I don't think I've ever seen you get like that before," Hemi continued. "Not even with some of the more colorful customers that come in here."

I huffed a laugh. "After you tell someone there's no way for me to add another temperature button between regular and extra hot enough times, you become a little numb to the argument."

Hemi chuckled, but bringing up one of the many inane arguments we'd had to deal with over the years wasn't enough to distract her completely. "I didn't realize you knew that guy."

"Which one?"

Hemi shrugged. "Both, I guess."

I finished stacking the last few cups before I settled on saying, "Yeah, Ryan and I used to be close. Knowing Dave came as part of the friendship package, unfortunately."

Why hide it? Especially now that Ryan and I would be working together on his Fall Fest appearance, Hemi was bound to find out sooner or later. Might as well nip it in the bud before she could accuse me of being a liar, at worst; a truth-omitter, at best.

She reacted the exact way I knew she would. It was the same as everyone else when I'd been more open to admitting I knew *the* Ryan Caldwell. "Close, huh?"

"Don't say it like that," I chastised, a hand on my hip as I leveled her with a glare that screamed *don't start.* "You know that's not what I meant."

"How do *I* know what you mean?" Hemi shrugged, adopting an air of innocence. "I hardly know you at all, apparently."

"You literally know my period cycle."

"Yes, so I can make sure you have the day off and save our customers from the raging lunatic you become when you have your first day of cramps." I tossed a dish towel at her, and Hemi laughed, removing it from where it landed over her face. "Come to think of it, maybe we should make sure you're unleashed on Dave during your next cycle."

I rolled my eyes, the mention of Mr. Caldwell washing all the cheeriness away.

Hemi noted it immediately.

"Wow, it must be bad."

"It's… complicated," I admitted reluctantly. If I dove into the grand history of Harper and Ryan, we'd be here all day. We'd have to close up shop, and there was no way in hell the town would appreciate that, especially at such short notice.

"Sounds like it."

"Do you really not need me to help you with the Festival?" I asked when Hemi went to flip the CLOSED sign to OPEN. A few minutes late, but it was better than nothing.

Now it was my turn to note the sudden change in character. Hemi, for all the toughness she liked to display, wore her heart on her sleeve.

I placed my palm flat on the counter and tracked her with my eyes, waiting for my stare to finally break her.

"You're not as scary as you think," she told me when she was standing behind the counter again.

"No, no, no—you don't get to coax personal information out of me, then shut down when it's my turn."

"You told me nothing."

"I told you enough," I argued. "Why the sudden sad face?"

"I'm not sad. See?" Hemi plastered on a tooth-filled smile that stretched from ear to ear. "Happy as can be."

"Don't make me cuss in the shop. I know how you don't like it."

"Why do you need to cuss?"

"Because I'm calling bullshit."

The normally quick-to-reprimand-my-foul-language Hemi was quiet. That's how I knew I'd caught her.

My sass deflated, replaced with genuine concern. "Is something wrong?" I basically whispered. We were still alone in the shop, but I couldn't muster anything more. Getting shy when things got serious was my specialty. "Are you okay?"

"I'm fine," Hemi assured me. "But…" She shook her head. "You know how I've been traveling a lot?"

I nodded. I'd been left in charge of Sunrise a handful of times over the last few months. It's why Hemi had hired on a few more part-time baristas, too, that we called in as needed. I knew plenty about running the books and making sure stock was good, but I couldn't do that *and* successfully run the front on my own. And during tourist season? Definitely no chance.

"I've been going back to India," my boss admitted. "My mom is sick."

"Hemi…" I reached for her hand, but she pulled it away. She was never one for sentimentality, but in a situation like this, I wanted to offer whatever comfort I could.

"It's fine. You don't need to worry."

"Of course, I'm gonna worry," I said. "Why didn't you say anything sooner?"

"The same reason you're not telling me everything about this Ryan boy," Hemi challenged; some of her usual spark returned to her eyes. "You don't need to concern yourself with everything that's going on in my personal life."

"Yeah, sure, fine," I agreed. She held a very valid point. "But all this time I thought you were—I don't know. Like, going on a bunch of vacations or something."

She huffed a laugh. "I wish. I could use a vacation, that's for sure."

"Do you have to go back again during the Fest?" I asked. "Is that why you won't need my help?"

Her face grew somber again, and after a few moments of silent contemplation, she finally said, "I'm selling Sunrise."

"*What?*" I screeched just as the bell above the back door jingled to announce our first customer of the day.

And what a customer it was.

Ryan paused, midway through the door he held open with a crutch, and stared down Hemi and I like a deer in headlights. Couldn't say we were giving him a much better welcome. Even if I'd wanted to, I wasn't sure I could form any coherent thought after the bomb Hemi had just dropped on me.

Having been privy to the information for more than three seconds, the owner of the coffee shop—though for how much longer she'd hold that title, I wasn't sure—composed herself enough to say, "Welcome in. What can we get started for you?"

She nudged me as she walked up to the register, offering a stare that very clearly communicated to drop our previous conversation so long as customers were present.

Especially this one.

Until yesterday, I would have believed her if she'd told me she had no idea who Ryan Caldwell was. Hemi had never bothered with American sports, finding more of an interest in soccer and cricket. She might have been the only person in this one-road town who didn't give a shit who this man was.

She probably still wouldn't, honestly, if it hadn't been for my connection to him.

I eyed Ryan as he hobbled his way over to the counter before I turned and busied myself at the espresso machine. It already sparkled with a fresh polish, but I wiped at it anyway. Anything to avoid interaction.

"I'll, uh, take an Americano with a pump of no-sugar vanilla. Room for cream. Extra hot—but, like, not too hot where I can't drink it right away, you know?"

Hemi's eyes slid away from the tablet where she punched in the order to meet my waiting side-long stare.

"Alright…" Hemi said, drawing out the second syllable as

she finished inputting Ryan's requests. "Go ahead and pay here," she added, turning the screen so Ryan could tap his card—AmEx Black Card, of course. "And Harper will get that right up for you."

A small strangled sound came from my throat, but it did nothing to stop Hemi from smiling politely at her customer as soon as the payment went through before hurrying into the back room.

Oh, we were *so* in a fight.

At least this would be over quickly. I didn't know why I'd thought Ryan would be a latte drinker. Maybe because when we'd grown up, he'd hated the smell of coffee, let alone the taste. And the one time he *had* decided to have a cup while we'd studied for finals our junior year, he'd spent a solid hour in the bathroom afterwards.

Yet here he was now, drinking essentially straight espresso. It just went to show how much I actually knew about him anymore.

The music hadn't been turned on for the day. That was usually my job, but I'd been a little distracted, to say the least, since I'd come downstairs. Without its presence in the background, I was forced to concentrate even harder on my task, lest I give into temptation and steal a glance at the customer.

Where in the heck were all the tourists? They usually flooded through the doors as soon as we opened.

The same nervous energy from the town hall meeting had

returned. I desperately wanted to say something—do something—but I didn't know what. This wasn't Ryan Caldwell, my friend, anymore. This was Ryan Caldwell, the athlete.

"One Americano. Extra hot," I said when the drink was finished.

I'd been forced to turn around to place it on the counter, and the moment I did, my self-control went out the window.

He'd been dressed casually for the town hall meeting, but now, Ryan wore a pair of gray joggers that were perhaps a size too small. Maybe that was because of his brace; he needed something that would fit beneath it. But I couldn't deny the wonders these too-small pants did to show off the quad muscles he'd developed during his years of athletic training.

Ryan had always been a fit guy, but now I could only imagine the kind of routine he went through regularly. He probably had a personal trainer. Or two. And a personal chef. No more late-night fast-food runs here. If his thigh muscles weren't an indicator of that, the biceps that were practically bursting through his t-shirt were.

And that... holy shit, Ryan had tattoos now? A half sleeve on his right arm, a full on his left from the looks of it.

The muscles on the arms I was shamelessly staring at strained as he crutched over to the spot on the counter where I'd set his order.

"Thanks," he said, and once again that one syllable had my heart dropping to my stomach.

Then it turned to something like nausea when a small smirk curled the corners of Ryan's lips.

He knew I'd been staring.

"Mhm," was all I replied before I turned, trying to hide the redness that colored my cheeks after being caught.

I thought—and hoped—that would have been it, but of course it wasn't.

"So," Ryan went on. From the corner of my eye, I saw him put his full weight on his armpits, the crutches somehow supporting his large frame, as he held his drink in both hands. "Barista, huh?"

"We can't all be millionaires," I said, my voice flat.

"I guess I didn't expect you to still be here, is all."

"Yeah, get in line," I half mumbled as I cleaned out the cup I'd just used for his drink's espresso. "Anything else I can get for you today?"

Even though it was a line I used with all our customers, nothing about my tone indicated I actually wanted to help. In fact, the message to get out came across clear as day. Except Ryan didn't listen.

"I figured we should probably talk at some point. About the Festival?"

I bit my tongue. Yes, the Festival. Obviously. Because we, of all people, had *nothing* else to talk about.

"Yeah, sure."

"You… come here often? Seems like a good place to get stuff done."

"Well, I work here, so…"

"Right." He cleared his throat. "When do you get off?"

"I don't know. Whenever Hemi stops needing me for the day."

A fresh grin appeared on his lips. "This place doesn't close at any point?"

"We do."

Ryan nodded. "So… would you want to meet up when you're off?"

"Today?"

Ryan shrugged as best he could without one of his crutches dropping. "Or tomorrow. Soon, though, since we only have a month or so to get this together, right?"

"You got your people's approval?" I was genuinely curious, but it came out with some residual iciness.

"We're going to talk with them now. Heading to the library to make sure the Wi-Fi is more stable."

"We?"

At that moment, a car horn honked. I lifted myself onto my toes to see out the front window where a shiny black pickup truck was parked. There was no chance of me seeing who sat in the driver's seat through the intense window tint, though.

"My, uh—my dad," Ryan said. "I'm staying with them—my parents—while I recover."

"Fun." I lowered myself again. "Couldn't hire someone for that?"

"My mom insisted I come back. Seemed easier than dealing

with this in San Antonio, anyway."

"There's no place like home, eh, Dorothy?"

A fresh sparkle lit his eyes at my unexpected joke. "Right." The car horn sounded again, and this time was accompanied by someone shouting, "I love you, Ryan!"

My brow furrowed as I lifted onto my toes again and found the answer to my question about the lack of other customers. Two police officers were standing on the path that led to the front stairs. Another was standing at the back door. He must have followed Ryan to the handicap-accessible entry. All of them were holding back anyone who'd wanted to come to get their coffee, I assumed, until Ryan was finished.

"You've, uh, got quite the fan club out there," I commented.

"And a pissed off dad," he added. Ryan adjusted the hold on his cup so he could maneuver his crutches. "Thanks for this. It's really good."

"It's literally espresso and water."

Ryan grinned again. "It's really good espresso and water." He pivoted, and a part of me wanted to ask if he needed any help, but that would mean admitting that somewhere, deep down, I still cared. I wasn't ready to let Ryan have that win quite yet— if ever.

The car horn honked again, and Ryan cussed under his breath.

"I'll let you know where to meet up?" he asked over his shoulder, halfway to the door. The cop posted there opened it for him and took the drink from his hand.

"Sure."

Ryan paused in the doorway, taking advantage of the assistance the officer gave him. He smiled at me as he said, "It's good to see you again, Harps."

My mind couldn't work fast enough to think of something to say. *Goodbye* would have more than sufficed, but even that was too hard. Instead, I stared as Ryan let the door close behind him, and the boy who knew me as Harps was swallowed up by his fans, reminding me of the man he'd become.

"So," Hemi said, drawing out the word, as she finally re-emerged from the back. "How'd it go?"

I narrowed my eyes at her. "If you thought that problem would distract from the other one, you're sadly mistaken."

"I didn't think that at all. I know you well, remember?" The bell above the front door jingled, and all the people who'd been standing outside flooded in. One glance out the window, and I could see that Ryan and his dad had pulled away. "But now we have to get to work. There's no time for talk."

As much as I wanted to argue, Hemi was right. This rush would keep us busy for at least a few hours, and after it passed, I wasn't sure I'd have the mental capacity to handle a heavy conversation. Especially not with the knowledge that I very well might have another one coming, too.

CHAPTER FOUR

HEMI TOSSED HER apron on the floor as soon as she locked the door behind our last customer for the day. I couldn't say I was far behind her, exhaustion-wise. My ass was ready to hit my couch and stay there for a long, long time. Never mind it being a Friday night and me being in my prime for socializing. There were exactly five people I cared about spending time with lately anyway and one of them I was mad at, two—Tori and Jackson—used Friday nights as date night, and the remaining options were my parents, which, loved them, but I didn't need to see them *every* week.

That's what the routine had felt like it was becoming lately. It wasn't like the town was in abundance of people my age. There were definitely some options, but I needed to handle them in doses. When you grew up with the same twenty people for two decades, breaks were necessary.

Besides, if I asked my parents to hang out one more time, my mom was sure to ask me why I was wasting my time with them rather than, say, going on a date.

Again. Twenty people. She knew that, but asking me about my love life was still her favorite pastime. Like she wasn't completely aware that there were approximately three decent options left in this town—and I'd already slept with all three of them.

Mom didn't know *that*; we were close, but not so close where I disclosed details of my sex life. But if there was one thing I'd learned in my so-called adventures, it was that the men in this town were good enough for short-term entertainment. Marriage, though? Co-habitation? *Reproduction?*

I cringed at the thought.

That wasn't to say I didn't want that one day. Marriage had been something I'd wanted since I was a teenager. Thoughts of kids had come a little later, but they'd shown up nonetheless. Especially after I'd met my niece. If one of my idiot big brothers could somehow manage keeping a tiny human alive, I figured I could, too.

I just needed to find the person I wanted to do all those things with.

"If you need me, I'll be sleeping until tomorrow's shift begins," Hemi said, kicking her apron along with each of her steps as she returned to our haven behind the counter.

I nodded as I hung my own up on its regular hook, then

added Hemi's when she picked it up and handed it to me.

Her hand found my shoulder while my back was to her, and tears welled in my eyes. I figured it was partially due to the residual stress of the day, maybe even a little pent-up anger from the town hall meeting. But a lot of it was definitely from knowing what was coming next.

"I would have told you eventually, Harper. You know that," Hemi said, her voice soft. The edge she usually carried—the one she'd been forced to adopt as not only a woman who needed to prove herself, but as an immigrant—gone for the time being. "I'm still trying to figure things out myself. I wouldn't even consider selling if I thought there was some way to—"

After all that had happened the last few days, the break in Hemi's voice as emotions overcame her was the biggest surprise.

I turned to face her, and she tilted her face down, trying to hide the signs of her sadness.

"You're right," I told her. "I know you would have said something. I mean, heck—you would have had to when you fired me."

I'd meant it as a joke, but apparently the sarcasm didn't come through.

Hemi lifted her head, her fire reignited. "Anyone in this town would be lucky to have you on their staff. If it comes down to it, I promise I'll be a reference for anyone who might—"

"Hemi, don't worry about me. We need to worry about *you*. What can I do to help?"

The way Hemi's face softened made me wonder if anyone else had ever offered their assistance before. If she'd ever *let* them.

"Nothing at the moment," she assured me with a squeeze. "Just keep showing up here and making sure this place runs smoothly."

For now were the two words missing from the end of that statement. But maybe, just like she hadn't wanted to tell me yet, Hemi wasn't ready to admit what most likely lay ahead in the future of Sunrise Brews.

Her exhaustion, from the day we'd just survived and from the conversation, was starting to show, so I offered a small smile and placed my hand over hers. "I can do that."

Moment over. Hemi pulled her hand back, forcing me to do the same.

"You sleeping for the rest of the day, too?" she asked as she whipped out a rag and spray bottle and began to wipe down the counter.

"I don't know about sleeping," I replied, then made my way over to the little storage cubby where I stashed my phone during the day. "But I'll probably end up ordering take-out from Ziggy's and watching more of this new show I found. I swear I'm, like, so obsessed with it, and I'm only three episodes in. Have you heard of—?"

Popularity was far from my middle name, so I rarely found notifications on my phone. Maybe a few automated ones from various apps. A stray text here and there. A distant relative liking something I posted on Facebook three years after the initial share date during a not-so-subtle social media stalking sesh. So, when I found a text from an unknown number asking, *Meet me at the library?* I was definitely thrown off.

"Have I heard of…?" Hemi repeated.

I shook my head, my brow scrunched and eyes still on my phone. "Sorry," I said as I simultaneously typed back, *Who is this?* "I, um—it's called—holy shit."

The reply from the mystery number came back almost instantly: *Ryan*

Hemi stared at me with wide eyes. "They're allowing shows to be called that now?"

"No, no. It's not—" I shook my head, a bit dumbfounded by the situation I'd found myself in. "No, I'm distracted. Sorry."

"By what?" Hemi passed by me to put her spray bottle back and craned her neck to try to sneak a peek at my screen. "Special someone?"

"It's Ryan," I told her.

Unsurprisingly, Hemi looked even more confused. "So?"

"He kept my number."

After all he'd done—all the people he'd met as his career progressed—I hadn't thought I'd have made the cut to remain in his contacts list. I couldn't seriously believe that the moment his first ad spot or Pro Bowl appearance came around he didn't go through everyone he had saved and wipe out the entire population of Timberland Creek.

What was the point in having them? He'd moved on to bigger and better things outside our little town. Although, if there was one thing I'd heard over the years, it was plenty of bragging that people had Ryan Caldwell's number, followed by a huge resistance to actually do anything with it. *Don't want to bother him; he's probably busy* was the biggest excuse I'd heard from guys who name-dropped Ryan like they'd been best friends.

I was the only one who could make that claim, and all the guys knew it. Funny how the comments never came up when I was part of the conversation, only an innocent eavesdropper. Even funnier how I had probably been the single person in this whole town who could have texted him, but had deleted his number instead.

I'd hung onto it for as long as my heart could allow it. Then, after a certain point, seeing it was too hard of a reminder of what I'd lost.

Apparently, the same hadn't rung true for Ryan. Or he simply had so many contacts now that he hadn't come across *Harper* too often.

Another text came through. *I'll be there in ten. Just come whenever your shift is over.*

"That's a… bad thing?" Hemi asked, reading my tone.

"Yes," I said. "Or no. I mean—" I shook my head and all the jumbled thoughts within it. "It's not great since I got rid of his, and now he knows that."

Hemi let out a low whistle. "I sense a bit of drama, perhaps?"

She had no idea…

"I think I have to go," I said, trying to evade the conversation I knew I was being dragged into. "He'll be at the library in ten. I can—" I looked around the café, trying to figure out a few closing tasks I could do in record time.

"Go." Hemi nudged me with her hip. "I'll handle it today. You have a boy to meet."

I tilted my head, giving my boss a cut-that-out look, which she followed with a suggestive wiggle of her eyebrows.

"It's not like that." It never had been, not even when Ryan and I were at our closest.

"He kept your number, didn't he?" Hemi fired back.

Instead of trying to think of some argument that made sense, I texted Ryan back, letting him know I'd be there soon, then saluted my boss.

"You get more info when I get more info," I said.

"Pizza night at the cabin tomorrow?" she suggested.

"It's on."

And with that, I made my way out of the café.

CHAPTER FIVE

I PROBABLY HADN'T needed to rush out of Sunrise as quickly as I had, considering the library was a two-minute walk up the road. I'd been influenced by shock, more than anything, and now I was paying the price as I waited in the parking lot.

September in Wisconsin was a fickle beast. One day it could be seventy-five and sunny, the next fifty and rainy. Today was the latter, minus the rain, thank god, because my ratty old Packers sweatshirt that had been passed down since the 90s was barely holding up against the wind as it was. I didn't need to be wet on top of that.

A strange sense of déjà vu overcame me when I heard the rumble of what I knew would be the large black truck from earlier. Unlike when we were younger, now the announcement of Ryan's arrival wasn't so much an, "Oh, what poor soul has to drive that hunk of junk?" as it was, "The driver of this car means business."

Then the joyous, quick honks—like the driver was trying to orchestrate a song with one note—rang through the air.

"Hey, sweetie pie!" Gina Caldwell called out the open window as she turned into the parking lot.

The saying opposites attract could not have been truer when it came to Ryan's parents. Where his dad was… well, he was a dick. No point in sugar-coating it. But his mom was an angel on earth. Still, to this day, I'd met fewer people as kind and welcoming as her.

The car came to an abrupt halt a few feet from me, and Gina lurched forward. Beside her, Ryan let out an *"Oof,"* as he had no choice but to do the same. His hand flew out to stop himself from crashing too hard into the dashboard.

There were also few people I knew who were worse drivers than Gina Caldwell. The day I'd gotten my driver's license was the day my parents breathed a sigh of relief, knowing I didn't have to rely on her for rides anymore.

"Oh, would you look at this!" she said through an excited squeal and hopped out of the car. Like, literally hopped. The woman was five-two on a good day. The truck looked like it could eat her and still want more.

"Hey, Mrs. C," I said with a smile, but way less enthusiasm as I waved.

"Stop that!" Gina mock-scolded. "You know I'm not letting you out of giving me a hug!"

"I don't know if—*oof!*"

I hesitantly returned the embrace. Gina was surprisingly

strong for her size.

Over her shoulder, I caught sight of Ryan trying to maneuver his way out of the car without bending his injured leg. Once he hopped down onto his good one, crutches under his arms, he gave me a shy smile.

He kept your number, Harper. Don't fall for the charm, I reminded myself.

"I saw you at Piggly Wiggly last week, Mrs. C," I finally said, patting her back. She took the hint and released me. "And I made your pumpkin spice latte the week before."

"I know," she replied with a dismissive flick of her wrist. "But this is different. It's like old times—me dropping Ry Guy off for a little play date with his BFF!"

She meant it innocently. I wasn't stupid. But, out of everything she'd just said, something about my brain couldn't help but snag on the word *date.*

"We're just business partners," I clarified. "Working on the appearance for the Fest and all that."

"I heard." Something about her enthusiasm deflated, likely after catching my attempt at reestablishing the standards of Ryan's and my relationship. One quick glance at him, and I saw his smile had faded, too. "Ryan's team was thrilled to hear he was doing this."

"Were they now?" I asked, more to Ryan than his mom.

Ryan stopped at Gina's side. "They like when we do voluntary things. Makes it easier on them, but has the same result."

"No such thing as bad press?"

Ryan shrugged. "Depends who you ask."

I stuffed my hands into the front pocket of my hoodie, not sure how to respond to that.

Ryan's throat bobbed as he swallowed. "Should we, uh, get inside? It's a bit chilly out here."

"Oh, sweetie, this is nothing!" Gina said through a chuckle. "Just wait until the winter hits."

"I know, Mom. I used to live here, remember?"

"But then you got all used to the Texas heat," Gina reminded him. "You have to build up that Midwestern resilience again!"

"You're gonna be here for the winter?" I asked.

"It'll all depend on his physical therapy," Gina answered before Ryan could get a single sound out of his gaping mouth. He closed it quickly and his attention strayed to something on the ground. "We're hoping there's only two more weeks on these crutches, then he can begin proper rehab. Be back out on the field mid-season or so, right, honey?"

"Yup."

My eyes narrowed briefly as I watched Ryan, waiting for some sort of explanation, but that was all he offered.

Gina rubbed her son's arm. "At least it happened early on in the year. We have to count our blessings, even if it feels disappointing right now."

"Yeah, sure," Ryan agreed and adjusted his stance on his crutches. "Can we get going? My team's expecting a few updates. They have to know if they need to mail anything else."

"Else?" I asked, brow lifted. "What are they sending to begin with?"

"Oh, you know," Gina said with another dismissive wave. "Cardboard cutouts, headshots. I think I heard something about that neon sign you had at your last big appearance, didn't I, Ry—"

"Let's go, Harper," Ryan interjected.

He hopped forward, and, as best he could, tried to usher me away from his mom.

"Just like old times!" she repeated as we made our way into the library. I cast a glance back over my shoulder, almost tripping while trying to keep up with Ryan's impressive speed on his crutches, to see Gina waving. "Text me when you're ready to be picked up, sweetie! Good to see you, Harper!"

I gave a half-hearted wave and smile in return. Better than before, but still not necessarily friendly.

My attention settled on Ryan when I faced forward—or almost forward—again. He was watching the door to the library with all the determination of a man mentally preparing to be walloped by a linebacker, his mouth set in a straight line.

I didn't think I'd been so desperate to be able to read his mind again, like I'd been able to all those years ago, than I was in that moment.

"SO, I HAVEN'T had a ton of time to think about the float," I started once we'd breeched the supplies conversation, flipping the page in the notebook Mrs. Klein, our town librarian, had let me take from the stash of supplies usually reserved for forgetful students. "But we should probably go with Stallions colors. I mean, duh, right?"

Ryan didn't say anything. He twirled a pen through his fingers. Ever since we'd come in here, he'd been distracted. It had been like pulling teeth just to get him to contribute the list of items his team could supply us.

"And then, uh, it might be cute if we did Timberland Creek High colors, too. Not that we're going for cute. Maybe sentimental is the right word? Show where you came from and where you ended up and all that sort of crap—"

Ryan's phone vibrated on the table, and the noise and light naturally caught my attention.

His eyes drifted that direction, too, and he decided the person who'd texted him was important enough to get a reply back right away.

"Uh, yeah," I said while he typed. "So, anyway. Maybe we could talk to Coach Fitz about getting some of the current team on the float with you. They'd love that, and—"

"Fitzgerald is still coaching?"

I nodded. "Twenty-five years or something crazy like that. There was a big celebration for him at the homecoming game last year. Maybe the year before?"

A noncommittal hum was Ryan's response as he finished his text and set his phone on the table. When it lit up again, rapidly vibrating with the sequential texts that came in, I got a glimpse of who he decided was more important than our planning.

Madeline with a tongue-sticking-out emoji and the water droplets emoji.

Classy.

Ryan picked up his phone and began to type again. Maybe this was why he'd been distracted. He'd been waiting for her to text him.

Trying to pretend I hadn't noticed how he'd decided to degrade that particular contact, I said, "I think the boys would really like to be included. I'm not sure how much standing room we'll have, so maybe we can see if we could borrow the seniors for—"

Ryan's low chuckle and first genuine smile since we'd arrived had me slamming my palms on the table.

"*Shhh!*" Mrs. Klein hissed from her desk, as if the three of us weren't the only ones in the whole building.

I gave her an apologetic wave before I turned back to my companion who had the decency to look ashamed. And a little surprised, honestly.

"*You* invited *me* to a planning session, remember?" I said. "So why am I the only one planning while you text your—your booty call or whatever she is."

"I *am* planning," Ryan argued. He reached across the table and tapped my open notebook. "Remember that last page? All me."

"All *your team*," I retorted. "Unless you plan to order and ship everything?"

He rightfully grew quiet, knowing there was no chance of that. The fiery pits of hell would open before Ryan Caldwell lifted a finger. After sitting so close for the last hour, I was beginning to wonder if he got manicures. Actually, the more I paid attention, he had really nice hands. Big. Strong. Football-catching hands.

Strictly football-catching hands. Obviously. Although Madeline might say differently.

As if he'd read that thought, Ryan said, "She's not a booty call, by the way." I leveled a stare at him, which caused him to add, "I treat women with more respect than that. Geez, Harps."

"You seriously think I don't know what those emojis mean?" I might not have left Timberland Creek, but I didn't live under a rock. The internet still existed here, even if it was pretty spotty.

"That was Navarro," he explained, referring to one of the wide receivers on the Stallions. "He did it after our first pre-season game. Stole my phone while I was going through massage therapy."

As much as I wanted to accuse him of lying, I'd seen enough videos of Rafael Navarro to know he was definitely a well-known prankster in the league.

"Well, he had to get his inspiration from somewhere," I said as I lowered my head, my attention returning to the blank page of the notebook.

My pen had hardly touched paper when said paper was pulled

away.

"Hey!" I hissed, which earned me another reprimanding from Mrs. Klein. We were *never* going to be let back in here.

Ryan flipped the notebook shut and held it up by his head, well out of my reach. Like the mature, grown woman I was, I pouted and crossed my arms over my chest, knowing temporary defeat when I saw it.

"Give it back," I tried anyway.

"I will when you stop thinking I'm some sort of man-whore."

"First of all, I'm not shaming you for having sex—if that's what you are, in fact, doing with Madeline."

It took a beat, but Ryan finally admitted, "It was."

I tried not to let me surprise at the past tense show. So she was an ex, then? Or maybe he was just referring to the fact that he couldn't do much of anything right now—let alone fuck someone—with his injury. That as soon as he was healed, those emojis might very much become a reality for the two of them again.

"Good," I said, trying to sound nonchalant despite the sudden urge to flip the table overcoming me. "Go at it."

"You're still mad."

"I don't like the idea of you using her for your entertainment."

"Who says that's what I'm doing?" Ryan lifted a challenging brow. "What if I told you she means a lot to me?"

"Why don't you get rid of the emojis then?"

His following silence spoke volumes. Boys will be boys and

all that jazz, except I wasn't going to let him get away with it.

I refused to break his ocean-hued stare, and if he'd learned anything at the town hall the night before, he'd know how long I'd keep it up if necessary.

But he wasn't breaking either. He watched me, still holding the notebook in the air. Maybe my eyes were playing tricks on me, but every so often his brow would scrunch as the result of whatever he was thinking. And from my peripheral… was he actually grinning right now? It was infinitesimal, but I could have sworn the corners of his lips were curled up—or desperately wanting to.

Ryan sighed.

Victory.

I reached for the notebook as soon as he placed it on the table, and had barely begun to pull it towards me when his hand slammed down on it again. When I tried to tug, it went nowhere.

"What are you—?" I tried to ask, but the moment I met his gaze again, I was struck silent.

Those same blue eyes I'd just been staring into were watching me again, except this time, there was nothing playful about it. A storm had taken over the ocean, and I couldn't help the way my whole body tingled knowing I was the subject of their focus.

"For the record," Ryan said, his tone matching his stare. "I have more respect for women than you'll ever know. The other guys might treat them like toys, but that will *never* be me. That goes for in life *and* when I fuck them. I will *never* leave a woman hanging."

Holy shit. Hadn't seen that one coming. Not just the bluntness, but the direct reference to how he pleasures women.

At no point, not even when we were at our best with our friendship, had the topic of significant others—namely what we did with significant others in private—ever been breached. Sure, we'd each had our own handfuls of partners, but outside of the casual, "So how are things going with insert person's name here," we never really got into more detail. I'd never wanted to. Knowing what Ryan was doing in private with someone… it had always been a hard pill to swallow. That there was someone out there who would know him better than me.

He could divulge his deepest darkest secrets to me, but having sex? That was an intimacy we'd never experience with one another. I'd always be missing that part of him.

So, I nodded, once again not breaking the stare he'd restarted, even though this time I desperately wanted to. There was no way my body's sudden heat hadn't made it onto my face.

When I tugged again, he relented the hold on the notebook, and after a few more seconds, he freed me from his gaze as well.

"So," he said, by all accounts sounding and acting normal. "The float. Football seniors."

"Um," I said, still half in my daze. I shook my head, trying to clear my mind. "Yeah. Do you have any other ideas? Things your team might be able to provide?"

Thankfully, he talked more this time around, his phone and Madeline forgotten, even though it vibrated more than once. Then it went blessedly silent as Ryan continued to list what the Stallions could and could not provide us with for the float.

I let him keep going, my mind still not fully back to its normal state. I wasn't even sure I heard everything he'd said.

I was too busy watching his lips, how they moved as he spoke and how he wetted them as he thought things through. How his hands flexed on the table every so often. How even through the long-sleeve shirt he'd changed into since I'd seen him that morning, his muscles were perfectly visible, straining against the fabric.

I will never leave a woman hanging.

"Harper?"

My attention lifted from Ryan's lips to his eyes only to find him watching me with a furrowed brow.

"You good?"

"I—yeah. I'm fine. Just…" I sighed. "Sounds like we have a lot of work to do."

Ryan nodded slowly. The tension in his forehead eased. "We do. Probably gonna be seeing each other a lot over the next few weeks."

"Yeah," I agreed. "Probably."

And that's what killed me the most inside.

CHAPTER SIX

"WOO, AM I *parched!*"

Every single head in Sunrise Brews turned to see who'd joined us, and the present locals were not at all surprised to find Tori entering. Her husband, Jackson, was attached by their intertwined hands, chuckling at her usual antics and flair for making her presence known.

"You know coffee dehydrates you, right?" I asked.

"It's half water," she argued. "It can't be all that bad. Besides, I'm getting decaf."

"That's still—"

Hemi burst in from the back room, her eyes wide and set on Tori.

"I was right?" she asked.

A slow smile spread across Tori's lips until all her teeth showed. Jackson leaned down and kissed the side of her head before his wife nodded the confirmation to Hemi's question.

I'd never in all my years working here seen my boss actually squeal, but there she was, doing just that and rushing from behind the counter to give Tori a hug.

That's when it clicked. Holy shit.

The embracing women broke apart, giving Hemi the chance to pat Jackson on the arm, too.

"Surprise," Tori said, smiling, then placed her hands on her stomach.

Hemi pointed an accusatory finger. "I knew something was up when you stopped ordering your regular at Ziggy's a few weeks ago."

"Ugh," Tori groaned with pout. "It's tragic, but baby doesn't seem to like patty melts. Or red meat at all, really."

"When are you due?" Hemi asked.

"Next spring," Tori said.

"And do you know the gender?"

"Not yet." Tori looked adoringly up at her husband. "I know this one wants a girl, though."

Jackson shrugged when Hemi's confusion showed. "I'm not sporty enough for a boy."

"Total girl dad," Tori agreed.

I couldn't help but smile at their excitement. Hemi, on the other hand, had a word or two for Jackson about parenthood and why it didn't matter either way what they had; babies were miracles.

Tori placed her arm on her husband's shoulder and muttered something about being right back. He might have escaped the argument if it wasn't a well-known fact that Jackson Albrecht needed to prove himself correct in every situation. Hemi might have just booked him for the whole afternoon as he started his rebuttal speech.

"Hope he's not on deadline," I joked when Tori came to the front counter. "He'll be here all day."

"He'll get her. Don't worry." She cast a loving glance back over her shoulder.

"I'll bet you a free drink on the winner," I challenged. "Your payout will be convincing Rosie to cover something for me next time I'm at Ziggy's."

"Why do you think I have any sort of pull with Rosie?"

I tilted my head at her, knowing as well as anyone in this town that Rosie had practically adopted Tori and Jackson the moment they'd shown up in town just over two years ago.

"All right, fine," Tori said and extended her hand.

I shook it, even though I was secretly rooting for Jackson, too. His excitement was cute. "While we wait to see who wins the wager, what can I get you?"

"Decaf of my regular and Jackson's caffeinated regular. Oh—and make his a large. He *is* unfortunately on deadline at the moment."

"That's rough," I said as I punched in the order then turned the tablet around for her to pay. "Hey, did you ever ask him about the Fest?"

Tori nodded. "He's all in. I sent Jordi a text too. She said she's gonna check with Alfie, but right now their calendars are clear."

"That's awesome. Like, can you actually believe a celebrity might come here?"

"Eh." Tori shrugged. "Alfie's kinda lost his luster for me. He's like an annoying little brother at this point. But, hey—what about your little celebrity?"

I turned over my shoulder from where I'd started to prep the drinks to find Tori wearing a suggestive grin. "Who? Ryan?" She nodded, and I huffed a laugh. "Yeah, no."

"Why not?" Tori practically whined. "He's a hottie."

"Hey," Jackson piped up, mid-sentence. "I'm right here."

"I'm married, not blind, babe," Tori retorted. "Go back to verbally annihilating Hemi. I bet on you to win."

One blown kiss from his wife later, and Jackson did just that.

Tori shook her head as her body trembled with silent laughter. My own smile was plastered on my face.

"No, but for real," she said when she decided to pick our conversation back up. She tapped the counter excitedly, making sure she had my attention. "Give me the lore. What's up with him?"

"He's a football player who used to live here."

Tori rolled her eyes. "Not the basic lore. The lore that involves *you*."

I was thankful I was busy making their lattes. It made hiding my emotions that much easier when I said, "There is no lore involving me."

"I'm calling—sorry, Hemi," Tori called out preemptively to

the owner of the shop. Then with all the flair of a cheerleader, finished with, "Bullshit."

"I mean, we used to be friends," I said with a shrug. "But there's not much more to it than—"

If Tori's entrance could have been compared to the first warm, sunny day in the spring, the entrance of our latest patron was exactly the opposite.

It was like all the joy had been sucked from the room, every single patron falling into a hush, their eyes tracking the new foreboding presence before they went back about their business. Even Hemi and Jackson drew a temporary truce as they watched Dave Caldwell approach the front counter.

Tori stepped off to the side, her smile gone, replaced by the other side of my friend: the mama bear. I could only imagine how *that* was heightened in her current condition.

Watching from my peripheral as I finished up the Albrechts' orders, I saw Dave place his hands on the countertop, drumming his fingers, and sighed.

He turned just enough to catch sight of Tori—and jumped as if he hadn't realized there was more than one person present. It was his world, and we were simply pests within it.

Dave lifted one hand, his index finger aimed her way and face scrunched as he tried to place her.

"You," he said. "You're the one with the celebrity friend?"

Jackson ambled over to his wife's side, his argument forgotten in favor of protecting her. Not that Tori needed it.

As much was proven when she placed a hand on her hip and

said, "And you're the asshat who touts his son for clout."

Ouch. But I heard no lies.

Dave clearly hadn't been expecting that, though. His eyebrows rose into his hairline. He turned to Jackson. "This your wife?"

"Yep."

"You gonna, I don't know, teach her how to show some respect?"

Jackson's grin was the most beautiful thing I'd ever seen all day. "Nope." He wrapped his arm around Tori's waist. "She can decide who does and doesn't deserve her respect on her own."

I had to physically bite my tongue to keep my smile from showing when I placed their lattes on the pick-up counter. "Here you go," I said.

My widened eyes that came with the delivery were enough for Tori to get the hint. She didn't need to bother herself with this nonsense. As much as I appreciated her in my corner, I'd handled Dave Caldwell for most of my childhood. I could handle another month or so while his son and I were forced to work together.

"Let's go, babe," she said to Jackson even though her narrowed eyes were still on Dave. "We should get back to the store."

I'd never thought Jackson could be violent, but something about the way he stared down the other man made me wonder if he'd listen to his wife. The moment Tori's hand found his, however, they made their way out of the café.

"Good to see you've made some new friends in Ryan's absence," Dave commented when the front door clicked shut behind the couple.

I plastered on a forced smile. "What can I get for you today?"

"One of those pumpkin lattes for Gina. Ry wants that American thing—extra shot of expresso." I blinked slowly, hoping that when my eyelids opened again, I'd find out this whole interaction had been a nightmare. No such luck. "And I'll take a black coffee. None of that fancy crap."

I punched in the order as Hemi, having heard the whole thing, started with the more complicated drinks.

"We'll get those right up," I said, another one of my tight-lipped customer-service smiles making an appearance.

I'd almost finished filling his coffee when Hemi leaned over. The espresso machine was making enough noise that no one else could hear her when she said, "If you spit in that, I wouldn't fire you."

I grinned. "I'm afraid he'll have my DNA and use it for a voodoo doll or something."

She chuckled, no one any wiser to her antics, and I lidded the drink.

"So," Dave said, when I slid his coffee across the counter to him. "Sounds like you and Ry made some good progress yesterday."

I didn't know what about our most recent interaction made him think I'd want to engage in small talk. He probably just liked hearing the sound of his own voice, honestly.

"Yup." I wasn't wasting more than one word on this pointless conversation.

"Don't know what he told you, but his team wasn't too thrilled he's doing anything while he's here." Dave leaned a hip against the counter and half-crossed his arms over his chest with his drink in hand. "They want him resting up. That's why they thought he was coming here, and all that. We had to really play up the charitable deeds crap to convince them, but they still might send people out here to do check-ups."

Yup. He definitely just liked talking to talk. I didn't bother giving him further ammunition by letting him know Ryan had already told me how his team had reacted. It wasn't at all like Dave was describing. And despite my hesitation with Ryan, I still trusted his word over his father's.

"He should have just listened to them and never come home in the first place," Dave continued. "Now when he eventually goes back, he's gonna have to get in the right mindset again. Like when he first started in the league. Christ." He scoffed. "Kid played like shit. It was like he'd never seen a football before, let alone been nominated for a Heisman."

I grabbed the finished latte from Hemi, our eyes locking in the briefest moment of pity on our own behalf, and placed them on the pick-up counter.

"It was nice of Ryan to make Gina happy," I said.

Dave's brow scrunched. "Gina?" he asked. "What does Gina have to do with—?"

The bell above the back door jingled, and the *click-thud-squeak* of crutches on the old hardwood floor of the café followed.

Whatever confusion my comment had caused Dave was replaced by his son's sudden presence.

"There you are," Ryan said before his dad could speak. He checked the labels on the drinks then picked up his order. "Was wondering what was taking so long." His eyes darted between Dave and me, but the usual soft smile I'd noticed Ryan wore in public was missing. "You two catching up a bit?"

"If that's what you want to call it," I replied.

Nothing about that seemed to ease Ryan's apparent worry.

His dad slapped a hand on his back. "Harper and I were just talking about all the good work you two are doing," he said. "Your booth is gonna be a big hit."

"Hopefully," Ryan agreed. He lifted his drink to his lips when, suddenly, he startled.

"It's extra hot," I said in a panic. "I thought after the last time—"

"No, it's not the drink," Ryan assured me, and it was only then that his smile returned ever-so-slightly. "I just remembered—I forgot my notebook in the car. I wanted to show you what other ideas I came up with last night after we met." He turned to his dad. "Would you mind getting it for me?" He tapped his crutches. "Might take me a bit longer."

Dave opened his mouth—probably to argue—when Ryan, through gritted teeth and a tight-lipped smile, said, "Cameras."

I hadn't taken my attention off the Caldwell men to notice

that Ryan was right. While not everyone in Sunrise was paying attention to the hometown celebrity in their midst, plenty were. Two little boys sitting with their parents in the enclosed porch space up front were practically jumping out of their seats, doing nothing to hide their excitement about being so close to Ryan Caldwell.

"I'll be right back," Dave said with all the enthusiasm of a kid who'd just been told their parents ate all their Halloween candy.

"Should be on the console," Ryan called after him. Only when the door shut behind Dave did he turn to face me.

"What did you come up with?" I asked.

"A couple of things," he said. "But there's no notebook."

"Then why did you—?"

"Are you okay?"

I straightened my posture, leaning back from the counter. "Uh, yeah. Should I not be?"

He gave a one-shoulder shrug. "I could see you two talking through the front window. Thought it might be best to come in and prevent a potential World War III before it broke out."

"Why do you think that?"

"Well, given how the town hall went…"

Ryan's wide-eyed *yikes* face was enough to get me to crack a smile.

"Mr. Caldwell?"

We both turned at the sound of the tiny voice, finding the boys from the front room standing timidly beside Ryan. The smaller of the two clutched a phone in his hand like his life depended on it.

I could tell Ryan wanted to crouch down, seem less intimidating. The bravery these boys had shown by not only approaching an actual football player, but a football player of Ryan's stature, was pretty impressive. I didn't know if I'd have been able to do that at their age, no matter who it was.

So instead, he did the next best thing and put on the biggest smile possible. "Sup, bud," he said, addressing the one who had spoken. Then to the other boy added, "Hey there, dude."

The boy with the phone released it for the briefest moment to tap his tiny knuckles against Ryan's extended fist, wearing a shy smile.

"Do you mind if we get a picture, Mr. Caldwell?" the bigger one asked.

"Not at all," Ryan said, then, as if remembering himself, found the boys' parents. They gave their nods of approval, looking as though they appreciated Ryan's silent request for permission.

Nothing like some good, old-fashioned Midwest manners to further win over some fans.

"Why don't we come over here, alright?" he said, ushering the kids as best he could towards a nearby table. "I'm an old guy who needs to sit."

"You're not old!" the small boy exclaimed. "You run too fast, and old people can't do that!"

Ryan sat down, gently placing his crutches on the ground beside him, and now at a better height, had no trouble ruffling the boy's hair. The kid jumped away, laughing, and Ryan's smile was enough to make my heart melt. I'd never seen him interact with kids before, but I imagined he had to pretty regularly with all the league-sanctioned camps and appearances he went to.

He was a natural.

"Here," he muttered, extending his hand to take the phone. Once he had it, he turned to me. His smile turned into a full-fledged smirk when he realized I'd been watching.

Ryan lifted the phone. "Do you mind?"

I didn't bother giving Hemi any attention as I shuffled past her and took the phone from Ryan's hand. He muttered something to the boys, and they inched closer as a result until both of them were tucked comfortably under Ryan's arms.

"Say cheese," I instructed, earning two higher-pitched and one baritone echo.

And one bell jingle to ruin it all.

"What's this?"

Ryan twisted in his seat, and the two boys' smiles fell. As soon as they saw Dave, the smaller one ran back to his parents, finding solace in his mother's hug.

"Hey, it's alright," Ryan called after him. He waved the boy back. "Let's get the picture, then you can—"

Dave marched forward, and I reared back when he stopped between Ryan and me, extending his hand to block me from taking any more photos.

"You know you aren't supposed to be doing this for free," he hissed at his son. Then to the little boy—who looked like he was on the verge of tears—added, "Sorry, bud. Ryan's got stuff to do right now. No bugging him."

"He's not—" Ryan tried.

It was too late. The boy sheepishly stepped away from Ryan and offered a quiet, "Thanks, Mr. Caldwell," before he scurried over to me to retrieve the phone. I passed it to him, heartbroken at how crestfallen he looked.

"I got one," I let him know.

But not even that did anything to lift the boy's spirits. He simply took the phone and ran back to his parents. Dave was oh for two with the mama bears today, that was for sure.

"The fuck, Dad," Ryan said through gritted teeth, careful of his volume.

"You know what your agent said about taking unsolicited photos," Dave said. "Besides, aren't you supposed to be charging people for shit like that in a few weeks? No one's gonna wanna pay if they know you're giving it away for free."

"It's one picture," Ryan argued. "It's not that big of a deal."

"Tell that to Scott the next time we talk with him." He finally lowered his arm, and I wondered if he'd kept it up to prevent me from interfering. "There was no notebook, by the way. Looked all over the damn truck."

"Must have forgotten it at home, then."

I'd always had a weird fascination with old western movies, where the good guy and bad guy have a standoff in the town saloon. I mean, how realistic was it for them to just air their dirty laundry in the middle of town?

Now, I understood it wasn't all that odd as the Caldwell men stared each other down. In all our years of friendship, Ryan and his dad had never gotten along perfectly, but it had *never* been like this.

"Let's go," Dave finally said, his voice laced with ice, when he grew tired of his son's behavior. "Your mother is waiting."

The tightness in Ryan's jaw made it appear even more defined than it naturally was. He bent to pick up his crutches and only then, when he was sure his son would follow orders, did his dad make a move.

"I'll be in the car," he announced.

It wasn't until he'd made his way out of Sunrise again that I went to assist Ryan.

"Here," I said, then guided his hand to my shoulder as a support while he got out of the chair. He hopped on his good leg until the crutches were back under his arms.

"Thanks." He tried to smile, but it didn't reach his eyes. He must have known it, too, and cut the act, sighing. "I'm sorry you had to see that."

"And to think you came in here to prevent *me* from getting into a fight with him," I tried, hoping to bring some sort of ease back into the conversation—and room as a whole. The tension in the entirety of Sunrise could be cut with a knife. "Are… are you okay?"

"I'll be fine," Ryan assured me, but I wasn't sure I believed him. Not while he sounded so broken. "Before I go, I know the notebook was a lie, but I was serious about the new ideas."

"That's good. Wanna text them to me?"

"I was thinking maybe we could meet up again." Was it me, or did he sound embarrassed to suggest such a thing? "What're you up to tonight?"

"She's busy," Hemi called from behind the counter.

"Employee-employer pizza night," I clarified—as if that was a perfectly normal way for someone in their upper twenties to spend a Saturday night—when Ryan's confusion became evident.

"Oh… kay." He cleared his throat. "Then what about tomorrow morning?"

I paused, my face twisted in thought like I was going through a mental calendar. Ryan didn't need to know how utterly unexciting my life was.

"Yeah, I think that should be okay."

He knew I was full of shit. I could tell from the playful grin he wore.

Thankfully, he saved me from the embarrassment—or rather the blaring car horn outside did.

"Jesus motherfucking…" Ryan muttered under his breath. Then to me, he said, "I'll text you."

"Yeah. Alright."

The world record for speed crutching was broken by Ryan as soon as the car horn went off again. I watched, making sure he didn't accidentally trip in his haste.

"Looks like you two are getting along now."

I eyed Hemi sidelong as she replaced the chair Ryan had used at the table where it belonged.

"Kinda have to." When I noticed her suspicious expression, I added, "What's that face for?"

"Oh, nothing." Her sing-song tone told me it was definitely not nothing going on in that devious head of hers.

"You're worse than Tori," I accused.

"Better hope we don't hang out anytime soon then," Hemi said with a wink. "We might start match-making."

Before I could argue that, my boss gave me a little nudge. "Now get going," she said. "There's mugs to unload."

CHAPTER SEVEN

"OKAY, FESS UP," I said by way of greeting when I entered Hemi's home that night.

The tiny studio cabin was the perfect display of all that was Hemdeep Batra. Statues of Hindu gods and goddesses meshed perfectly with the bohemian-style furniture, statement pieces, and multitude of plants she used to decorate her space. Candles and a tapestry I knew she'd brought back from one of her visits to India—because she'd gifted me an identical one that I'd hung in my apartment—brightened the otherwise neutral room with some warm tones.

Hemi was at the island in her kitchen, pouring two glasses of wine—bless her—and looked up at my boisterous arrival.

"What could I have possibly done in the thirty minutes since you last saw me?" She gestured to the glasses in front of her. "Other than give myself a slightly larger pour."

Oh, so it was *that* kind of night. One where Hemi ignored the rules of her religion and went for a drink. Very few things—

most of them named Rosie Donahue, because no one could say no to sweet old Rosie—could make that happen.

I almost felt bad as I strode through the living room into the kitchen, where I set the pizza box I was carrying down with a slap on the wooden countertop. The moment I lifted the lid, the scent of melted cheese, onions, peppers, and Italian seasoning filled the air.

"Rosie put extra sausage on my half," I pointed out. "She *never* puts extra sausage unless you pay for it." I narrowed my eyes at Hemi. "What have you told her?"

"Nothing."

"Hemdeep…"

Hemi sighed. "Fine. I might have let it slip to her and Tori during our weekly get together that I'd—well, that I'd let it slip to *you* about Sunrise."

"*And?*" I goaded.

"And so she might be taking pity on you in the form of extra pizza toppings."

I narrowed my eyes, but they widened again almost instantly. "Is that why Tori was being so cheery with me today?"

"Tori's always cheery."

"Except for when she's scary," I countered. "And today, she was definitely rah-rah Harper—until Mr. Caldwell showed up."

"For the record, I also want you to experience nothing but happiness," Hemi said, passing me one of the wine glasses then a paper plate. "Which is why I called this after-work-hours pizza party."

"Parties are fun. I feel like this won't be fun."

Hemi groaned. "Your generation is just miserable."

"Only when we're left in the dark." I took a sip of my drink then said, "Spill the tea."

"Get your pizza," Hemi said, nodding toward the box. "Then you can join me in the living room."

"Can I have the bean bag?"

"You think my knees let me get out of that thing anymore?" Hemi asked. "You're the whole reason I keep it around."

A giddy chuckle escaped me as I pulled at the first slice—but it quickly turned into a gasp that had Hemi jumping back.

"There's extra cheese, too?" I exclaimed. Narrowed eyes found the woman standing opposite me. "I'm losing faith in you."

"Pizza. Bean bag," Hemi instructed, pointing at each respectively, and once we were both settled in our chosen seats, plates full of greasy food balanced on our laps, she sighed, ready to begin.

"So, you know the gist of what's happening," she said. "My mom is sick. I don't have many relatives left in India, and my brother is absolutely useless. I've had to go back when she has her treatments. Blah, blah, blah."

I quickly tore off the bite I'd been taking and lifted my hand to cover my mouth. Around the unchewed food, I said, "It's not 'blah, blah, blah.' That's your mom you're talking about."

"I know. But… it's complicated. In Indian culture, families are very tight-knit. Many move in together in order to be closer as our parents get older. It's easier to take care of them. But that was part of the reason I wanted to immigrate to America. I'd always been more independent, wanted to start my own business—that wasn't something I could accomplish as easily if I'd stayed."

"But because of your brother not being involved…" I prompted.

Hemi rolled her eyes. "I love my brother—I really do. But Nirmal is just like me in the sense that he doesn't necessarily follow traditional values."

One of my eyebrows lifted. "Meaning?"

"Where I don't follow the traditional collectivist mindset, he's not terribly keen on doing the whole take-care-of-the-elderly thing."

"How old are your parents?"

"It's more the principal of it than my parents actually being the standard definition of elderly," Hemi explained. "Regardless, Nirmal isn't doing a thing. So, I've been spending the money that should be going towards Sunrise on frequent trips to India. Making sure my mother has company—in addition to my father, of course."

Shit. Well, that explained a lot of it right off the bat, I supposed. Not that I knew anything about the cost of international travel—I'd barely traveled the continental United States, let alone the rest of the world—but I'd learned a thing or two about the cost of operating Sunrise. It was… not cheap. And that was putting it lightly.

"What about tourist season?" I asked. "Did that help with things at all?"

Hemi shrugged. "To an extent, but then I turned right around and spent it on a flight. Or do you remember when the espresso machine was down that one day?"

A high-pitched, trauma-laced laugh escaped beyond my control. How could I forget one of the most chaotic days of the entire summer? We'd ended up closing by noon because we couldn't handle the complaints, despite the clear signage and many announcements I'd shared via social media.

"It's just one thing after another," Hemi continued. "And I've unfortunately gotten to the point that, if I want to continue to run my business, I have to make some tough calls."

"Hemi." I set my plate of uneaten food to the side. "I know I was all pissy about losing a job—or potentially losing a job or whatever—but, like… this is your *mom*," I said, repeating the sentiment from earlier. "I can find somewhere else to work. It's not the end of the world. Do I want Sunrise to close? Fuck no—sorry for the cussing. But…" I shook my head, not really sure where I was going with that.

Somehow, Hemi knew exactly what my brain couldn't figure out. "But is losing my business a greater tragedy than losing my mother?"

I nodded.

This was a sensitive topic, considering I was in her employ, so I knew Hemi's hesitance to answer wasn't because she actually thought her mother's life was of lesser value than

Sunrise Brews.

I extended a hand, placing it on Hemi's foot since it was the only part of her I could reach. The bean bag chair was comfy, but the convenience it offered could be better.

"Family comes first. Always," I said.

"I know. Trust me—I know." Hemi sighed. "But do you know how hard it is for me to even consider having to close down? I'm not married. I have no children. This community has become my family while my own is in another country. And shutting down this business that so many people have told me they love—"

The moment her voice broke, I was out of the bean bag. It took seconds for me to place myself beside my friend on the couch, and a strangled laugh escaped her as she fought against her emotions.

"See?" she said, grabbing onto the hand I offered, palm-up, for her without argument. "I never could have gotten out of that thing so quickly."

I smiled, but ultimately decided to ignore her attempt at diffusing the tension. "Hemi, this community won't be mad at you. I promise everyone around here wants to help just as much as I do."

Hemi shook her head. "I know. Deep down, I know. But then I go to these town halls and hear about the businesses that are closing because they can't get any traffic, and I'm here complaining knowing full-well I'm going to be busy from open till close."

"You're allowed to complain." I huffed a laugh. "Heck, you're *more* than allowed to complain. I'm pretty sure I started bitching and moaning today when someone left a straw wrapper on their table after they left."

Hemi laughed, though it sounded different than her normal cheery cackle. The emotions were still too heavy.

"You've been put in a situation that you never thought you'd have to handle," I said. "I mean, maybe one day closing Sunrise Brews would have been inevitable, but not yet. You're in your prime, lady—even if you can't get out of bean bag chairs in less than five minutes anymore."

The next sound out of Hemi was a squeak as she leaned back, clutching my knee, her eyes squeezed shut.

"Stop," she pleaded. "You're going to make me cry."

"From laughter, I hope."

"I'm afraid it will be a mixture of a lot of things," she said on an exhale, opening her eyes and dabbing at the corners.

We fell silent as she composed herself, and only when I was sure she was okay again—as okay as she could be, anyway— did I speak again.

"You know people wouldn't be mad if you took the money from the Fall Festival fundraiser. They'd want to help you just like they want to help any other business."

"I can't." As one of the strongest people I knew, Hemi truly sounded defeated. "Not knowing what I know. My income from Sunrise is triple—if not quadruple—what some of these other businesses asking for funds are seeing. It would feel like stealing if I took anything away from them."

In that moment, I knew I was a shit person because I would have felt no guilt at taking from the funds that were raised. That was the whole point of the fundraiser, after all—to help the businesses in need.

It wasn't that I didn't care about any of those people. Many I'd known for most of my life. Hemi had been right about that; the Timberland Creek community was like one big blended family. The last thing I wanted was for any of them to suffer.

But I couldn't deny there was a little bias when it came to Hemi's situation, no matter how hard I tried to keep it suppressed.

"You're a good person, Hemdeep Batra," I said. "I'm glad I get to have you as a mentor."

"You're the one keeping me strong, Harper." The surprise confession was enough to get my eyes welling with tears, too. "I couldn't have kept things running for even this long if I hadn't had you around."

And that was it. The one thing I needed to hear. That would spur me forward.

I didn't care what Hemi said. She'd worked too long and too hard for her dream to come true only for it to come crashing down before she wanted to call it quits on her own terms.

We'd worked together long enough that I knew when Hemi said something, she meant it with her whole heart. There wasn't time for wasted breath. So, from the two conversations we'd had on the topic, I knew two things for certain: Hemi was truly at the point where she saw no other choice but to close down the business and she refused to get any financial help.

The thing was, she didn't need to take from the Fall Fest fundraiser—or at the very least, she didn't know that she was going to.

Because I *was* going to help her, whether she liked it or not. And I had the perfect tool at my disposal when it came to doing just that.

CHAPTER EIGHT

A DAY OFF work couldn't have come at a better time. After the night I'd had at Hemi's, I needed to step away from Sunrise. I still couldn't wrap my head around the fact that—according to what I'd learned later, after the two of us demolished half a pizza and a bottle of wine—within a year, a place that meant the world to me could simply cease to exist.

Sunrise Brews. My friend. My job. My apartment. They'd all be gone in the next twelve months.

Too bad I had a say in it. A secret say, but a say nonetheless.

That's why I was rumbling up the still-familiar road in my old car before nine in the morning.

Thankfully, the Caldwells appeared to be awake. Or at least one of them was. When I pulled up to the house, Gina's silhouette was visible through the giant front window, my view from outside stretching from the living room, further into the house towards the kitchen of the old two-story. Despite Ryan's newfound riches, it looked like his parents hadn't decided to use any of it to update their home. Though there was a nice, shiny white Audi in the driveway. The truck was blessedly missing.

It had been years since I'd come to this part of town, but then again, driving past anyone's house was just a random occurrence more often than not. Subdivisions weren't really a thing around here, namely because so much of the land in Timberland Creek was still devoted to farming.

When developers did decide to build, it was for the purpose of tourism, anyway. They'd make way more money on yearly rentals during busy season than they would on a one-off purchase from a townie.

So, the rest of us took what we could find, some people living *miles* away from their next neighbor.

The Caldwells weren't quite that secluded, but enough so where I was surprised to see a few other cars pulled off to the side of the road across the street.

I put my car in park and got out, eyeing the unfamiliar company over my shoulder as I made my way to the front door. A bell chimed a familiar *ding-dong* within the home when I pressed it.

Muted conversation came from the other side of the door— a deep timbre and a chipper, higher-pitched voice. So, Gina wasn't alone, and her male companion made himself known when the door clicked unlocked and opened.

Ryan leaned on a crutch, wearing nothing but some plaid pajama bottoms that hung low on his hips. I couldn't stop myself from stealing a glance at his well-toned abs and the trail of light hair that disappeared beneath the waistband.

I definitely didn't remember that from the many trips we'd made to the beach during summer breaks in high school and college. The collage of black-ink tattoos that adorned his arms, shoulders, and pectoral on his right side had also definitely not been there.

"Harper?" he asked, his voice still rough from disuse. Given the state of his tousled hair, too, there was a good chance he'd just woken up. "What are you doing here?"

"I, uh…" I tried, realizing I needed to actually speak, not just ogle him. No—I wasn't doing that. I was simply taking in all the changes to the man that had once been my best friend. The surprising and, what some might call, attractive changes. "Didn't you say you wanted to meet up this morning?"

"Yeah, but I didn't realize this morning meant"—his eyes strayed past me to the sun peeking over the field across the street—"when the sun has hardly even risen."

"It's almost nine. The sun's been up for a bit."

"Okay, then when *I've* hardly even risen," Ryan argued, proving my assumption about him just waking up correct.

"I texted you I was coming." As soon as the words left my lips, I unlocked my phone to make sure I hadn't just *thought* about sending the text and actually did it. Wouldn't have been the first time that had happened in my lifetime.

"I put my phone on silent when I sleep."

"Oh, well." I peeked around him into the house where I could just barely make out the sound of bacon frying, if I were to guess based on the accompanying scent. "I can go grab coffees and come back. Americano extra hot again?"

"You're already here," Ryan said. "Why waste the gas?"

I couldn't help but grin. "We're in Timberland Creek, not San Antonio, dude. It'll take me approximately five minutes to get to Sunrise Brews and back."

"You're not going to work on a day off, even as a customer." He opened the door wider, providing more room between it and his crutches. "Come on. Bacon's almost ready, and I got Mom a Nespresso for Christmas that you can teach us to actually use."

One of my brows lifted. "You can't use an espresso pod?"

"Stop being a smartass and accept my invite. Jesus," Ryan said through a smile that faded as soon as he looked across the street again. "Hurry."

His sudden urgency had me following orders. As soon as I was within the Caldwell home, Ryan closed the door and locked it again—with both locks.

"Mom, I'm closing the curtains," he called out as he hobbled over to the front window. Seemed like he'd forgone his leg brace as well as the second crutch, but if the grimaces he made—and tried very poorly to hide—with each step were any indication, he was still in a lot of pain.

"Are they back?" Gina shouted from the other room.

Ryan waved for me to follow him, and during the slow journey to the kitchen, I took in the sights of the Caldwells' house. Just like the outside, the inside hadn't changed much. They'd painted, falling into the popular neutral-wall trends, but the same décor and family photos from the last two decades remained where I'd last seen them.

Mrs. Caldwell was at the stove, flipping that bacon I'd smelled with tongs, when Ryan and I entered. He pulled out a seat for me and I gave him a look. If one of us was sitting, it definitely wasn't the person with two working legs.

"I think they were recording this time," Ryan said. His eyes darted to the chair and back to me.

I placed my hands on my hips, and he grinned.

"We'll have to call Sherriff Walters again and get another one of his boys out here." Gina shook her head and tsked. "It's such an invasion of privacy."

"Wait," I said, looking between the Caldwells—and giving Ryan a particularly stern glare as my eyes mirrored the motion his had just given me. "Those are just random people parked out there?"

"They've been showing up ever since reports started sharing I was working on my rehab at home." Ryan's eyes narrowed at me as he spoke. The poor bastard actually thought I was gonna cave. "Doesn't take a rocket scientist to find out where that is."

No, it did not. Ryan had been the so-called Cinderella story of the league when he'd first been drafted. The boy that had come from "nothing" and gone on to make a name for himself.

Newsflash: coming from a small town didn't mean coming from nothing. Just because we didn't have twelve Starbucks and two half-vacant malls, didn't mean we weren't thriving here.

But the PR move was basically handed to Ryan's team the moment those stories had started showing up. They took that poor small-town boy image and ran with it—all the way to the playoffs his rookie year, actually.

One quick Google search of "Ryan Caldwell hometown" and probably a million articles about Timberland Creek would pop up.

How they'd found his actual childhood home address, though...

I took a step forward and extended my hands, placing them on Ryan's shoulders. For a moment, he seemed very unsure of what I was doing, and honestly, same. This was the first time I'd touched Ryan so casually since we'd been reunited, and of course it was happening while he was shirtless. But he vibrated with quiet laughter as I tried to push him into the chair.

"We think they come from out of town; no one from around here would bother Ryan like that," Gina said. "But I don't care what you and your father have been telling me, Ry. I still think—oh."

In the midst of battling with a man twice my size, I'd admittedly gotten myself into a questionable situation. Ryan didn't seem to think so, now sitting on the chair, grinning like a fox. But I could see from where I stood with my legs on either side of the seat and my hands on Ryan's bare shoulders, where Gina was probably shocked.

It wasn't *my* fault he was so big. Or that gravity was at fault for me toppling forward when Ryan spontaneously decided he was done standing. His body had been the only thing available for me to catch myself on, and straddling the chair had been the only option unless I'd wanted to land directly on his lap.

And there was *no way* that was happening. Dumping the bacon grease over the top of my head sounded more appealing.

"So." I waddled backward until the chair was no longer an obstacle and tried to lean casually against the side of the kitchen table. "They just, like, watch you all the time?"

I needed them to take the diversion. With Ryan still grinning and Gina's eyes darting between the two of us, though, I wasn't sure I'd get that. She knew Ryan and I had never been interested in each other the way her stare was suggesting. Hell, we hadn't even kissed each other before. Not even to just try it out and confirm that we were definitely-one-hundred-percent-without-a-doubt destined to remain friends. Nothing more. Nothing less.

Well, we were nothing less for a minute. But I couldn't deny part of me was definitely warming back up to the familiarity of Ryan Caldwell as a part of my life.

It was Ryan who saved me from impending doom when he said, "They'll stake out the house for a few hours. Wait for me to come out. Say 'Go Stallions' or some shit and try to ask for a picture." He gave an annoyed shrug. "It happens."

"At your place in San Antonio, maybe, but not here," Gina added. It seemed like she'd thankfully decided whatever she'd been thinking—*incorrectly thinking*, might I add—wasn't worth perusing. "Did you speak with your community security about that by the way, sweetie?"

Ryan rolled his eyes, and in the most teenager-y way possible, groaned, "Yes, Mom."

"Good. They shouldn't be letting random people through the gates in this day and age."

"It's not like I don't have plenty of security systems at my house," Ryan mumbled.

Oh, so he owned a house. In a gated community.

The football salary was showing.

"I hope those weirdos don't ruin whatever it is you kids have planned today," Gina continued as she removed the cooked bacon and added some raw slices onto the skillet. "Ryan won't tell me a single thing about your plans, Harper. Can you believe it?"

Ryan was already waiting for me when I eyed him sidelong. "Doesn't sound like him at all."

"He did bring something home yesterday after our little family outing. You make a *delicious* pumpkin spice latte, by the way. I thought Dave was gonna throw it out the window if I talked about how yummy it was one more time."

That definitely sounded like Dave, but I wasn't about to admit that out loud. Instead, I changed the subject. "What did you get?"

"Here." Ryan put a hand on the kitchen table for a support, then hoisted himself out of the chair. Damn. All that work for nothing. "Mom, how long do you think breakfast will be?"

"Another fifteen minutes or so. Still have to cook the eggs. Oh, and Harper, maybe you can show me how to make that latte with my Nespresso!"

Ryan's grin reached his eyes when our stares met again.

"Yeah, sure. I'd love to," I said, knowing the odds of them having the proper ingredients were slim, but I'd still teach her how to make a latte in general. Teach a person to fish, and all that.

"I can show you what I got while she finishes up here," Ryan said, then abruptly turned over his shoulder. "Unless you need the help?" he added to Gina.

His mom harrumphed. "I can do this with my eyes closed after so many years of cooking for you boys. You and Harper need to get moving with this little project of yours if you want it done on time."

She wasn't wrong about that. Ideas were fine and dandy, but I wouldn't lie that pulling everything off was my biggest fear. Even with the help of Ryan's team sending us supplies, there were still only a few weeks to accomplish everything. And I needed this to be a success now more than ever after the conversation with Hemi.

"We'll be back to help you set the table," Ryan said. "Call for us, like, five minutes before you're ready."

"Thanks, sweetie. You two go have fun."

Ryan hopped once on his good leg until he could reach his crutch. I took up looking for the other, thinking maybe he'd left it behind in a rush to get the front door when I'd arrived, but it was nowhere to be found.

"Only one for now," he told me, as if he'd read my thoughts. "C'mon. The surprise is in the garage."

CHAPTER NINE

RYAN SWEPT OUT his free arm, encouraging me to enter the dark garage. That didn't last long, however, before he flipped on a switch and a soft hum accompanied the fluorescent light that filled the room.

It smelled like the cut grass that I saw in bags on the wall opposite where we'd entered. A plethora of sports gear—primarily football—hung on hooks and had been organized in some contraption of what looked like Dave's making. Maybe he'd used all the tools in the fancy metal cabinet that was right beside it.

None of that had been there when I'd frequented this house before. Seemed like after Ryan moved out, Dave and Gina had taken it upon themselves to do a little bit of tidying up.

But the light not only gave me the ability to see all the new changes, but also a new addition.

"What the hell is this?" I asked.

I approached the flatbed trailer taking up the entirety of the garage, and ran my hand along the rail. It was in pretty decent condition, actually. A few scrapes and scuffs, but nothing too bad.

Ryan stuck his single crutch on the floor and used it for balance as he hopped down the two steps that led to the garage from the house. Once he was on solid ground, he came to join me. Again, he grimaced each time he put pressure on his injured leg.

"That," he said, clearly trying to sound cheerful, but it came out tight, "is our float. The base of it, anyway."

"Where did it come from?"

"You remember Mr. Cochran?" Ryan asked. When I nodded, he continued, "It's his. We went to pick it up after the whole… ordeal yesterday."

"Right," I said with a nod, my eyes drifting from Ryan to the flatbed again. "It's nice. That was kind of him to let us borrow it."

"My team overnighted some stuff that we can use to decorate it, but I thought maybe today we could work on some little stuff? Polish her up. Put up some streamers or something."

"Streamers?" The idea of Ryan Caldwell going from celebrations hosted by the NFL to riding on a float with cheap birthday party decorations we bought at Piggly Wiggly seemed incomprehensible at the moment.

"Or something," he repeated. Maybe he realized how odd it sounded, too. "I think we'll get some official Stallions décor in the boxes when they arrive."

"You think it'll match whatever we manage to get around here?"

Ryan's lips pursed as he surveyed the trailer. "I tried to explain what the Fall Fest is. Sent a few pictures my mom had from last year's event."

"And?"

He sighed and sat down on the back of the flatbed, his face finding his hands. For the briefest moment Ryan's elbows rested on his knees, but the added pressure to the already injured area had him jumping back immediately.

"Truth be told, we might not need this trailer," he said, slapping a palm down on the surface. "For all I know, the team's marketing department will send a full fucking display. LED lights. Confetti cannons. I don't know. I still don't know how I convinced them to support some rinky-dink parade."

"Your dad said something like that," I said. When Ryan's attention popped up to me, I clarified, "Yesterday. Before you came into the café."

His following expression was one of anger. A little annoyance was definitely in there. And I definitely couldn't miss the embarrassment, too.

"I'm sorry he's been such an ass to you," Ryan said.

"He's always been an ass," I countered. "I was just too young to realize it—or fight back."

Ryan huffed a laugh. "Yeah. That was his first mistake. Thinking you'd sit back and take it."

A silence fell over us that, for the first time since I'd known him—even in these awkward few days where we were getting reacquainted with one another—made me feel uncomfortable. Like if I didn't break it, we might never speak again.

The only problem was I had only one question on my mind.

"He, uh—your dad mentioned something else yesterday. About your team not wanting you back here at all."

Ryan stiffened, but didn't say anything, so I went on.

"I thought it was kinda weird how he gave me this look when I said you were just being a good son and all that." He still hadn't looked at me, his gaze still trained on something by the garage door. "Didn't you say your mom asked you to come back? So she could take care of you or whatever?"

Finally, Ryan showed some sign of life and shrugged. "She's happy I'm here, that's for sure."

That was a roundabout answer if I'd ever heard one.

"I bet," I said, trying not to let the frustration starting to bubble within me show. "It's definitely been a while. Since you've been in Timberland Creek, that is."

I wanted to pull the words right back into my mouth the moment they left, but I couldn't help myself. The desire to call Ryan out on leaving us—leaving *me*—behind had been burning in me since he'd first crutched into the town hall meeting.

But if I was to look on the plus side of finally letting my feelings show—albeit in a pretty passive aggressive way—it was that Ryan finally turned to me.

"I mean," I continued before he could think of any excuse. I was on a roll and needed to keep going before whatever had kept me quiet the last few days came back to shut me up again. "I feel like it would've been pretty well-known if you'd shown up—even for Christmas or, you know, your parents' birthdays or something."

Ryan leaned back on the trailer bed, resting all his weight on his palms. "What are you trying to say, Harper?"

Oh, good—now we were both annoyed. Although, I didn't really understand why he had any right to be. I wasn't the one who'd disappeared. Or kept the other person's number and never used it. Or failed to realize that maybe it *could* be used to warn his supposed best friend that he was finally coming back home after being gone for half a decade. Then when we were finally hanging out again act like nothing had fucking happened and everything was perfectly fine and normal and I hadn't been shattered into a million pieces when he decided I wasn't good enough for—

"Shit. Harps."

His crutch was forgotten, his pain ignored but very visible as Ryan limped over to me. His hands went up to my face. In all my internalized rage, I hadn't realized tears had started falling.

He wiped them away with his thumbs, but he never stopped holding me—forcing me to look up at him.

"You still had my number and never called," I whimpered when I could finally find the strength to form words again. "You never even *texted*, Ryan. I haven't heard from my best friend in five years, and then suddenly you're just… here." I shook my head in disbelief. "*Why* are you here?"

Ryan's throat bobbed as he swallowed. "I needed to rest."

"Then why are we doing this?"

His whole body rose with his inhale, and the sharp focus in his stare somehow got stronger. "Doing what?" he asked, his thumbs making a minute movement. It was more of a twitch, really. Like he was holding himself back from brushing them across my cheeks again.

"This stupid fucking project," I said, and Ryan exhaled, that intensity that had been so obvious exiting his body with his breath. "Am I just being stupid agreeing to help you with this? Are you going to disappear again when the Fall Fest is over?"

In all the years I'd known him, Ryan Caldwell had never been one to hold back. At the beginning, maybe, but not once we'd gotten to know each other. He told me every thought that ran through his mind, but now? Now, it was clear as day that he was restraining himself. Sometime during the last five years, he'd unsurprisingly lost that trust in me.

"Harper, there's…" He trailed off, then sighed, closing his eyes. "There's more that you need to know."

For the briefest moment, hope ignited within me that I might finally get the answer I'd wanted for the last three days of playing into blissful ignorance.

But then the door to the house opened.

"Well, whatcha think?" Gina said by way of greeting, a bright smile on her face.

Ryan's hands had already dropped to his sides, and I took the newfound freedom to move, angling myself away. Gina didn't need to see my remaining tears.

"It's great," I somehow managed to squeak out. "Can't wait to get to work."

Ryan's stare burned into me, but I didn't dare look up at him.

"I just know you two are going to have the best float in that whole parade. Now, who's ready for some breakfast?"

"I, uh, actually think I might head out." I hastily wiped at whatever tears were still present, then tucked a piece of hair behind my ear to disguise the action. "Sorry for dropping in, I just forgot that I had this… I'm meeting someone at Ziggy's for the games later."

"Isn't the first game at noon?" Gina asked.

"You can stay," Ryan said. All my hard work getting rid of the tears was almost undone when his hand brushed against mine. "Please."

"Yeah, sweetie. Don't feel like you're intruding; Ry Guy and I are happy to have you here. And hey—you still have to teach me how to make a pumpkin spice latte, remember?" Gina added.

"Rain check?" I asked. Mrs. Caldwell's smile faded as soon as I finally allowed her to see my face. "I really—I have to go."

"Harper—"

"I'll text you later, okay?" I put on a brave face as I looked up at Ryan. I couldn't miss the way his hand lowered, as if he'd been reaching out to hold me back.

Dejected. That was the only word I could think to use to describe the way he was watching me. We both knew we weren't done here, but there was no way I'd be able to sit at the kitchen table in the Caldwells' home and pretend like everything was alright.

Besides, we had a float to build. We'd have to reconnect at some point. Regardless of where we ended up, I'd have to put on my big girl pants and buck up. He was my last hope of helping Hemi, and even if I was mad at him, I needed Ryan.

He watched me silently for a moment before he finally nodded. "Have fun at Ziggy's."

I knew I'd been the one to insist I leave, but a small part of me deflated at the ease with which he let me.

It made me wonder if it was simply that painless for him to be without me.

CHAPTER TEN

IT WOULD HAVE been a bit excessive, even for a football lover like me, to camp out at Ziggy's all day. I knew there were plenty of guys in town who'd be there, but that almost made sitting alone at the bar worse.

I had a lot of confidence, but not nearly enough to subject myself to the "poor Harper; sitting all alone" comments that would make their way through the grapevine as soon as the guys made it home to their girlfriends and wives.

So, I called in back-up.

Dad sipped on his beer, his eyes glued to the TV and a game that wasn't even featuring our team of choice. In fact, it was the Bears. Around these parts, some might argue that he should be charged for treason. Bill Bennett versus the State of Wisconsin. Crime? Giving the enemy *any* sort of attention.

I pursed my lips, trying to find something I could bring up, but I was pretty sure I'd exhausted my options. This was how

Dad got when things were busy at the shop and he was pulled away. As the town's only regular mechanic, people relied pretty heavily on him. Combine that with being a people pleaser? Not even Hercules couldn't carry the amount of pressure Dad placed upon his own shoulders.

"Did Cam say if he's coming home for Thanksgiving this year?"

"Huh? What?" Dad mumbled as he set down his drink. Just in time, too. "Picked off! Those stinkin' Bears could only dream of having the legacy of QBs Green Bay's seen."

"Dad." I didn't normally snap at people, but I felt I had no other choice in that moment. "Cameron. Your second son?"

"What about him?"

Dear Lord.

I sighed and wrapped my hand around my own pint glass. "Never mind…"

There was no denying I was Dad's little princess. He'd do pretty much anything for me as soon as I asked—hence his presence at Ziggy's. His attention span, however, rarely got the memo.

"Harper?"

Ah, shit.

I turned in the barstool, a smile ready as I greeted, "Brent. Hey. What's up?"

Brent Taylor was handsome by conventional standards, and it was showing now. His dark hair swept in a side-part—I didn't think he had any other choice with how long it was getting—

and his brown eyes shining as bright as his smile.

"Brent," Dad said. He extended his hand. "Good to see you again, son."

There wasn't a doubt in my mind that if I hadn't just said his name, Dad wouldn't have remembered it. Never mind that Brent had been my first real boyfriend and a frequent flyer as my date to dances in high school.

Plus, Brent was the manager at Piggly Wiggly. It was hard for anyone in this town who bought groceries not to know him.

"Good to see you, too, Mr. Bennett," Brent said, accepting Dad's hand. Then he turned his smile-lit face to me. "How've you been, Harper? It's been a while."

No, it hadn't been. I'd seen him the week before—surprise, surprise—while I'd been grabbing some more peanut butter. And he'd stopped by my table at Ziggy's when I'd watched the pre-season game where Ryan got injured with Derek and Sarah.

What he'd *actually* meant to say was, "It's been a while—since I've seen you naked."

It wasn't that I was purposely avoiding Brent. He was reliable as ever anytime I needed a good lay. It was just that he wasn't good *enough* for me to be begging on my knees for him to constantly fuck me.

"Things have been busy, I guess," I excused with a shrug. "Lots of work. You know. The usual."

"I get that, but hey—at least I got to see you here, right? I won't keep you two, though. Don't want to interrupt father-daughter game day."

"No, no." Dad picked up his drink and downed what was left. "You two have fun. I have to get back to the shop as it is."

Brent snapped his fingers. "I've been meaning to bring my car over, actually. It's been making some clinking sound?"

Dad's face scrunched, immediately going into Mechanic Mode. "Change your oil lately?" When Brent shrugged, he said, "Bring it in next week. I'll check that for you. Otherwise, it might be your brakes. Nothing some new fluid can't fix."

"You're the man, Mr. Bennett." Brent beamed.

Dad slapped a hand on Brent's back as he got up from his stool. "We'll catch up more when you bring your vehicle in," he said. "And I'll see you soon, Harps." He planted a kiss on the side of my head. "Have fun, princess."

"Bye, Dad."

If he'd noticed the plea in my tone to stay—save me—he didn't comply. He was out the door of Ziggy's in record time, full of beer and free from watching the Bears.

Brent's hand found the back of the stool Dad had just vacated.

"This seat taken?" he asked, then chuckled at his own joke.

I tried to do the same, but it came out flat. Just like Dad, Brent didn't pick up on my misery and took a seat beside me.

"So," he said, his voice lower now. "I've missed seeing you."

Brent's hand found mine, and his thumb brushed along the back. A chill went up my spine—and not the good kind. Not like the one that had shot through me as soon as Ryan's hands had found my face earlier. When his thumbs had caressed my cheeks. When he'd stood so close that I'd been wrapped in his body's warmth.

Not like now, as my heart started beating faster just thinking of it all.

My eyes lifted from where I'd watched Brent's hand stroke my skin. He was still grinning.

Dad was officially getting one less Christmas gift.

THIS HAD TO be some bizarre form of torture. Never in all my life had I thought I'd learn so much about the grocery business as I had in the last hour.

I didn't remember Brent ever being so damn talkative. Then again, I didn't remember the last time I'd hung out with Brent and we'd done anything more than exchange pleasantries, have sex, and say, "Do this again soon?" before one of us left the other's home.

Even in high school, I couldn't recall Brent being so hyper-fixated on his job. He'd started his role at the Main Street Market as soon as he'd turned sixteen. Maybe it was his management position that had changed things? His pride at working up the ladder? Working for a chain rather than a local grocer?

"So then, this guy goes and asks me if we carry this… this—you know, I don't actually even know what it is." Brent drummed his fingers on the bar top as he tried to recall the detail. "Have you ever heard of Waggy?"

I raised a curious brow. "Waggy? Is it, like, a dog food?"

"No, no. He was at our butcher counter. But he kept asking for it, and I had to keep telling him we don't have any Waggy beef—"

"Wagyu."

My whole body tensed at the single word spoken in the deep voice I thought for sure I wouldn't hear again today.

Brent didn't know any better, though, when he pivoted in his seat to face Ryan. "What was that?"

"Wagyu beef," Ryan repeated. "It's a Japanese cattle breed. Really tender meat."

I lifted my beer—my third—to my lips, hoping the cold amber liquid would help cool the heat that had suddenly overcome me.

"Leave it to the hotshot to know all the lavish meats," Brent said through a chuckle. "Ryan fucking Caldwell. How are you, man?"

He extended his hand, but Ryan stood there unmoving, his hands clutching the grip of his crutches. I turned just enough to catch his eyes dart down to where Brent and I's thighs were touching. Where Brent's other arm was wrapped around the back of my stool.

I brought my legs tighter together, trying to prevent any sort of contact with my companion in the crowded bar.

A sly grin spread across Ryan's lips. "Mind if I take a seat?"

"Yeah, yeah, you betcha," Brent said, the Wisconsin boy

coming out.

I couldn't tell if it was the Midwestern politeness that had been instilled in all of us since childhood, or his desire to please the local celebrity that had Brent moving at the speed of light. But within seconds he was out of his barstool, and Ryan was seated beside me.

"So," Brent said, a bit too enthusiastically already. It was no secret that Ryan had been avoiding a lot of people around here. His outings to Sunrise and the library had been the most public appearances I was aware of. Anyone in Ziggy's would have a field day getting the chance to chat with him, and here he was, plopped down right in the middle of the chaos—on game day, no less. An open invitation. "What's up, man? How've you been since—"

"I actually wanted to talk with Harper alone, *man*," Ryan interrupted.

Any hope Brent had shown since he'd first arrived at Ziggy's faded. Here the guy had been thinking he'd get laid *and* talk with an actual professional football player. Ryan crushed that dream with one sentence.

Because there was no freaking way anyone would dare challenge the tone Ryan had just used. He'd left no room for argument.

"I..." Brent was clearly thrown off but, bless him, was he trying to keep his composure. "Yeah. Sure. You two probably have a lot of catching up to do while you're in town, right?"

"Right." Ryan spoke as he lifted a hand to wave down a

bartender.

And then, as casually as if he'd done it a million times before, Ryan's other arm replaced where Brent's had been, resting on the back of my stool. My breathing picked up as soon as I felt the press of his muscles against my shoulders.

I swallowed, forcing myself to hone in on the game.

"Well, then." Brent's eyes moved between Ryan and me. "I'll, uh, see you around, Harper."

The acknowledgement that he'd never talk to Ryan again was clear. "Yeah. I'll see you."

Brent shuffled off with one more backwards glance at my new companion who was still more intent on getting a bartender's attention than bidding our old high school buddy farewell.

He'd been paying closer attention than I'd thought, though, because the second Brent wandered out of earshot, Ryan said, "So Brent Taylor, huh?"

Oh, this absolute ass.

"How's Madeline?" I shot back.

I'd expected him to show some sign of remorse, but instead, Ryan grinned. "I deserved that," he admitted, removing his arm and the warmth I hadn't realized it had brought me. "But seriously, Harps. I know you two have a history, but you can do better."

"Just because we dated for a bit, doesn't mean we have history," I argued.

His eyes slid my way, his playfulness fading. "You and him

did a bit more than date, if I remember correctly."

I turned, trying to hide the color that found its way onto my cheeks. I forgot he'd known that. It had been at Brianna Howard's homecoming after party. I'd gone with Brent as my date since Ryan had just started seeing someone and we therefore couldn't instate our we're-each-other's-dates-if-we-can't-find-anyone-else pact.

I'd never imagined losing my virginity that night, let alone to Brent Taylor. But it just… happened. One minute we were kissing in a corner like everyone else—as high schoolers do—then the next I was asking him if he wanted to go somewhere more private.

Ryan had watched me go, stopping his own activities with his new girlfriend to do so. An hour later, when I'd shown back up in the barn where the party was taking place, he'd been the first to confront me.

He'd said something similar back then, too.

You can do better.

"But you're still involved with him?"

"There aren't a whole lotta options around here," I muttered. "And, what? Did you think I'd just stay celibate the rest of my life?"

It would have been impossible to miss the way Ryan's jaw tensed before he said, "Not at all."

I might have questioned him on his behavior, but that was the moment Rosie finally decided to pay him some attention.

"Sorry 'bout the wait, darling. What can I getcha?" She

pointed to my half-empty drink. "You want another one while I'm here, sweetie?"

I nodded. "Thanks, Rosie."

"And I'll take whiskey on the rocks," Ryan said.

"Any preference?" Rosie asked as she poured my fresh beer.

"You have Macallan?"

I couldn't help but snicker at the face Rosie made.

"Honey, I can introduce you to my friend Jack or my friend Jameson," she said as she set my drink in front of me. "Take your pick."

"Do they have a third friend named Makers?"

"He should be around here somewhere."

"I'll go with that," he told her.

Rosie cast me one more look before she said, "Coming right up, Fancypants."

If that's the nickname she'd settled on for Ryan, I didn't want to know how much the liquor he'd tried to order cost. Probably a month's wages for me. Maybe more if it wasn't included in the impressive collection of bottles located behind the bar.

As if the day hadn't already reminded me of how far Ryan and I had drifted apart, the allusion to his wealth certainly did.

I finished off the beer I'd started and set the drink to the side.

"So, was there any reason why you came here? Other than to chastise me about my sex life."

"Nope, that was pretty much it."

Any other day, I might have punched him in the shoulder. Glared at him. Flicked him on the side of the head. And given his grin, it seemed that's what Ryan wanted out of his little quip, too.

Not today. Especially not after crying in front of this man less than five hours ago.

It didn't take long for him to catch on.

Ryan sighed.

"I wanted to make sure you were okay."

"Fine and dandy," I replied in a tone that implied I was *not*, in fact, fine and dandy. At all.

Rosie returned with Ryan's drink, and I made sure my attention was set intently on the TV in front of me, now filled with post-game interviews and sportscaster analyses before the next match-up started.

"Do you… want to talk about it?" Ryan asked once Rosie was gone.

"I believe you were the one who admitted to having some explaining to do." I watched him sidelong. "How many whiskeys will it take to get you to start blabbing?"

"None," he said, much to my surprise. That must have been evident, because Ryan's brow scrunched. "You really think I need to be drunk to tell you what I'm thinking, Harps? You know me better than that."

"After five years?" I huffed a laugh. "I hardly feel like I know you at all anymore."

I could have picked up a fork and stabbed Ryan right in the eyeballs and he would have looked less pained than he did in that moment.

It only got worse when his attention strayed and he caught sight of the TV.

The Stallions were running onto the field, their home stadium packed with fans adorned in deep teal and gold. The camera panned to one particular fan dressed in a horse mask and cowboy hat. The guy next to him help up a giant gold chain with a horseshoe attached to it.

The camera went back to watching the team as warm-ups began, and a little graphic appeared in the bottom corner of the screen.

Stallions without Ryan Caldwell.

We were only three weeks into the regular season, but apparently that was enough to significantly lessen the team's total yardage and pass completion percentage. Their quarterback had also been sacked more in those two games than he had in the entire second half of the previous season.

Sometimes I forgot how much importance a tight end held on a team. Especially one who played at the level Ryan did.

He sipped on his whiskey beside me, eyes never leaving the screen. I knew he was reading the same graphic as me, except he had the advantage of personally knowing every single player on the team. Where I could try to analyze the stats all I wanted, he'd know why they were happening. How each man's play would be affected by his absence.

"You miss it?" I asked.

To my surprise, Ryan shrugged. "It's complicated."

That was a far different response than I'd been expecting.

Particularly because the last time the two of us had talked about his football career—soon after he'd had his first professional game—he'd sounded so heartbroken at the idea of never playing again.

"You'll be back out there in no time," I tried.

"Six to eight weeks," Ryan recited, probably having heard it a million times from doctors, physical therapists, and even sports broadcasters, then took another sip of his whiskey.

I drummed my fingers along the side of my glass. "I, um, noticed you weren't using both crutches this morning."

"I'm told to use only one while at home. It's still a little painful, but they're trying to speed up the recovery."

"And at all other times?"

"Both crutches in public—for now. Give it another week or two once I start PT, and I'll probably be walking around here on my own again."

As if the timeline for the Fall Fest wasn't already making Ryan's stay here feel rushed, hearing his recovery timeframe definitely did. Granted, I'd heard most of the same stuff he'd just told me on social media already, but I always took those reports with a grain of salt. Hearing it straight from the horse's mouth left no room for argument.

Ryan continued to stare at the TV, watching as everyone prepared for kick-off. He was so dialed in that it surprised me when he said, "I really do want to talk, Harper. Just… here might not be the best place for it."

"Why? No one's paying attention to—"

"Caldwell!" came a loud call from across the bar.

It didn't take long for Ryan and me to find its origin, given the group of guys were now making horse noises and galloping in place. Beer sloshed over the sides of their glasses, but none of them seemed to mind the mess. No one from Timberland Creek disrespected Ziggy's in the way they were. Out-of-towners, then. Ones who had recognized Ryan in the crowd. Not that he was hard to miss, even in his every-day clothing, no Stallions merch in sight. His crutches made it even worse.

His eyes slid back to me. A single brow lifted.

"Okay, I see your point," I conceded, then eyed both our drinks. "Want to head out?"

I'd expected him to down whatever was left of his whiskey and take me up on the offer. Not that I knew where we'd go. Any restaurant with a TV would be packed on a Sunday afternoon. Not to mention it was the perfect fall day outside: crisp and cloudy. Even more reason for everyone to cram inside and enjoy the comfort a dive bar brought on game day.

If privacy was what he was after, that wouldn't happen anywhere in town. Besides, the idea of him hobbling around on his crutches all afternoon in pursuit of somewhere satisfactory didn't sound like a fun time.

"Nah," Ryan finally said, shocking me once again. "Let's stay here. It's been a while since we've watched a game together." He nudged me with his elbow, a bit of his liveliness returning. "How about you ask anything you want about my team, and I'll tell you if you're right or not?"

He officially had my attention. But I wasn't one-hundred percent sure he was telling the truth.

My eyes narrowed. "Is it true Landon Reid missed that field goal last season because his brother-in-law placed a massive bet on the opposing team while he was drunk in Vegas?"

"Okay, I was thinking more general gossip, not legal issues."

"But is it true?"

"I signed an NDA."

I gasped, and Ryan sat back in his stool, hands up in defense.

"I neither confirmed nor denied," he argued.

My O-shaped mouth slowly transitioned into a smile. "It's true. Holy shit, I told Connor that's what happened but he said it was still too close to making it through the goalposts that he didn't believe it was—"

The rest of my words were cut off when Ryan's hand clamped over my mouth. His other arm wrapped around my shoulders, pulling me closer so he could say through gritted teeth, "NDA, Harps."

His eyes darted around the room, checking to see if anyone had heard, but everyone was way to engrossed in just about anything else. Even the obnoxious frat bros who'd called to him earlier paid us no mind.

"Your secret's safe with me," I said when my mouth was freed. "But I'll try to keep it more lowkey from now on. Or just general opinions. Starting with that shit-head Navarro."

"Navarro's a great guy."

"Not according to your phone contact list he's not."

Ryan chuckled. "I fear the day you two meet. You'll never let him hear the end of it."

"It's a good thing we don't have to worry about that happening then, huh?"

Maybe it was a trick of the light—the TV screen's constant changes shining onto his face—but I could have sworn Ryan's smile faltered. I didn't have time to dwell on it too long, however.

"Yeah. That'll never happen," he said, then downed the rest of his whiskey.

CHAPTER ELEVEN

"THIS ONE'S GOING. This one too. What the fuck were you thinking for *him*?"

I tried to snatch my phone back from Ryan, but toppled forward a little too far and missed. He giggled—big, bad Ryan Caldwell actually *giggled*—as he held the device out of my reach.

"Gimme," I half-pleaded, half-laughed. My hand swiped fruitlessly through the air again.

In fairness, this wasn't an even fight. I'd been drinking since the early afternoon when Dad and I had gotten to Ziggy's. Ryan, even though he'd been drinking hard liquor the whole time, hadn't shown up until the late afternoon game.

Still, it hadn't stopped him from catching up, which resulted in the walk from Ziggy's to my place becoming one of the most entertaining events of my life. Large, injured man plus many glasses of whiskey plus his insistence he can still use his crutches equals hysterical Harper. I'd laughed so hard I'd nearly peed myself in the bushes out front of Turning Pages.

Not wanting to risk another near career-ending catastrophe, I'd suggested we pop a squat on the steps that led up to Sunrise and, by default, my apartment.

And that's when Ryan had stolen my phone and done the only thing any logical, twenty-seven-year-old guy would do.

Evaluate my fantasy football team.

"You don't even have me on here," he said with a pout, my phone once again lowered so he could finish reading the members of my team.

I placed my hand on his leg brace. "With good reason."

"I could've been on your bench."

"I'm not wasting a seat on my bench with your injured ass when there's bye weeks starting soon."

"Yeah, well you'll regret it in four to six weeks when I'm back on that field *kicking* ass."

My snort was so aggressive I lurched forward, shoulders hunched.

"That was so bad," I said.

A slow smile spread on Ryan's lips as he drawled, "I'm pretty drunk."

I snickered. "Worse than when Harry Bukowski threw that pool party junior year?"

Ryan mumbled something that sounded a whole lot like, "Oh shit," as he ran a hand down his face. "I fucking forgot about that."

"I don't think anyone else did," I said with a smile. "Better hope no one has pictures they can sell to TMZ."

"Still not as bad as senior prom when you were plastered and went up to Avery Morgan and accused her of stealing your dress."

I gasped. "You *know* she bought hers, like, three weeks after me!"

"She saw the pictures you were showing in the locker room after P.E. and copied you," Ryan mocked.

"It's true!"

"I believe you." Then, for whatever reason, Ryan decided to shout, "Because Avery Morgan was a *bitch*!"

My hand was over his mouth almost instantly.

"*Shhhhhh!*" I hissed, but the reprimand was much less threatening than I'd hoped, considering it was accompanied by my laughter. "Hemi will hear you."

I cast a nervous glance back at the cabin behind the main Sunrise building. The lights were off, but that didn't mean Hemi wasn't up. She was a minimal light kind of person. Candles in lieu of the overhead, and all that. She only turned them on when I came over because I'd tripped on a pothos vine one time. That was apparently enough to lose aesthetic light privileges.

Ryan pushed my hand away before he craned his neck and whisper-shouted, "Sorry, Hemi!" in the direction of the cabin.

"Don't spit in my coffee!"

Another too-powerful-for-my-tipsy-state snort escaped me and my head landed on Ryan's shoulder. Damn, it felt nice to not be spinning so much anymore. Not to mention, with the chilly fall air sneaking through what I'd thought had been thick-enough clothing, his body heat was the equivalent of being wrapped up in a nice warm blanket.

It got even better when, while laughing, Ryan wrapped his arm around my back, keeping me close.

And then it all stopped. The laughter. The silliness. It was like we'd both sobered instantly, staring off across the street and into the darkness that waited there. Realistically, I knew it was the waterfront, but the lack of light pollution made it impossible to see beyond the streetlights.

A car whizzed past, the hum of its tires on the road coming to a crescendo in front of us, then fading as it disappeared down the road, out of downtown. A few crickets that hadn't yet gone into hiding chirped. In the distance—maybe from a vacation rental or a campground across the water—a dog barked.

We sat as still as the world around us.

And I couldn't even make it thirty seconds without ruining the moment.

My hand shot up to my mouth to try to disguise the sound that had just escaped me.

"What?" Ryan asked. He leaned forward, head tilted, trying

to find my face.

"It's nothing," I said. Then another squeak snuck out.

"What is it?" Ryan repeated, the tease of his own budding laughter coating his words.

"It's just—" I shook my head. "No, it's embarrassing."

"I wanna know." Ryan's arm tightened around me. "Tell me."

My current state of mind wasn't conducive to arguing. I sighed.

"You're just so warm, and it got me thinking back to earlier when you were all—" I twisted just enough to look at him and lifted my hands. Ryan's eyes widened as I reached for his face, but I stopped right before my palms would have made contact with his cheeks. They shook in place as I said, "Ugh!"

"I'm afraid my Harper is a little rusty," he teased. "Care to translate?"

"When you grabbed my face in the garage and…"

Normally, my lips got pretty loose when I drank, but for whatever reason, talking had become an almost impossible task. Maybe because of what I was admitting. Maybe because of the way Ryan was watching me, and even in the dark, I could see the way his eyes shone. Bright. Curious.

"And what?" he prompted when I failed to find the end of my thought.

"Don't laugh, okay?" When Ryan nodded, I said, "I thought you were gonna kiss me."

This time, I knew I didn't imagine it when Ryan's eyes widened with shock. Not enough for me to take offense at his reaction—kissing me would be a freaking *honor*, thank you very much—but enough to know he held some sort of opinion on the matter. Unfortunately, I couldn't tell if it was positive or negative.

My head fell, my eyes trained on my shoes.

"It was stupid, right?" I shrugged. "I mean, obviously that wasn't your intent."

The silent trance Ryan had fallen into broke. He let out a huffed laugh. "Yeah, right? I don't just go around kissing all my friends."

"Exactly."

He went quiet again, his arm falling away from my shoulders and letting the cold seep back in. I watched as he played with something on his leg brace before he snuck a glance up at me.

"What?" I asked, taking my turn to question his weird behavior this time. His sudden shyness was kind of charming. Cute.

Ryan shook his head. "If you thought *your* crazy idea was embarrassing, I don't want to tell you mine."

"Try me." I leaned into him briefly, trying to encourage him. "Then we'll be even."

His face angled up just enough for me to catch the sparkle in his eyes. "Have you... have you ever thought about it?"

My eyes widened when I figured out what he was implying.

"About… kissing?"

"More specifically, kissing each other."

There was no denying the way my heart rate picked up as he spoke. I wondered if he'd noticed in the darkness, how my chest rose and fell a little heavier than before. That would have been the only outwardly visible sign of my body's reactions. He thankfully wouldn't be able to tell a fresh heat had started to burn low in my stomach. The chill that started taking over when he released his hold on me was no longer a problem.

I shifted, hoping to disguise the way I pressed my legs together as best I could. What the fuck was my body doing? This was Ryan, for god's sake.

But…

"Yeah," I admitted softly. "I've thought about it."

How could I not have thought about it over the course of our friendship? Maybe not when we were little—he'd definitely had cooties way back then. But as we'd gotten older, and I'd noticed how well he was growing into his features, it definitely became something that crossed my mind on occasion.

Besides, pretty much everyone that had known us growing up used to ask if we were secretly hooking up. It was hard not to think about the possibility of something when it was constantly being brought up to you.

Yet, we'd never crossed that line. Ryan and I had always been strictly friends. And I'd done my best to ignore any possibility of it ever happening.

"Have *you* thought about it?" I fired back at him. When he nodded, the heat in my core increased.

"Would you…" My lips pursed when I chewed the inside of my cheek. I couldn't believe I was actually going to say this. "Would you want to?"

"Seriously?" Considering he was the one that had brought the topic up in the first place, Ryan sure seemed surprised by my suggestion.

"I mean, we don't have to," I said quickly. "I just thought since you asked you might want—never mind. You already told me you don't go around kissing all your friends."

"You're not just one of my friends, Harper," Ryan whispered. "You're my best friend."

His hand slid over where mine sat palm down on the stairs, supporting my weight.

"So, what you're saying is you only go around kissing your best friends?" I tried joking. This was getting way too intense for my comfort, yet I didn't want it to stop.

"Well, I haven't kissed you yet," Ryan retorted.

"Are you going to?"

Somehow, his whole face softened, yet his eyes maintained an intensity unlike anything I'd ever seen before. "I'd like to. Yeah."

Holy shit.

He was leaning in slowly, testing, seeing if I'd take the bait. If I'd consent to what he'd just admitted.

"We probably should," I whispered, leaning in ever-so-slightly as well.

"Get it out of our system," he agreed.

"Then we never have to do it again."

"Exactly."

His lips hovered so close to mine that they briefly touched when he angled his head. Our breath mingled, hot and heavy, as anticipation overcame us. And when Ryan finally let his eyes drift closed, I followed his lead, leaning in to fill the miniscule space that separated us.

For all the strength I knew he showcased on the football field, I never would have guessed how gentle Ryan Caldwell's kisses would be.

It was nothing more than a lingering peck, and when he pulled back, I exhaled, not realizing I'd been holding my breath. But I didn't move.

When I opened my eyes, I found Ryan watching me, waiting for any sort of reaction. His pupils were so dilated that, in the darkness, his eyes looked like nothing but black voids.

Which made it less of a surprise when his hand cupped the back of my head, fingers tangled in my hair, he brought his lips to mine, and—

Oh. *Oh.*

This was more along the lines of what I'd imagined Ryan's kisses would be like. Rough and wanting. *Greedy.* Yes, that was the perfect way to describe the way he took control, his hands on my body, his tongue licking my bottom lip to get me to open for him. As soon as I gave him that access, a deep moan rumbled out of him.

Whatever heat had been building in me earlier was nothing compared to the infernal blaze roaring now.

Ryan turned as much as he could, one of his hands landing on my hip before it moved to my ass, trying to pull me closer. As the only one who could really do anything in this situation, it was time for me to take over.

I swung one of my legs over his hips, holding my weight somewhat uncomfortably on my knees. The wood of the stairs dug into my skin through my leggings.

"What are you waiting for?" Ryan panted, both his hands planted firmly on my ass now. I found I didn't mind one bit.

"I don't want to hurt you," I said, then moaned when one of his hands cupped the side of my face, fingers pushed into my hair again, and his lips found my neck.

"You won't hurt me," he assured me against my skin. "I want to feel you, Harps."

I wanted to feel him, too—and that I did the moment I lowered myself completely onto his lap.

Fuck. Me.

My hips instinctively rolled, and a whimper escaped me when my center ran across his length. Even from what I could feel through his jeans, I knew Ryan was *huge*.

"Fuck," Ryan mumbled, taking a break from where he

sucked on the spot where my neck met my jaw. "Keep going. Keep fucking doing that."

As if I planned on stopping.

Each roll of my hips brought a new bought of pleasure. I'd thought I'd graduated past dry-humping in high school, but here I was, absolutely relishing in the feel of Ryan through our clothing.

I ached in places I didn't even know it was possible. The desperate need for Ryan to touch me anywhere—everywhere—other than my ass was immeasurable. If I wasn't so concerned with making sure I didn't accidentally put too much weight on his bad leg, I might have palmed my breasts myself. The friction of my bra against my hardened nipples was almost unbearable.

"Look at you," Ryan whispered. His teeth found my earlobe and tugged. "My cock doesn't even need to be inside your tight little cunt to make you come."

I couldn't form any words, but I wanted to let him know that was very much the truth.

Instead, I kept going, my back arched as I ground against him. Between the way he was touching me—kissing me—and the hardness pressed between my legs, I was building fast.

"Ryan," I gasped.

His hands tightened on my ass, helping guide me. I was right on the brink—my orgasm so close to taking me over.

"Get it, Caldwell!"

I'd never been turned off so quickly in all my life.

Ryan's hands moved instantly to pull me against him, one splayed on my back, the other on the back of my head, holding me close. Protecting me.

The car drove past, a collection of guys hooting and hollering out the window. The driver took the liberty of honking excessively, until all their hoopla faded with the increasing distance.

The world grew silent again, Ryan and my breathing the only sound I could make out in the still night. The steady rise and fall of his chest calmed me, my own pressed tight against it.

"I, um—maybe I should go," he finally whispered.

I nodded as best I could with my head still cradled in his large hand. A large hand that had just shown me a tease of what, exactly, it was capable of.

That's when he released his hold, and I pulled back enough to see his face. Just like before, Ryan's eyes were dilated, except now, his cheeks had taken on a flushed pink tint. What had once been relatively tamed hair stuck out in odd directions from where my fingers had tangled in it.

I couldn't imagine I was much better.

"Maybe if you just—" he tried, eyes darting down.

"Oh, right. Yeah. Let me—"

In twenty-six years, I'd managed to have my fair share of awkward moments.

The fumbling and mumbling and utter lack of coordination

that Ryan and I endured as I tried to ease myself off his lap was probably close to the top of the list.

Once I finally found my feet, Ryan hoisted himself up on the stair railing. It took every ounce of my strength not to glance at his crotch where I knew his bulging erection would still be visible.

The one *I'd* caused.

"So." Ryan cleared his throat as he situated his crutches under his arms. "I'll, uh, just make sure you get to your apartment alright."

My eyes slid sideways towards the remainder of stairs that stood between me and the front door of the apartment above Sunrise Brews.

Clearly sensing that I thought he was being overdramatic, Ryan added, "I need to, um, wait a second before I get in my ride."

Right. Raging hard on.

"Well, in that case"—I pointed both my thumbs up the stairs—"I'll just head on up."

"Get home safe." When he realized how stupid he sounded, Ryan shook his head. "Not that I don't think you will. Stairs are pretty easy. Unless you're me. Right now, at least. All other times, I'm a stair *master*."

"Oh, I don't doubt you climb them like a champ."

"A real… real winner."

I'd never wanted silence to be broken so badly before in my

life.

"Well," I drawled. "Good night."

"'Night."

The same time Ryan leaned in for a hug, I extended my hand for a handshake.

A *fucking handshake.*

With a nervous laugh, I pulled it back, running my fingers through my hair like a cliché from a tween movie. Really, this whole ordeal felt like a cliché from a tween movie. And to think I'd always made fun of them for being unrealistic.

I gave Ryan a quick smile. "Bye."

I'd made it halfway up the stairs before he had the chance to say anything back, and when I reached the door, I'd never been more grateful for not remembering to lock it.

My butt met the floor just inside the entryway when I slid down the door.

And that, kids, is why you shouldn't kiss—no, why you shouldn't *dry hump*—your friends.

CHAPTER TWELVE

I'D BEEN THREE seconds away from texting Hemi that I wouldn't be able to show up for my shift the next morning before I decided to buck up.

My head was *pounding*. And even as I made my way downstairs—because I'm a team-player, dammit—it still hadn't stopped. The tightening tugs on my ponytail probably weren't helping the Advil I'd taken work any faster.

"I don't know if Rosie has some deal with the brewery to up the ABV or something," I said in lieu of a proper *good morning* to Hemi, "but I swear I only had, like, six beers yesterday and I feel like I'm—"

I stopped talking. I stopped walking. I just flat-out *stopped* because at the end of my wide-eyed stare, sitting in the front room of Sunrise Brews—before we opened, might I add—was Ryan.

It wasn't particularly cold out, but there was enough of a chill for me to notice the sudden increase in my own temperature when I spotted him sitting at his table, flipping through a Timberland Creek dining guide.

My shoes squeaked on the hardwood floor when I spun to face Hemi.

"Um, what's he doing here?" I asked in a hissed whisper.

She tilted her head just enough to sneak a peek at Ryan before she went back to stacking the mugs from the dishwasher. "I thought you'd be excited to see him after all the fun you two had last night."

Holy shit, we'd need to turn on the air conditioning if this room got any freaking hotter.

"We didn't do—" I tried, but didn't get to finish because Hemi leveled me with a knowing stare.

"I might not get a lot of action myself these days, but I've been around the block a few times," Hemi said. "You two weren't as subtle as you probably think you were."

My mortification levels just hit a new high.

I turned slowly over my shoulder to see if Ryan was paying any attention and found him still engaged with the dining guide. Or pretending to be engaged. I mean, there was a half-wall that separated the two portions of the café, but that didn't mean he couldn't pick up bits and pieces of the conversation. It wasn't like there was anyone else in here to dilute it with their own chatter.

"Looks like you took my advice to go for it," Hemi continued.

"I didn't take anyone's advice," I challenged, facing her once more. "It just… happened."

"Mhm…"

I crossed my arms, not appreciating the sass. "That still doesn't answer the question of why he's here."

"He slept on the bean bag."

"What?"

Hemi nodded. "Showed up at my door around ten? Eleven? Probably eleven because he said his parents weren't answering. Seems more reasonable that they'd be asleep at that time."

"Why'd he need his parents?"

"Needed a ride home, apparently." Hemi finished with the mugs and got to work on the espresso machine, the air filling with the aroma as she made a fresh shot. "Kid thought he'd get an Uber around here."

Oh, that poor city-tainted boy.

"When that didn't work, and he couldn't get ahold of anyone, he apparently decided to come knocking on my door," Hemi explained. "Gave him a blanket and a pillow off the couch, then told him the bean bag was the only place I had that would fit him. He didn't seem too bothered."

I stole another glance at Ryan. He was texting someone now—maybe Gina or Dave? But one thing I hadn't noticed in the midst of monitoring his activities was that he was, in fact, wearing the same clothes he'd worn to Ziggy's the day before.

And somewhere beneath those clothes—beneath his jeans in particular…

I blinked myself out of that daze. The last thing I needed was to break out into a full-blown sweat because I couldn't stop imagining how big Ryan Caldwell's dick was.

Although, it wasn't entirely a work of my imagination anymore.

"Surprised he didn't spend the night at your place," Hemi said, pouring the shot of espresso into a cup. "But I could see where the stairs would become an issue."

"It's not like that," I mumbled, half saying it to convince myself it was the truth.

We'd agreed last night: once and done. Get it out of our system and forget about it. Now, we were just like every other co-ed friend pair to ever exist. We'd shared our experimental kiss, and we went on with our lives like normal.

Well, as normal as we could be. I, unfortunately, believed my mind would jump to the memory of how his lips had felt on mine—on my skin—for the foreseeable future.

Hemi turned, the mug in her hand filled with steaming coffee. "Mhm," she repeated as she passed it to me.

"What's this?" I asked. I never got espresso drinks during my shift.

Her eyes darted to the front room and back. "Go deliver it to our customer."

My eyes narrowed when her lips curled into a sly smile. "I'm beginning to think you might hate me."

"On the contrary." She pushed the mug harder into my hands. "Go on."

Our stare-down lasted approximately three seconds before my headache forced me to concede. Hemi's smile grew as I yanked—okay, forcibly grabbed; didn't want to spill anything—the mug from her and made my way to the front room.

Ryan's immediate attentiveness made me wonder if he'd been using the dining guide as a ploy all along.

"Hi," he greeted.

"I'm not sure what she made you," I said as I set the cup down in front of him. "But it has espresso in it, so that's all that really matters."

Ryan chuckled, and his hands wrapped around the mug, putting his long fingers on display. "I needed this. I'm running on, like, two hours of solid sleep."

"Hemi said you slept on the bean bag?"

"Yeah."

"Didn't like it?"

Ryan shrugged. "It was fine. A bit rough with the brace, though."

"Right."

Ryan lifted the mug and blew on the coffee in an attempt to cool it. "You had anything yet?"

"Nah, I'll go pour myself some of whatever Hemi put in the dispenser today," I said, pointing my thumb back over my shoulder in the direction I'd come from. "Which, I should probably go make sure that's ready before we officially open."

"Sorry to crash the party before it starts."

"You're fine." I motioned to his drink. "Enjoy. Let me know if you want a refill."

I'd hardly turned away when Ryan said, "Harper." I aimed a raised, curious eyebrow at him, and he continued with, "About last night."

My heart dropped into my gut. We hadn't even talked about what had come between us over the last five years, yet he already wanted to talk about the night before? I'd hoped that his disinterest in bringing up important topics would have carried over into all aspects of our acquaintanceship—renewed friendship?—but apparently not.

"Yeah?" I asked, hoping the break in my voice hadn't come out as loud as I thought it sounded.

"I said some shit." Ryan shook his head. "I'm sorry. I get a bit crass when I'm… you know. Caught up in the moment, I guess?"

You and me both, dude. While I hadn't said anything, I hadn't exactly hidden how I'd felt either.

And damn, had I felt good. *Really* good.

My cock doesn't even need to be inside your tight little cunt to make you come.

My core tightened at the memory of his words.

The heat must have made its way onto my face, too, because Ryan raised a brow. Or I'd just been silent long enough, lost in the recollection of the night's activities, to make him uncomfortable.

"D-don't worry about it," I managed. "It happens."

"Yeah," he said with a shy grin. Clearly, he was just trying to be nice. The level to which we'd taken our experimental kiss—the things he'd said to me—didn't just *happen*. "Totally."

I rocked from my toes to my heels, my teeth working the inside of my cheek.

"Okay," I said when it was clear Ryan didn't have anything further to contribute. "I'm gonna head back."

"Yeah, don't let me keep you."

And keep me he didn't. Ryan didn't so much as look at me again as I returned to the front counter.

"How'd it go?" Hemi asked, wiggling her eyebrows.

She got her answer when I crouched down, hiding my face in my hands.

I definitely should have called in sick.

"THANKS. THAT'LL BE right out."

The customer returned my polite smile as they slid to the side, allowing the next person in line to come forward. Despite the pounding still occurring in my frontal lobe, I couldn't deny it had been nice having a steady morning at Sunrise. I'd made more pumpkin spice lattes than I'd ever thought possible, but still, distractions were very much wanted.

Especially since Ryan still hadn't left.

His presence was like a magnet that desperately sought my attention, but I refused to give in. On the few occasions I'd fallen to temptation, my heart lurched so dramatically that I actually worried it might have popped out of my chest.

"Thanks. That'll be right out," I recited as the next customer followed the same path as the last one.

And as soon as they were gone, my heart might as well have flown across the room.

"Hey," Ryan said, giving me a smile.

"Hi." I swallowed whatever apprehension his sudden proximity brought over me. "Need a refill?"

"Actually, I hate to do this, but I was wondering if you could give me a ride."

My eyes widened. "Huh?"

There was no way I'd heard him correctly. I mean, I knew we were both completely, one-hundred-percent aware of what had transpired the night before, but being so outright about it was a little—

"Back to my parents' house," he clarified.

Oh. Of course. Because I hadn't thought he was asking me for sex. Nope. Not at all.

"Mom is at her monthly book club brunch today and Dad's…" Ryan sighed. "He's being himself."

"An asshat?"

"You said it, not me." I smiled. At least some things never changed. "He's being stubborn. He didn't see my texts from last night letting them know where I was—and that I needed a ride about twelve hours ago—so now I'm being punished."

"Maturity is a wonderful virtue."

Ryan rolled his eyes as he said, "They apparently almost called the cops to file a missing person's report this morning when they learned I wasn't in the house. Then Mom checked her phone."

I let out a low whistle. "Talk about making headlines."

"The papers around here would have had a field day," he agreed. "But do you think it's possible?"

Hemi wasn't with me behind the counter—she'd probably gone into the back to get something for one of the many orders waiting to be made—so she hadn't heard the request. Even if she had, I wasn't sure she'd oblige in the same way she normally did. Again—many orders waiting and, currently, no one was handling them.

"I'll, uh, have to check with Hemi," I said. "And it might have to wait until we have a bit of a break in—"

"Go." Hemi burst through from the back room, three giant bottles of flavor syrups hugged in her arms. "I can do this."

"Are you kidding?" I asked. "There's, like, ten orders in line."

"Then finish up with the current customers, help me fulfill the drink tickets, and be on your way." She schlepped the syrups onto the counter with the rest of our supplies. "This one needs a fresh shirt," she added, nodding in Ryan's direction.

If he'd tried to be inconspicuous when his chin tilted down so his nose was closer to his armpit, he'd failed.

"You don't smell," I assured him. "But can you wait, like, thirty minutes?"

He nodded, and I watched as he crutched back over to his table. My fingers worked almost on auto-pilot at this point as I typed in his regular order in the system, applying my special employee discount to allow it to go through without payment.

"You take the rest of the day off when we're done here," Hemi said as walked over to the work-station portion of our behind-the-counter sanctuary. I removed the last three order tickets and hung them up on the line to be prepared. "This seems like our late morning rush. I don't think it'll be too busy the rest of the day now that the weekend's finished."

"You sure?" In the three years I'd been working for Hemi, I could count the days she'd let me go early on one hand. Not because she didn't want to, but because she'd genuinely been unable to due to demand. "I don't mind coming back. It should only take, like, ten minutes to get him home."

"You've been working hard. Take a break." Hemi stuck a metal cup filled with cream under the frother. "Don't you two have a project to work on, too?"

I supposed we did. And the success of the project—really, it's general appeal—would play a big role in the plan I had for making sure this place kept its doors open.

Taking off might not be the worst idea…

"Fine," I agreed, trying to sound disappointed. "But you're not paying me for a full day."

Hemi grinned. "Deal." She nudged me with her hip. "Now go take orders. We don't want these people waiting."

CHAPTER THIRTEEN

I WASN'T NAÏVE enough to expect that things between Ryan and me would ever be completely normal again. Between the separation the last five years and what had transpired on the stairs of Sunrise, I didn't foresee us ever going back to what we used to be.

We'd survived well enough at the café—well, aside from when he'd tried to apologize for talking to me about his dick— but this awkward tension that radiated between us during the car ride was more than I'd expected.

The negative energy only heightened when we approached his parents' house, and the rigidity in Ryan's body somehow got worse.

The car jostled as I rolled over the little lip at the end of the driveway. Normally, I would have parked on the street, but I didn't want the police to come by and think I was one of the frequent stalkers. At least there were none of those today—not yet, anyway—which only added to my confusion over Ryan's behavior.

He wasn't moving, not even when I put the car in park and expected him to get out.

"Hemi gave me the rest of the day off," I said. "I was gonna go grab something for lunch really fast, but then I thought I might come back? We can get started on the float. Or keep planning or something."

Ryan didn't respond.

"Want me to grab you anything? I was thinking sandwiches from the Main Street Market. Nothing fancy," I tried again.

Still nothing.

"Hey."

His hand tensed on the console when I slid mine over it. I immediately pulled back, and he seemed to realize what he'd done.

"I'm sorry." Ryan sighed and his eyes squeezed shut. "I—it's not you."

"What's wrong, then?"

I was beginning to think that question was cursed. The universe clearly wanted me to receive no answers from Ryan at any point. And just when I thought he might finally deliver some sort of information, I caught the front door of the house open in my peripheral.

"Nice of you to finally show up," Dave called out, his voice cutting across the driveway like a knife, loud enough to penetrate the closed windows of my car.

Ryan's jaw tensed, his glare locked on the man standing on the porch.

Okay, maybe he'd been telling the truth about his weirdness having nothing to do with me.

"Well? Are you coming or not?" Dave snapped, gesturing sharply toward the house.

It wasn't immediate, but that did finally get Ryan moving.

With a sharp push, he shoved his car door open and stepped out. The brace on his leg made him a bit clumsier than he probably would have liked given the attention he was getting, but he moved with a determination that dared anyone to pity him.

"Do you need any help with—?" I offered when he opened the back door to get his crutches.

But he cut me off with a stern, "I'm fine," that he once again looked like he regretted as soon as the words left his lips.

My eyes cut back to Dave who stood on the front stoop with his arms crossed. If the Caldwell men were competing for most unapproachable, I honestly wasn't sure who'd win.

At least Ryan made an attempt at civility, as he took in a deep breath and let loose an equally heavy exhale.

"I'm fine," he repeated, and this time when he set his eyes on me, some of the softness had returned. "I promise. I'll text you my order from the Market, and then we can—"

"What the fuck is taking so long?" Dave shouted, then must have decided he'd had enough waiting around.

I clutched the steering wheel as he stormed down the path that led to the front of the house. My attention only strayed from the approaching man when Ryan slammed the back door hard enough to rattle the whole car.

For over ten years of my life, I'd been certain that Ryan had shared all his secrets with me, but in this moment, I wasn't so sure that was the case. Because there was no way in hell this sort of behavior was coming out of nowhere. No—the way Dave yelled in front of my car was the result of something that had been brewing for weeks, if not years.

Having grown up in a male-dominated house myself, I'd witnessed a lot of pointless testosterone-driven arguments. But no matter why they'd started, they'd always dissolved just as quickly.

This? This was not like that. Dave's face had turned a shade of purple-red so deep I wondered if he was even breathing while he continued to shout at his son.

And Ryan took every word of it, staring stoically back at his father, white-knuckled hands clutching the bar of his crutches.

If it hadn't been for my experience with my brothers, I probably wouldn't have cut the engine and gotten out of the vehicle when Dave took a step forward and thrust his index finger at Ryan's chest.

"Hey!" I shouted, slamming my door behind me. "What the

fuck is wrong with you?"

"You stay out of this!" Dave yelled right back, turning to aim that same finger at me instead. I reared back, scowling. "This is a family matter!"

"Don't you fucking dare!"

Ryan's crutch clattered on the asphalt of the driveway at the same time his hand connected with Dave's arm, the resulting slap echoing in my ears.

"You don't speak to her with that tone, and you sure as fuck don't invade her space," Ryan roared. "You have a problem with her, you take it out on me."

"You know damn well my problem is with that girl as much as it's with you, boy," Dave said through gritted teeth. He took another menacing step towards his son. "So, if you think I'm gonna sit back and let her mess with your head again—"

"Dave?"

Even though it was the patriarch of the Caldwell family that had been addressed, I was the only that turned at the sound of Gina's voice. Amid everything else going on, I hadn't even noticed the Audi pull up along the side of the road, its driver watching the on-going argument with concern, but not a whole lot of surprise.

"Boys?" Gina's heeled booties *click-clacked* on the pavement as she hurried up the driveway. "What's going on?" she asked when she stood beside her husband.

"Dad's being a dick."

"Ryan!"

Dave huffed a laugh, ignoring his wife's protests altogether. "Maybe I wouldn't have to act like this if you showed a sense of responsibility and started behaving like an adult."

"Excuse me?" I knew I should have stayed quiet, but asinine comments like that were where I drew the line. "Weren't you the one who refused to pick him up this morning because you were too busy throwing a hissy fit?"

"What did I say about staying out of our family's business?"

"Alright, alright!"

Gina, in all her five-foot glory, squeezed her way between Dave and me. Honestly, thank goodness it was her instead of Ryan. If that look on his face was any indication, I wasn't sure Dave would have walked away with his nose in-tact should his son get involved.

Gina aimed a narrow-eyed glare at her husband. "You," she said. "In the house. *Now.* I have no idea what's going on with you boys, but this is ridiculous."

"Same shit, different day," Ryan muttered.

"Why you ungrateful little—"

Gina put both her hands on her husband's chest and pushed when he tried to advance on Ryan again. Even I took a protective step towards him, though I wasn't sure what I would have actually done to stop any altercation.

"House," Gina repeated. "Go."

When her husband remained rooted in place, she gave him

another little shove. I doubted she was actually strong enough to move him herself, but it got Dave to finally take a step away from Ryan. It did nothing to stop the way the two men were staring at each other, though.

I took another step in Ryan's direction, keeping my eyes on Dave until he finally relented. Gina hurried behind him as he trudged back up to the house, the both of them speaking in hushed, unhappy whispers.

When the front door shut behind them, the warm presence beside me disappeared.

"Ryan?" I asked, but he was already halfway to the garage. "Ryan!"

I picked up the crutch still on the ground and hurried over to where he was punching in the code for the garage door opener. The old mechanism creaked and moaned when it finally began to open, and Ryan ducked under before it was even halfway up.

I would have argued with him that he needed to take his crutch back and stop putting so much pressure on his injured knee when I froze.

"What's all this?" I asked as I scanned the garage.

My memory was definitely not perfect, but I was pretty sure I would have remembered seeing the insane number of boxes stacked around the trailer when I'd been here the day before. There had to be at least fifty of them.

"The shit my team sent," Ryan explained, his tone

monotonous. He grunted as he bent at the waist and fumbled, one-handed, with a box the size of a carry-on suitcase. "They got here after you left."

By some miracle, he managed to finagle the box into the crook of his arm, but that was about as good as it got.

"Shit," I cussed under my breath as I rushed over to steady Ryan when he started to lean to the side, his bad leg finally giving out. The box toppled out of his arm and back onto the floor, the contents inside rattling.

I didn't care to check if they'd broken. In that moment, all I was worried about was the man in front of me. This close, it was easier to tell just how hard he was breathing, his eyes squeezed shut again.

"Hey," I whispered. My hands went up to the sides of his face. "Hey, look at me, Ry."

His jaw trembled under my touch, and when he finally obeyed my request, there was nothing but pain shining amongst the blue.

My face twisted in concern. "Are you hurt?" I asked.

"No." I didn't doubt he meant it in regards to his physical well-being. But emotionally…

"What do you need me to do?" I looked around at the boxes surrounding us. "Do we need to move these?"

"I need to get out."

"What?"

"I need," Ryan repeated through gritted teeth, "to get out."

"I-I don't—"

"Get me *the fuck* out of here!" he boomed in the direction of the door that led into the house.

The sudden volume startled me, but I had enough cognizance of the situation to know that if this shouting match began again, there wasn't a guarantee Gina or I would be able to stop it for a second time.

"Okay. Okay—hey," I said, tightening my hold on Ryan's face, forcing him to hone in on me rather than the door to the house. Somewhere beyond it, I was sure Gina was going through the same motions with Dave. "We can leave. Where did you want to go? I'll drive you."

"Anywhere." The anger faded into pain again, and Ryan's hand lifted to grip my wrist. "Please, just get me away from here."

I'd never heard someone sound so broken—never seen such a look of utter defeat—and Ryan Caldwell was the last person I'd expected it from. For so many years, he'd been indestructible. The golden boy. The hometown hero.

But now I was beginning to wonder if more than just his knee had been shattered during his time in the pros.

"Okay." I nodded. "Get in the car."

CHAPTER FOURTEEN

WHEN I'D TOLD Ryan to get in the car, I'd assumed he'd know I meant *my* car.

So, when he got into the giant black pickup, I'd been a tad confused.

There was no way my little sedan would have been able to accomplish everything he had in mind, though. Only a few of the boxes would have fit in the trunk, and the trailer wouldn't have even been an option. If it were any other day, I might have argued a bit more when Ryan had insisted we bring it all to begin working on the float. Clearly, the dude needed a minute to calm down. Decompress. But he'd reiterated that working on our Fall Fest project would be better.

"If we're doing nothing, I'll keep thinking about it."

Since I hadn't been able to come up with any sort of argument to his logic, I'd ended up loading as many boxes as I could into the truck—Ryan was *not* allowed to help after he'd nearly hit the ground during his first attempt at lifting one—latched the trailer on the back, and fulfilled Ryan's request to take us far away from his parents' house.

Well, as far away as a town the size of Timberland Creek would allow.

With a more-equipped car than either of us had before, I was able to get a little bit closer to the destination I'd picked. It was the first that had come to mind, honestly—as if seeing Ryan in distress had triggered some sort of instinct in me, despite not having come back here in over five years.

The barn was just as we'd left it. A little bit more worn-down after enduring a few additional brutal Wisconsin winters, but it was still standing.

My eyes slid over to Ryan briefly as I navigated the bumpy land that led up to Our Spot, the trailer rattling behind us. As soon as we were close enough, coming to a slow stop at the side of the slightly dilapidated structure, I put the car in park.

This far removed from the rest of the town, the silence hit harder than usual. I didn't dare break it first.

Ryan's throat bobbed as he stared out the windshield at the old, red barn.

"I haven't been here in years," he whispered.

"Neither have I," I admitted. "The last time I came was with you."

On the day that he'd confessed he'd gotten an offer from an agent. The day I'd told him to go for it, unwittingly knowing what it would mean for the two of us.

Ryan seemed to recall that last visit, too. He blinked twice and swallowed again. That same distant look in his eyes hadn't faded since we'd left his parents' house. In fact, it looked even worse now.

"Should we head out?" I suggested, my voice soft in fear of startling him.

Ryan nodded, and without a word, unbuckled and got out of the truck.

I followed his lead, realizing I wasn't entirely sure I knew what I wanted to do now. At the pace he was moving, it seemed Ryan didn't either. Though that could have also been because he'd forgone taking his crutches with him. They probably wouldn't have boded well on the uneven ground, anyway.

It took a minute or two of slow, distracted wandering, but he finally settled himself on the back of the trailer with a sigh. Still, his eyes had hardly left the barn.

I made my way around the truck and took a seat beside him, my legs dangling off the end. Even lifted two feet off the ground, Ryan didn't suffer the same problem.

"Did you come here for a particular reason?" he asked in a whisper.

I shrugged. "No, not really. It just felt right, I guess."

Ryan leaned back, putting his weight on his palms. For the first time since we'd arrived, his blue-eyed stare landed on me. "Trying to trick me into finally giving you those answers I owe you?"

"You don't have to talk if you aren't ready to, Ryan," I said, and meant it. "I just wanted to get you away like you asked."

Ryan hesitated, his attention going back to the barn before he asked, "Would it be okay if I did?"

"You know you can tell me anything."

That had always been the rule, but especially here at our barn. I didn't care how much time had passed. That wasn't going to change.

The huffed laugh that escaped Ryan surprised me almost as much as his hesitant smile. "Where do I even begin?"

"Wherever you want."

He went quiet again, thinking, then said, "The beginning might be good."

"That's a pretty popular option, usually."

I was grateful when he chuckled at that. After the day we'd had, the sound warmed me even more than usual.

"Alright," he said through a smile that slowly faded as he prepared to start his tale. "I don't know if you know this, but I became a pretty successful football player."

I punched his shoulder, and Ryan laughed again.

"Cut the bullshit, Caldwell," I chastised.

"I'm done, I promise," he said. "I just wanted us to be even."

I narrowed my eyes at him as I mirrored his posture. "Fine. Go on."

The moment he broke our stare again, I knew he was going

to. He'd never been able to maintain eye contact when shit was about to get serious. Apparently, that hadn't changed.

"My dad was right. Just a little bit, but he was," he said.

My brow furrowed. "About what?"

"That you're at fault for a lot of what's gone on," he clarified. Before I could ask why, he quickly cut in, "But not for the reasons you probably think."

No, probably not, because at that moment I was wracking my memory for any sort of reason why I'd be to blame for anything that had happened to Ryan over the last half-decade. Aside from encouraging him to sign with the agent and enter the draft, I'd had essentially no involvement.

"I don't think I'd anticipated what a huge change it was— playing college ball versus professional," Ryan admitted. "Those first few months with the Stallions were *brutal*. Not to mention it was the first time I was living outside of Wisconsin, so my life was absolute chaos as I adjusted. I'd half-expected to be cut from the fifty-two-man roster, but when Scott let me know I'd made it…" Ryan shook his head. "I almost declined."

"What?"

Ryan tilted his head in my direction, a brow raised. "You sound surprised."

"Well… yeah," I admitted. "I used to ask you all the time how you were doing, and you never told me any of this."

While we'd lost touch over time, those first few months after Ryan had moved to San Antonio had been normal. We'd texted almost every day, even if just to check in and say hi. I hadn't expected him to have oodles of time to spend chatting with me—it's like he'd said, pro football was a hell of a lot different than the college level—but I liked to let him know I was thinking of him. That I missed him.

"How was I supposed to tell my biggest cheerleader—the person who'd encouraged me to go for it—that I wanted to give up my dream?"

"Uh, just like that?" I asked.

"Hindsight's always twenty-twenty," Ryan countered. "Back then, I was embarrassed I was even considering it. I mean, my rookie contract was *incredible*, Harps. I was getting things that some vets on the team haven't even been offered. Most people would have told me I was a fucking idiot for thinking about turning it down."

"So, that's why you signed it?"

Ryan shook his head. "I still didn't want to at first. But I called my parents—"

I didn't mean to groan out loud. My hand went up to cover my mouth as soon as I realized I had, only to quickly pull it away to say, "Sorry."

Ryan chuckled. "It's fine. Especially after what you just saw."

"Your mom's great," I interjected.

"And she was during the call, too. She told me to do whatever I felt was best. They'd let me move back home, live with them until I figured my shit out. Get a job. All that."

"And your dad?" I asked, already dreading what I might learn that would sway the scale further in favor of Dave Caldwell being punched in the face. Perhaps even by me at this point.

"He told my mom she was crazy for giving me that sort of advice. Then he told *me* I was even crazier for bringing this up to them." Ryan shook his head. "In his eyes, there was no reason why I shouldn't accept."

"Even if you were miserable?'"

"'The money will be worth it,'" he quoted in a mocking tone. His lips turned in and unfolded after he'd wetted them. "Then he brought you up."

Yup. My fist and Dave Caldwell's nose might become very well-acquainted in the near future. "Why me?"

"He asked if you were part of the reason why I didn't want to accept the offer. I told him no, but I'm not sure I told him the truth."

My mouth went dry, and a chill went down my spine.

"I hated being away from you, Harper," Ryan admitted. "And I know we were separated while we went to college, but at least we were in the same state, you know? We got to visit each other pretty much any time we wanted. This time I was in a totally different part of the country with an impending schedule that wouldn't let me come back—unless we played the Packers.

"Dad was adamant that I was losing focus because of you. All the years of hard work I'd put in for nothing. And—god, I don't know. Maybe he was right? Those first few games, I'd go out onto the field and expect to see you there like you always had been, and when you weren't..." He swallowed. "It was depressing as hell."

I remembered those games. I'd watched them, so excited to see Ryan out there living his dream, completely unaware that he'd actually been miserable.

But what followed after them also made a lot more sense now.

"Dad would call me after every game and go over everything, just like he did when we were in high school. But no matter what he said, I'd always go back to that comment about you. I mean, I was taking his advice about my performance. Got some extra time in with the coaches. Ran extra drills. Hired a personal trainer. Nothing I was doing was helping me get better. No matter what I did, I was still making too many mistakes I couldn't afford to make."

"So, you stopped talking to me," I concluded, my voice hardly audible as the truth set in.

Ryan closed his eyes and nodded slowly.

"I didn't know what else to do, Harps. I couldn't stop thinking about you. How much I missed you. How much I wanted you there. I'd walk out with the guys after the game and they'd all go and greet their families—their wives and fiancés and girlfriends—and I was just alone. The one person I wanted there, even above my parents, wasn't. I needed to cut you off because the pain of knowing that was getting to be too much of a distraction. So, I took my dad's advice."

He turned to me, moisture glistening in his eyes. "I would have quit, Harps. Honest to fucking god, I would have broken my contract—just up and fucking left—if I hadn't stopped talking to you."

"You could have visited," I said. "Or I—I would have come to San Antonio."

"I was never going to visit," Ryan whispered. "I'm not sure if you noticed, but my dad and I don't get along too well anymore."

"Yeah, I got that."

"It got to the point where even if I wanted to reach out to you again, I knew I'd burned that bridge, and it killed me. So, I took my frustration out on him. As far as I was concerned, my dad was the one who planted the idea that you were bad for me in my head. It was his fault I'd ruined what we had."

The Dave Caldwell Hate Club scale was toppling over at this point.

"Coming back here was like a double-edged sword for me. I not only had to live in the same home as the man who'd ruined the best relationship I'd ever had, but I also had to come back to Timberland Creek and be reminded of everything we'd done together. Those first few days I was home after my surgery were awful. The whole reason I'd gone to the town hall meeting was because my parents had forced me out of the house. They were tired of me sulking."

"Then why did you accept your mom's request?" I asked. "Why put yourself through that?"

"I didn't," Ryan said. "It was my idea to come back."

"Wait, wait, wait."

I sat up, waving my hands frantically in front of me. Ryan's brow lifted.

"*You* decided to spend your rehab period in Timberland Creek?" Even when he nodded his confirmation, I still didn't believe it. Especially not after everything he'd just told me. "Then why'd you say your mom asked you?"

"Because I'm a coward?" Ryan tried. "Because that was easier than admitting I came back in the hopes we might be able to mend our friendship? This was the first genuine extended period of time where I would have no commitments—at least until I start PT. It was now or never."

Now or never.

That statement echoed in my brain on repeat.

If Ryan hadn't gotten hurt, he *never* would have come back to Timberland Creek. I *never* would have gotten the chance to see him again. Hear his voice. Tease him. Hear his laugh. See his smile. A person whose life had become so intertwined with my own would have irreparably torn away.

All because of one terrible man's opinion that I was ruining his career. My involvement in his life was hindering his progress.

I chewed at the inside of my cheek. "Do you…" I started then trailed off. "Maybe your dad *was* right."

"Harper." Ryan sat up, his eyes wide with concern. "You've got to be joking."

"I'm not," I said, tears brimming in my eyes. "I mean, you did start to improve after we cut contact. Or after you did."

Ryan winced, but he didn't deny the truth of the comment. I'd been the one to keep reaching out. He was the one who didn't reply. I'd only been able to keep it up for so long before I realized I was never going to get the answer I wanted—until now.

"I only improved because I came to terms with the fact that I'd fucked up. *I* was the reason I would never see you again," he said. "How could I hold out hope for someone that I made sure would never be there? I needed to push through. And besides." He reached out to me, his hand finding mine and enveloping it. "All those years I *did* have you around, look what happened. We won state. I got a scholarship to Madison. I got drafted. *Missing you* was the problem. Not you being a part of my life."

A tear slipped down my cheek when I blinked. Ryan lifted his hand, his thumb brushing across my skin to wipe the drop away before he cupped the side of my face with his hand.

"I understand if you're mad at me," he whispered. "Fuck— I'd be furious. But I want you to know that the last few days I've been back in Timberland Creek with you have been some of the best I've had in a long, long time."

I sniffled. "You're just trying to butter me up because you know I'm pissed off."

"Not at all." Ryan's brow furrowed. "*Are* you pissed off?"

"Massively," I said. "Mostly at your dad, if I'm being honest, but a little bit at you, too."

A slow grin curled up the corner of Ryan's lips. "But only a little bit."

"Yeah," I said on a breath. I lifted my hand and placed it over his. "Because they've been some of the happiest for me, too."

There was no use denying it. I'd probably always be mad about the decision he'd made to cut me from his life, but the fact of the matter was it *had* been for the better. I'd obviously gotten the short end of the stick in the matter, but now… now he was back. And he had a storybook career to boot.

"Harps?"

I blinked, coming out of my daze. "Huh?"

"Nothing, I thought I lost you there for a sec." His thumb swept over my cheek again.

"No," I said with a sudden determination that shocked us both.

Ryan's surprise, in particular, heightened when I resituated myself on the trailer, one of my legs swinging over his hip so I straddled his lap much like I had the night before.

I grabbed his face in both my hands before I said, "You'll never lose me again," and brought my lips down to his.

CHAPTER FIFTEEN

UNLIKE THE NIGHT before, Ryan showed no hesitation. As soon as our lips met, his arms wrapped around me, holding me close. My back arched as I fitted against him, my hips bucking forward on instinct, grinding against his already half-hard length.

"Fuck, Harps," he moaned. "What happened to one and done?"

"I've decided the friendzone is overrated," I replied.

The vibration of his deep chuckle warmed me to my core. Or maybe that was his hands as they snuck under my flannel and t-shirt, fingers spread wide and claiming on my back.

Ryan's lips parted from mine so he could leave a path of kisses up my jaw to my ear.

"You have no idea how happy it makes me to hear you say that," he whispered. Then he nipped my earlobe. "I've waited years for it."

Just like that, five years' worth of nerves were erased from my body. Sure, I imagined I'd always be a little apprehensive—well, maybe not always, but at least for a little bit longer—until we figured out how our relationship had evolved.

But for now, I wanted to remain in the present. For once, I didn't want to have to worry about something out of my control. Not when I could be paying attention to the delicious way Ryan's tongue caressed my skin.

His hands moved to the curves in my sides, up my back, to my shoulders where he curled his fingers inside the fabric of my flannel and started to remove it.

A chill ran through me, and it had nothing to do with the brisk fall air now tickling my skin.

I lifted my arms above my head as Ryan tugged my t-shirt off, and when I was left in nothing but my bra, he licked his lips.

"Fuck," he mumbled, staring at my chest like he'd just found a buried treasure. His eyes lifted to mine, and when I nodded, he palmed my modest-sized breasts. "*Fuck*," Ryan repeated. "Your tits are so fucking perfect, Harps."

His attention shot upward again when an incredulous laugh escaped me.

"What?" he asked.

"You're cute."

Ryan's brows furrowed. "I'm serious." His thumbs ran

circles over my hardened nipples, and I sucked in a sharp breath. "Your whole body is so beautiful."

"Well, I'm no model, but…" I started. Because that's what he'd been enjoying lately. I wasn't above Googling "Ryan Caldwell Madeline" to figure out who she was.

An actual model. Lingerie, mostly. And in comparison, I was here in a bra I'd gotten as part of a three-pack on sale at the town bargain mart. I was pretty sure whatever underwear I'd put on wasn't much better.

Ryan was used to toned abs and tan, air-brushed skin. Perfectly proportioned bodies. Perky boobs. Firm asses.

I wasn't saying I lacked in *all* of the above, but magazine covers and national ad spots weren't things I'd qualify for, that was for sure.

Ryan's hands went up, cupping my jaw, and whispered, "You've always been perfect, Harps." He leaned in to kiss me. "So fucking beautiful."

And then, much to my surprise, I was flipped onto my back, Ryan hovering over me.

"What about your—?" I panicked, lifting myself just enough to make sure he wasn't putting any unnecessary pressure on his knee, but found him twisted at the hips. His braced leg was still extended, no weight on it.

"Don't worry about me," Ryan said. He kissed my lips again, then my neck, my chest right between my breasts. "We're focusing on you right now."

And focus on me he did as he folded the fabric of my bra back, exposing my peaked nipples, and took one into his mouth.

My back arched, my lower lip pulled between my teeth to suppress the moan that so desperately wanted to escape. When Ryan bit down, it did.

I found the fabric of his shirt, bunching it in my fist, desperate to cling to something. Anything.

But I lost my lifeline a moment later when Ryan sat up and shucked the fabric off, revealing the full extent of his athletic build, all the tattoos that adorned his skin.

I wanted to memorize every single one. All the artwork Ryan had deemed special enough to permanently mark his skin. But he didn't give me enough time to begin my studies as he sucked each of my nipples between his lips again, one after the other, and continued his descent down my body.

"Ryan," I moaned when he kissed just above the waist of my jeans, his hand cupping between my legs, rubbing me over the denim.

"I'm not letting these get in the way today," he assured me, then worked the button free.

I wiggled my hips when he tugged the pants down, trying to assist in any way I could. I was desperate. I'd never ached for anything as much as I was aching for Ryan, and I knew it showed on my panties given the way his eyes darkened as soon as his eyes settled between my legs.

"Look at this pretty little pussy," he groaned and ran a finger over the slickness seeping through my underwear. "All wet and ready for me to take it."

"Please," I begged, writhing on the trailer bed in anticipation.

Ryan's grin could be described as nothing but mischievous. This was a man that knew what he was doing. He'd told me already how he never left women wanting, but that was before I'd felt what he was hiding under his pants. Experienced what magic he could work with his tongue.

The longer he kept me waiting, the slicker I became, desperate for some sort of release.

Ryan's fingers curled into the waistband of my panties and pulled them down my legs. He tossed them carelessly on top of the growing pile of my clothes before he slipped off the trailer, his weight supported on his good knee. He bent it, resting it on the bed so his other could remain straight, before he grabbed my waist and tugged.

I slid closer, my eyes never leaving Ryan. One of my hands moved up to palm my own breast, my nipple pinched between my fingers. I knew he'd seen when he groaned, and then his arms were hooked under my knees, my lower body lifted off the trailer bed, my calves placed on his shoulders. My ankles instinctively latched around his neck, holding myself in place.

"You have no fucking idea how long I've wanted to taste your cunt," he growled, running a finger along my slick folds. My back arched when it disappeared within them. "So fucking tight. You're gonna feel so good wrapped around my cock, Harps."

"Ry—" I tried to plead, but was cut off by my own moan when he removed his finger and bent at the waist, replacing the touch of his hand with that of his tongue.

Oh. My. *God.*

It hadn't been his ego talking at all when he'd made his claims about pleasuring women. His tongue flicked over my clit, making the most beautiful feeling of ecstasy build. After being left on the edge of an orgasm the night before, it was a miracle I didn't shatter at the first stroke of his hand on me.

I was holding back now, needing more of this, not wanting to finish yet out of fear that Ryan would stop as soon as I did. If I let myself, I'd fall right over the edge of pleasure that very second.

Never had I ever been confronted with the issue of *holding back* my orgasm. Usually, it was the exact opposite problem. But Ryan was a man of his word.

And when he slipped two fingers back into me, still working my clit with his tongue, there was no way I could hold on any longer.

I clung to my breasts, writhing on the trailer bed as the orgasm overcame me. Ryan still hadn't stopped, pumping his fingers in and out of me while I clenched around them, his mouth still covering my clit, sucking.

"*Fuck,*" I said, voice quivering as I rode out the waves of pleasure that Ryan's work continued to prolong.

Only when my body turned to jelly did he stop.

Ryan lifted his head, a cocky grin on his lips, watching as I lay panting beneath him.

He placed a kiss on my soaked and sated pussy. "How was that?"

Half-breathless, I replied, "You know exactly how that was, asshole."

Ryan chuckled and placed a kiss on each of my inner thighs before he lowered me back to the trailer. With my body no longer obstructing my view, I could see just how hard he was in his jeans, the bulge straining against the fabric to the point where I imagined it was painful.

I sat up, already reaching for the button of his pants, when I said, "Let me repay the favor."

The button popped free of its hole at the same time Ryan's palm found my forehead and pushed me back.

"Hey," I complained with a grimace.

Two fingers pinched my chin and lifted my face just enough so I could stare up at Ryan from under my lashes.

He lowered himself so our noses were nearly touching, his hold never releasing.

"As much as I appreciate your enthusiasm to suck my cock," he said, "I'm afraid if you do that, I won't be able to stop myself from burying it so deep in your pussy they'll hear you shouting my name all the way in town."

"Why don't you then?" I challenged.

With his free hand, Ryan tapped his brace. "This. I don't want anything getting in the way." He somehow managed to get even closer, his lust-glazed eyes staring into mine. "I've spent at least ten years wondering what it would feel like to be inside you, Harper. So, when I finally get the chance to fuck you, I intend to fuck you right."

A shiver went up my spine. Or maybe I came a little again, just imagining what Ryan intended to do to me.

I nodded, speechless, and he chuckled. He placed a quick kiss on my lips.

"Now that that's settled…" Ryan lowered his good leg to the ground, making sure to keep his weight on it. "We have a float to build."

CHAPTER SIXTEEN

I NEVER THOUGHT I'd be able to look at Mr. Cochran's trailer bed the same way again, but over the course of the next week, as more and more of the Stallions-provided décor began to adorn it, a parade float slowly replaced the location of the best oral sex I'd ever received.

Then again, that title had been replaced with the backseat of my car, anyway. Followed by the backseat of the truck. And the bathroom at Sunrise. Oh, and Dave Caldwell's favorite chair in their family home. That one was actually my favorite, and not only because Ryan's cum might have left a stain after a little bit of titty fucking.

Whoops. Our bad, Dave.

What could I say? We'd been needing to get creative when it came to satisfying our needs—especially since Ryan was still adamant about wanting to wait until he no longer wore a brace before we had sex.

Besides, ruining a chair every now and then still seemed way less consequential than ruining five years of Ryan's and my lives.

It was funny, actually. This kind of behavior was probably what our parents had been afraid of when we were younger—two horny little teenage best friends sneaking around and getting each other off whenever we had the chance. I wasn't going to kid myself into thinking either one of us would have been as successful in the latter department at first; I'd had exactly one mediocre partner prior to college, and the sexual expertise to match. But as adults, we were undoubtedly worse. We had ten years of pent-up sexual frustration we'd both been in denial about, after all. Any minute spent making up for lost time was a minute well-spent.

Just because we'd grown up, though, didn't mean the sneaking around was any less at play.

I honked twice when I pulled into the Caldwell's driveway, as had become the routine. If I saw the truck when I showed up, I'd been told to stay in the car. The only time I was allowed in the house, per Ryan's request, was when his parents were out. Or at least his dad. I'd seen Gina a few times since the argument, and she'd gone on treating me the same way she always had, albeit with a little bit more obvious apprehension than before. Almost like she thought I'd mentally throw her in the same category as her husband.

Never. If I hadn't done it yet, I couldn't imagine it happening at any other point.

But Dave and I were now on a strict no-contact basis. Not that I was complaining. Life became much easier when you didn't find yourself constantly in defense against a misogynistic asshole all the time. Who woulda thought?

The front door opened, and Ryan's large frame filled the space. He'd been promoted to one crutch in public, and leaned his weight on it as he called back to someone in the house over his shoulder. Seconds later, Gina appeared at his side, passing off some sort of plastic container into her son's free hand.

I honked again when she waved excitedly to me, then lifted herself onto her toes to kiss her son's cheek.

"What's that?" I asked when Ryan made it into the passenger seat.

"She insisted we take some pumpkin muffins she made." He twisted and tossed the box gently into the back seat. "Thinks we aren't eating with all this work we're doing on the float."

"Well, she's not wrong," I said. "But I wouldn't say it's the float's fault."

Ryan chuckled, and that same nervous-excited feeling I always got when he gave me his attention lately bubbled low in my stomach.

"Hi," he whispered.

"Hey," I said back.

Then he leaned across the console to kiss me.

When he pulled away, his lips still within reach should either of us one want to pick back up again—and I knew I definitely did; his sweet, gentle kisses turned me on even more than the rough ones—I asked, "You ready for this?"

"Is anyone ever ready to go spend an entire afternoon being judged by teenagers?"

I laughed as I sat back, putting the car in reverse to get us started on our journey to Timberland Creek High School.

In hindsight, maybe Ryan and I should have waited before we put in the request with Coach Fitz about having his senior players on our float for the Fall Festival. Both of us had been so caught up in everything else going on that it had completely slipped our mind what time of year it was.

Homecoming.

Yeah. Fun. Dances. Whatever.

But around here, homecoming was a thing. Like, a *big* thing.

The whole situation was kind of funny once you left the town and heard about other people's high school experiences. I mean, really, the whole celebration was happening for under one hundred students. It gave everyone something to do, though, and it made the kids feel important. That's all that mattered, I supposed.

So, when Coach Fitz flipped our favor back on us and asked if Ryan wouldn't mind coming to speak as part of the homecoming festivities…

"I have a few notes," Ryan said, scrolling on his phone. "You don't think I needed, like, an actual speech, do you?"

"Probably not," I tried to reassure him. "Do you have something you can recycle from another event you've gone to?"

"Not sure the annual breast cancer awareness gala or Heisman acceptance speech I used in college will work for this one, unfortunately."

"You'll be fine." I put my hand, palm up, on the center console and Ryan's covered it almost immediately, our fingers lacing together. "Let's be so for real about it. The boys are gonna be fangirling. The girls are gonna be gossiping about how hot you are. No one's gonna be paying attention to what you say."

"Aw, you think I'm hot?" Ryan teased. When I tried to tug my hand away, he brought my knuckles up to his lips.

"Focus, Caldwell," I said through a smile.

"I am." He kissed another two knuckles. "Just not on what you want me to be focusing on."

"Oh, I love this line of focus, trust me." Ryan chuckled. "But you have about two minutes until we pull into the school parking lot. If you want a speech, you'd better think of it fast."

"I, uh, think I have less than two minutes, actually."

I was about to ask what he meant when I heard them. I'd been so zoned in on Ryan that I hadn't even noticed the cheerleaders and football players lining the road. As soon as they realized who was seated in the passenger seat of my car, idle conversations turned into excitement.

High-pitched wooing and voice-crack-riddled cheers surrounded our car. Pom-poms with metallic ribbons in the gold and black hues of Timberland Creek High sparkled in the mid-afternoon sunshine.

Ryan lifted his hand, offering the kids a few timid waves. I tried my best to avoid hitting them while turning into the school parking lot.

"Did they never learn to stay on the sidewalk?" I asked. I slammed on my breaks when a football player stepped off the curb, face twisted as he shouted and flashed a poster sign that read, "Once a Wolverine, Always a Legend!" A big, glittery eighty-seven finished it off, paying tribute to the number Ryan had worn since his peewee league days.

"I told you they're vicious," Ryan countered through his teeth, smile remaining intact as he waved at a gaggle of cheerleaders. They dropped into a huddle, all of them giggling and squealing.

"You said they're judge-y."

"Same thing."

A bright orange light stick caught my attention further down the way, and I followed it to the parking spot that had apparently been reserved for Ryan.

"Oh, Harper, sweetie, it's good to see you," Principal Morales greeted when I stepped out of the car. She'd been running this place as long as I could remember. "Ah, and there he is! Making his triumphant return!"

Considering I made her coffee almost every morning—caramel macchiato with an extra shot, no whip, and non-fat milk—being passed over didn't surprise me.

But the enthusiasm with which she greeted Ryan made me wonder if all those rumors about her having a crush on him when he was a student might have been true.

"Hey, Mrs. M," Ryan greeted, bending to hug the excited woman. I laughed when he grimaced over her shoulder at me. As someone who resembled the Latina version of Mrs. Potts from Beauty and the Beast, the strength of her hugs was never expected.

"Oh, don't you go worrying about formalities!" She pulled back from the hug and scoffed, flicking her wrists like calling her by the name we'd used for fifteen years was the most absurd notion. "Call me Lucia."

"Lucia it is, then."

I shook my head, lips pursed with a smirk. When Ryan noticed, he winked. And that's when Principal Morales must have remembered I was there.

"I should have expected you two to come together," she said. "Still the best of friends?"

"The bestest," I confirmed, my overly cheerful customer service voice coming out along with a bit of subtle sarcasm.

"That's so wonderful!" She clapped her hands together. "But onto the big news! Ryan—we're so grateful you could be here today. The students are looking so forward to meeting you. We invited the elementary school to join as well. Hope you don't mind."

"Not at all. The more the merrier, right?" Oh, his PR training was *good*. No one would ever know he was terrified of teenagers. "I'm glad Coach Fitz invited me."

"He's going to be in attendance, too, of course. We were thinking him and Mayor Turner could introduce you. And—oh, you know what? Why don't you just join me? We can meet up with them in the gymnasium. Most of the students are still in class, but they'll be let out a bit early so they can enjoy the…"

Principal Morales kept walking into the school. I doubted she knew that Ryan had stopped following. Instead, he'd stopped at my side.

"She's totally still got her crush on you," I teased.

"Isn't she married?"

"Oh yeah. Super married."

"Then why do you think she has a crush?"

"For starters, how come I don't get to call her Lucia?" I asked.

Ryan shrugged. "Because I'm hot?"

He let out a soft laugh when I scoffed and rolled my eyes. And even if he was being annoying, I couldn't stop myself from smiling, too. Just a little.

"She's getting regular milk in her macchiato next time. By accident," I added with air quotes.

Ryan's crutch-free arm wrapped around my shoulders, and I instinctively reached up to lace our fingers together. He kissed the top of my head.

"C'mon," he said. "Time for me to get ripped apart by some kids."

FOR ALL OUR kidding around, the students ended up being great. They listened patiently to Coach Fitz's long recounting of Ryan's history with the football team, then to Mayor Turner's life-lesson moment about why you should always give back to the communities where you grew up. By the time Ryan actually made it to the podium, I was pretty sure half of the student body was asleep, but they perked right on up again at the chance to ask a real-life football player some questions.

As expected, they were utterly profound. And by that I meant I was fighting back laughter as soon as I realized they were more interested in what kinds of cars Ryan owned—a Porsche for himself, then the Ford and Audi his parents drove—and the craziest vacation he'd been on—an adrenaline junky's dream trip to Australia—than anything actually pertinent to his career.

But Ryan answered them. No matter how absurd or completely unrelated-to-football the question might be, he charmed the pants right off everyone in the room with his smile and natural charisma.

And to think he'd believed these kids wouldn't like him. I was pretty sure the custodial staff member lingering in the corner was now completely obsessed.

"Okay, I think Mr. Caldwell has time for one or two more questions," Coach Fitz said. "Let's make 'em count." He pointed to a boy near the front row of the bleachers. "Aiden. You're up."

Aiden lowered his hand. The serious stare he aimed Ryan's direction made me wonder if we were finally going to get the first legitimate question of the afternoon. Then he asked, "Why do you keep staring at that girl?"

Apparently, this had been a topic of conversation among Aidan and his friends because the boys huddled around him started to snicker. He looked mighty proud of himself for being the one to take one for the team and ask what they'd seemingly all been wondering.

But while they were goofing off, the gymnasium bleachers filled with a sudden wave of hushed chatter. It didn't take long until they figured out who Aiden had been talking about. I was the only person other than Ryan—and a few others who were very obviously reporters for the *Timberland Creek Gazette*, given their notepads and cameras—who wasn't faculty.

Blush heated my cheeks, and I locked eyes with Ryan.

"Kids! Hey—everyone quiet down!" Principal Morales stepped in front of Ryan, waving her arms in an attempt to bring some order back to the homecoming week event.

Ryan reared back on the stool he'd been provided when she swiveled the microphone towards herself.

"QUIET."

The piercing screech was enough to make my eye twitch, but the command did its job. The chatter stopped. That wasn't to say they'd quit paying attention to me yet, though.

"I, uh…" Ryan started, when Principal Morales twisted the microphone holder back in his direction, giving it a gentle pat to match the smile she aimed his way. He huffed a laugh. "Well, right now, it looks like *everyone's* staring at that girl, huh?"

I widened my eyes as if to say *not helping*. He might be used to all the attention, but I most definitely was not.

Ryan cleared his throat. "The truth is," he said, returning his attention to Aiden, "I think she's very beautiful, and I keep getting distracted."

When Aiden grimaced, Ryan added, "I don't think he liked that answer."

Thankfully, the students laughed at that. Ryan cast me another quick glance, and I tried my best to give him a reassuring smile in return.

"Alright, onto the next one," Coach Fitz said. "Ella? What've you got?"

"Is she your girlfriend?"

Oh my god. This couldn't be happening.

Another round of whispers started, this time interlaced with giggles. But before Principal Morales could make it to the podium again, Ryan grabbed the mic.

"I actually don't know." He turned on his stool, and met my stare. "What d'you think? *Are* you my girlfriend, Harps?"

In the most high-school way possible, the gym filled with a challenging, prolonged "*ohhhh*" as if Ryan had just dropped the hottest tea anyone had ever heard. He very well might have with the way my face burned.

Ryan, of course, looked completely at ease. Scratch that—his grin was nothing but cocky. Teasing. It only got worse when he leaned back on his stool, arms crossed, clearly entertained by my reaction to being called out.

Asshole.

But still, that grin. My heart fluttered at the sight of it, knowing all the other times as of late that I'd seen it.

"C'mon, Harper," he teased, voice dipping low enough to send a ripple of giggles through the gym—and a ripple of something through me that had me crossing my legs.

The man knew exactly how to get me to react.

I swallowed hard, forcing my lips to curl into a smirk even as my pulse thundered in my ears. Two could play this game, I supposed.

"Well," I said, arching an eyebrow and tilting my head, unbothered, "considering I haven't been taken on a proper date yet, I'm not sure."

The students roared, their same reaction from earlier amplified tenfold at my bold call out. From behind me, I heard some of our old teachers mutter, "I knew it" and "I always thought they'd make a cute couple" as if I couldn't hear them.

Ryan held up his hands in mock surrender. "Fair point," he said, his grin widening. It very well might have been due to my worsening blush. "But it *has* been a while since I've been back here. I'm not sure I'd even know where to take you." Even from my distance, the mischief in his eyes was noticeable. "You got any suggestions?"

"Oh, no," I said, shaking my head and fighting back a smile. "This is your problem now, buddy."

Ryan laughed. Then he turned towards the crowd of kids, hands spread wide like he was addressing a jury. "What do you think, guys?"

I'd never seen hands fly into the air so fast, some of the more eager participants going as far as lifting themselves out of their seats to be seen easier.

"Corn maze!" one boy shouted when he was called on, earning a few nods and echoes of agreement.

"No, no—you have to go to a pumpkin patch!" another girl who'd been bouncing in her seat countered. "And then you can go home and carve them!"

"What about a haunted hayride?" someone else chimed in, their suggestion immediately sparking a chorus of oohs and gasps.

"And a ghost tour!"

"Alright, alright!" Ryan smiled as he waved his hands in a

gesture to get the kids to settle. They were all but chanting *haunted hayride* at this point. "Corn mazes, ghosts, hayrides, pumpkins—I'm taking notes." He mimed jotting things down, earning another round of muted laughter from the bystanders around me. Seemed the faculty was just as charmed by Ryan as I was right now. At least it was helping ease my nerves a bit.

"You *can't* forget to take pictures," Ella said, her tone much more serious than I thought someone as tiny as her would be capable of. "It's not gonna be official unless you post a picture!"

I pressed my lips together to keep from laughing as Ryan nodded solemnly. His eyes slid to the side, in the direction of the reporters who were feverishly scribbling on their notepads.

Oh, pictures would be taken alright. I was pretty sure they already had been, and it wouldn't be our social media where the news broke. All of Timberland Creek would know soon enough—if not the whole United States if any other reporters got wind of the article.

"Good to know," he told Ella, his eyes going from the reporters to me, a fresh sparkle lighting them, noticeable even at my distance. "So? Harps? Sound good enough for you?"

I crossed my arms over my chest. "I'm a bit of a baby with scary stuff."

Okay, note to self: kids do not like it when you can't handle the most basic parts of spooky season. Namely the spooking.

It was only a half-lie, though. Haunted houses and stuff

weren't usually my go-to. Not that I had a go-to to begin with. Fall—yes, the whole season—hadn't been something I'd participated in since I'd become so jaded. But now that the reason for that was also the one asking me on the date…

"Don't worry," Ryan said with a wink. "I'll keep you safe."

I curled my lips in to keep my smile from growing as large as it wanted to when the girls in attendance squealed in delight.

The boys had a different reaction entirely.

Aiden rose slowly in his seat, pounding his fists in the air with each beat as he chanted, "Go on the date! Go on the date!"

It didn't take long before his friend group joined in, followed by some of the girls, until the chant flowed through the whole crowd. I turned over my shoulder, surprised to hear it spread into the teacher section behind me.

Into the microphone, Ryan chanted, "Go on the date. Go on the date," and damn me if my heart didn't melt at his smile.

I let out a dramatic sigh. "I suppose I can go."

The gym exploded with cheers, but all I could hear was Ryan's quiet chuckle in the microphone.

"But it's gotta be good, Caldwell!" I shouted over the uproar. "Nothing's official unless it's good!"

Ryan's smile grew, and even above the continuing noise— that Principal Morales was now desperately trying to calm—I could hear him when he said, "Challenge accepted."

CHAPTER SEVENTEEN

HERE'S THE THING. I could preach about why staying in the small town where I'd grown up had been the best decision for me until I was blue in the face. I'd ramble on about the beauty of Timberland Creek for days. I could count on one hand the reasons why having a tight-knit community was a *bad* thing.

Unfortunately, I might have finally found a reason to move onto the next hand.

"Oh no…" I said, reaching for the stack of newspapers Hemi kept on hand at Sunrise Brews. All the local businesses had copies—right there next to the dining and shopping guides for tourists.

The last thing I'd expected when I'd walked into work that morning? To see my face on the front page.

It wasn't *only* my face, in fairness. Ryan was waving at the unpictured crowd of teenagers in the Timberland Creek High gym two days before. I stood at his side, smiling up at him, my hands frozen mid-clap.

Two more smaller pictures accompanied that one within the article: one of Ryan signing a football and one of him posing with the football team. The article, from what I could tell after skimming it, was really just a big promotion for the homecoming game happening later that night. As if everyone wouldn't be at it anyway. In a town like this, the degrees of separation from someone working at the school, volunteering at the game, or playing in the game were slim. Therefore, everyone went to show their support.

At least the part where the kids had planned our date for the weekend had been left out. The last thing I needed was for anyone to make comments about—

I jumped so high when someone knocked excitedly on the front door of Sunrise the newspaper flew out of my hand. Even Hemi, who I was sure knew the contents of the paper and was choosing not to comment yet, cussed under her breath at the sudden noise in the otherwise quiet café.

Somehow, I was still staring at the black-and-white photograph of Ryan and I when I looked to see who was here before open.

Tori popped out from where she hid behind the unfolded paper.

"What're you doing here to early?" I asked after I unlocked the door to let her in.

"I've been taking walks," she explained. "Trying to enjoy seeing my feet while I still can." Then she lifted the newspaper. "Um, so what's this?"

"I don't know what you're talking about."

I crouched down and picked up the copy of the newspaper I'd been examining before I stuffed it in the tray from which it had come. Then I turned my back on Tori, making my way across the café.

"Nope. You're not getting away that easy."

Tori followed right after me, and I prayed her unborn child never tried to sneak back in from a party or something. Jackson would be a pushover. Tori? No chance.

I caught Hemi's head swiveling to follow me as I moved around behind the counter, going about my everyday tasks, but I dutifully ignored her. Tori might have gotten the same treatment if she hadn't slammed the paper down, demanding it get attention.

"When did this happen?" she asked.

I shrugged. "A couple days ago."

"And he asked you to go along?"

"He needed a ride, so yeah."

"And do you look at all guys you give rides to like this?" When I gave her a look she clarified, "For once in my life, I legitimately mean a ride in a car."

"Can you blame me for checking?" I asked. But when she didn't respond, I sighed. "I mean, you wouldn't have been wrong either way, but—"

"Girl!" Tori leaned on the counter, eyes bugging and palms pressed flat to support her weight. A grin curled her lips, even as her mouth hung slightly open in what I could only imagine was mild shock. "Are you fucking with me right now?"

"Language," Hemi chastised.

Tori gave a little eye roll, then her face returned to the way it had been before. I'd argue there was even a little more eagerness as she awaited my answer.

"Not with *you…*" I said.

"But definitely with a certain football player?" When I nodded, she actually jumped. "Holy shit! I knew it! I. *Knew. It.*"

Somehow, amid all her excitement, Tori noticed Hemi's silence.

"You knew already?" she accused.

"Who said that?" Hemi fired back.

"You'd be *way* more vocal if you were just finding out about this for the first time." Tori put her hands on her hips. "Don't lie to a pregnant woman, Hemdeep."

"If you must know, I had no choice but to find out when they decided to have sex on those front steps," Hemi said with a nod towards the front door.

Tori gasped.

"We didn't have sex on the front steps," I argued.

"In the bathroom, then?"

"Not there either." Hemi narrowed her eyes at me. "We

didn't!"

"Mhm," she hummed, unconvinced. "You were in there a mighty long time…"

Tori reached across the counter and hit my arm before she mouthed, "Get it, girl."

"Just so you both shut up, I can promise you we haven't had sex. At all. I swear on Curly Lambeau's grave."

"Who the heck is Curly Lambeau?" Tori asked.

I narrowed my eyes at her. "I'll give you a pass because you're from Chicago," I said. "But regardless, I'm telling the truth."

"Well, are you gonna get on that?" Tori asked. "Literally and figuratively, of course."

"I mean, yeah. Eventually," I admitted. "But one half of the equation is a little out of commission at the moment."

Ryan had started physical therapy, though, which was promising. He'd only had a few sessions, accompanied by a trainer the Stallions had flown out here—much to the trainer's chagrin, according to his patient. I couldn't blame him. It probably sucked going from warm, sunny Texas to gloomy, po-dunk Wisconsin. But the Stallions had made it clear they wanted Ryan up and going soon.

Like soon-soon.

Like if he could become a superhuman and defy the six-to-eight-weeks recovery odds that were standard for his injury, they'd love that.

"You just *had* to pick the one with the long-lasting injury, didn't you?" Tori tsked.

"The heart wants what it wants," Hemi chimed in. "You know that better than anyone."

A wistful smile found its way onto Tori's lips. I hadn't known Jackson all that well, but I remembered he would come into Sunrise a bit before he and Tori were officially together. I'd actually helped Tori pick out the dress for their first official date when I'd still worked part-time at one of the boutiques in town. He'd been a stoic dude before that. A bit of a loner, it seemed.

Even though Ryan wasn't even remotely like that, I kind of understood the giddiness Tori showed at the mention of her husband. Now I did, anyway. It was the same reaction I had when I knew I was going to see Ryan. The same one I'd always had, really.

Weird how perspective could really make me understand my past. How I'd always loved Ryan, just maybe not in the way I'd once believed.

"He'll be back to normal in a few weeks," I informed them. "Until then, I'll just keep driving him around and helping with the parade float."

"And after he's better?" Tori asked with a suggestive wiggle of her eyebrows.

"Shut up…" I muttered, my chin tilted down. I was still smiling, though.

When Tori's fingers grazed my arm across the counter, I looked up to find her grinning, too. "I'm happy for you.

Seriously," she said. "You work so damn hard all the time. You deserve to take a moment for yourself. Enjoy some of life's pleasures."

"I'm trying." I wrapped my arm around Hemi's shoulders. "This one's giving me a bit of leeway with my schedule lately."

"That float of yours won't build itself," my boss added, her arm going around me in return.

The bell above the door jingled, and the chatter that came with our first actual customers of the day drowned out our trio of chuckles.

"Well, on that note," Tori said. "Mind if I grab Jackson's usual before I head out? I'll leave you two alone before it gets super busy."

"On it," Hemi said, not bothering to put the order in the system before she got to work.

Tori reached into the belt bag strapped across her chest and pulled out a ten-dollar bill. She stuffed it in the tip jar as she asked, "You going to the game tonight, by the way?"

"I wasn't going to," I admitted. "But then Ryan got asked to present the king and queen, and my brothers are all coming into town to see him so—" I shrugged. "It'll be fun, I guess. The team is good this year, supposedly."

"Maybe I'll see you there, then," Tori said. She nodded in Hemi's direction. "Ever since he got into it with that one, Jackson's been trying to pay more attention to sports. Wants to be prepared in case it's a boy or whatever." She rolled her eyes.

I chuckled. "I'll have some time after this float's done to coach him up on football."

"You *and* your beau," Tori said with a wink. She thanked Hemi when the latte was passed across the counter.

"I'll see ya later, ladies," she called back to Hemi and me as she made her way out of the café. And much to the horror of the elderly couple making their way up to the counter, didn't neglect to add, "Can't wait to hear about all the sex, Harper!"

THE GOOD PART about homecoming Friday? Locals were more involved in preparation for the game and the dance that would happen the next day than they were in their everyday activities. Which meant that Sunrise was blessedly slow. Not slow enough for my usual panic about Hemi's finances to flare, but enough so that I didn't miss when my favorite customer walked in.

Ryan beamed, holding up a copy of the newspaper that continued to haunt me. I rolled my eyes dramatically enough to make him laugh before I put my elbows on the counter. My face fell into my waiting palms shortly after.

"Is now a bad time to ask you to sign this for me?" Ryan asked when he reached the opposite side of the counter. He leaned his weight onto his good leg.

My head popped up, and I immediately clocked the mischief shining in his eyes.

"Just because *you're* used to being on the front page, doesn't mean we all are," I said. "How'd you get that, anyway?"

"Found it on the kitchen table this morning." The purse of his lips told me enough of how it had gotten there.

"Does your dad suspect?" I whispered.

"Probably."

"Has he said anything?"

Ryan shook his head. "Now that I've begun therapy, I think he's a bit more satisfied than he was before. My return to the field seems more realistic."

"Was it ever not?"

Ryan shrugged. "I suppose you never know with these things, right?"

I gave a one-shoulder shrug, but thankfully didn't have to say anything more on the matter when Hemi returned from the back room where she'd been enjoying her break.

"I was wondering when you'd show up," she greeted.

"Hi, Hemi," Ryan said back with a wide smile. The two of them had gotten mighty close lately, mostly due to Ryan's appreciation of my boss's no-shit attitude. And because, as she'd hinted, he showed up practically every day.

"You taking my employee away again?"

"Not this time," he promised. "I'm actually here to order and go. Mom's out in the car."

I followed the direction Ryan pointed his thumb, and sure enough the tiny frame of Gina Caldwell was just barely visible through the tinted windows of the Audi parked in one of the three spots out front of the café.

"Why didn't she come in?" I asked.

"I told her to wait in the car."

My brow furrowed. "Seems like more of a challenge for you to come in here than her?"

"Whoa now—I'm becoming a champ at walking again," Ryan defended. Then he grinned. "Besides, if she came in here with me, I wouldn't be able to do this."

I met him halfway across the counter when he leaned forward, our lips meeting.

"Not in front of the customers."

Hemi rolled up the paper Ryan had left on the counter into a cylinder and tapped us both on the head.

"I can't help myself," Ryan defended. "Your barista is too beautiful."

I rolled my eyes. "Did you just come here to compliment me? I mean, I'm not complaining, but it seems mean to drag Gina out here just for that."

Ryan grinned and aimed his index finger at me. "Tomorrow. Warm clothes are ideal. Nothing too fancy."

"Still not giving me anything else, huh?"

Honestly, I was happy I'd gotten that much out of him. Ryan had been radio-silent when it came to our supposed date. And I only said *supposed* because the lack of details I'd been provided—exactly zero—had me wondering if it would actually even happen.

The warning about warm clothing at least gave me some idea of what might be in store, even if I didn't know for sure what he had planned.

"Nope," Ryan said with a smile, popping the P. "Aren't surprises fun?"

"I hate surprises," I replied. "You *know* I hate surprises."

"Ever since your seventh birthday party when everyone jumped out at you."

"I cried for an hour." And had been traumatized by the mere idea of jump scares ever since. Come to think of it, that was probably why I wasn't too fond of haunted houses, either.

My eyes popped open at the thought. "You didn't take the kids' suggestion for haunted stuff seriously, did you?"

He thanked Hemi for the two drinks she'd prepared while we'd talked—the woman was good at learning the regular orders—then said, "You'll see tomorrow. I'm *full* of surprises."

"*Ryan*," I whined, prolonging the end of his name.

He opened his mouth to respond at the same time his phone started going off in his pocket. A soft cuss escaped him as he fumbled for it, trying to keep balance—of himself and everything he was holding.

Ryan muttered another soft thanks when Hemi took the drinks back and stuffed them into a carrying tray, at the same time he finally retrieved his phone.

"Shit," he murmured. "I have to take this."

"Who is it?"

"My agent," he informed me before he accepted the call, his phone balanced between his shoulder and ear, and said, "Scott. Hey, man—what's up? You have news?"

My brow furrowed, the voice on the other end of the line muffled enough that I couldn't pick up on what he was saying.

It wasn't like I expected Ryan to tell me everything that was going on with his career—most of it, at the moment, I was sure, was related to regaining his health—but the excited tone of his agent mixed with the soft smile and eager eyes he wore made me curious.

I knew he'd noticed my reaction when his gaze slid my way, his grin widening.

"Hey—yeah, no—that sounds great, just one sec, okay? I'm grabbing some coffee. One sec."

Ryan pushed the mute button before he retrieved the drink tray and aimed one more toothy smile in my direction.

"You look suspicious," I accused. "This doesn't have anything to do with our date, does it?"

"No," Ryan replied, leaning across the counter to give my forehead a kiss. "Hopefully another surprise, though."

He pivoted, angling himself toward the exit.

"Pick me up at six," he called back over his shoulder, the drink tray clutched in one hand while he maneuvered his single crutch with the other.

"I don't get to know what we're doing *and* you're making me drive us everywhere?" I already figured that would be the case. I was saying it more to give him shit than anything else.

Ryan grinned. "See you later, Harps."

He winked before he made his way out of the café.

CHAPTER EIGHTEEN

THE MODEST-SIZED football field—"stadium" if you asked the students, but then again, most of them had never had the opportunity to go to a professional game yet—was decked out in black and gold. Balloons, streamers, banners, posters of the players—you name it. It was there.

The marching band was making its way through a slightly off-pitch rendition of "Don't Stop Believin'" when my family and I finally made it past the ticket booth. We'd each forked over five dollars for a chance to see the Timberland Creek Wolverines take on the Golden Prairie Eagles.

"Can't remember the last time I was here," my youngest brother, Connor, commented.

"Probably Harper's graduation for me," Cameron added, holding onto his wife Hannah's hand while he pushed a stroller with my nearly one-year-old niece, Nora, in it. Said toddler was the primary reason why Cam hadn't been able to make it home in a bit. Couldn't say I blamed him. Flying from Columbus to Wisconsin with a baby didn't sound super enjoyable.

"What? You mean you losers *don't* want to spend a Friday night at your alma mater's homecoming game?" Derek teased. Sarah smiled at his side.

A bit of roughhousing and a few more verbal jabs later, Mom finally stepped in.

"Would you three cut it out?" She scoffed. "I swear these kids are more well-behaved than you three. And you're all in your thirties, for Christ's sake."

I pulled out my phone and checked for any new notifications in order to hide my grin. After two decades of living in a male-dominated house, Diane Bennett no longer gave a crap when it came to mincing her words. My brothers were going to get told exactly what she was thinking. She did the same for me, too, just less frequently.

"We need to entertain ourselves somehow before the main attraction."

"We purposely got here right before game time, so we didn't have to sit in the cold for too—" Dad tried, but Connor cut him off.

"Not *that* main attraction." Con looked down the line of our family until he found me. "Where's your famous buddy at, Harps?"

"He's here. Somewhere." I glanced at my phone screen again,

but there was still nothing. "I think he had to meet with the homecoming committee or something before the game."

I knew he'd been at the school since the afternoon. That's where his mom had been taking him after the detour at Sunrise. Filming some promotional videos for the admissions board. Getting interviewed by the school paper. All sorts of very long and boring activities I'd been grateful to miss.

"Is it for that thing you're doing?" Derek asked. "For the parade?"

"Wasn't that earlier today? Cam asked, referring to the annual homecoming parade that went through town.

What can I say—we liked our parades here in Timberland Creek.

"No, they're doing the Fall Fest," Mom corrected. "Did you still need my help at the tent, sweetie?"

"Huh?" I asked as I typed out a quick, *Where are you?* text to Ryan. "Oh. Um, sure. Gina's gonna be there, too, I think."

Connor nudged me with his elbow. "What's your float look like?"

"Is it at Mom and Dad's house?" Derek added.

That finally got Dad talking. "You think I have the space for a whole trailer in the garage?"

My phone vibrated with a new notification. *Fitz's office,* the text read.

Somehow, my family had managed to get into a mild argument about my and Ryan's project without me even getting involved.

"I'll show you guys progress pictures later," I said. "I'm gonna go snag Ryan really quick."

They'd really gotten into it, which meant I wasn't given much more than a few non-committal acknowledgements before I made my way into the school.

Compared to a few days before when the place had been abuzz with students, Timberland Creek High felt like a ghost town. My footfalls echoed down the hallway with each step I took on the vinyl tile.

I figured that's why Ryan was already staring in my direction when I turned the corner on my way to the locker rooms.

"Thought you said you were in Fitz's office?" I asked.

"I was. Then I got bored."

I chuckled as I made my way to his side. When I was close enough, Ryan wrapped an arm around my shoulders, his attention returned to the trophy case in front of us.

There wasn't much inside it, to be honest. Small schools in small towns didn't often get the kinds of student athletes that brought plethoras of championships. But there were a few plaques and trophies on display.

A third-place men's golf plaque from 1962.

A fourth-place men's track and field trophy from 1967.

A first-place women's swim team plaque—and a few other individual medals—from 1996.

Two second-place volleyball championship trophies from

1999 and 2004.

And, of course, the state championship football trophy sitting front and center. The school's most recent accolade.

As far as I knew, Ryan was the only winner represented in the trophy case that had gone on to have any sort of professional career in the sport he'd played.

Next to the trophy, a picture of the team had been mounted on a plaque, all the boys' names listed on gold plates below it. The board in the background showcased the winning score of twenty-seven to fourteen. Because he'd scored two of the team's three touchdowns, Ryan stood in the middle of the group, holding the trophy and smiling.

"You have such a baby face when you don't have facial hair," I commented.

"Girl I'm trying to impress likes stubble. Noted."

I chuckled as I twisted to the side, wrapping my arms around Ryan's torso. He leaned down and kissed the top of my head.

"I'm already impressed," I whispered. Then after another silent moment of us staring at the photo, added, "It feels like that game just happened."

"Ten years ago," Ryan said. "Eleven, maybe?"

"Damn," I muttered. My arms tightened around him. "And here we are again."

"Here we are," he repeated, kissing my head again, his lips lingering this time around. "Did you go with Brent to that year's homecoming dance, too? Or was that only junior year?"

"Why you wanna know?" I tilted my head up to see his face. "Jealous?"

The vibration of Ryan's deep chuckle made a tingle go down my spine. "Hardly. I'm just trying to remember who got the honor of being your date while you were wearing that green dress."

"You remember what I wore, but you can't remember I went with Peter Hanlon?"

"Harper, there are very few memories ingrained as deeply in my brain as the one of you getting out of your mom's car and seeing you in that tiny green dress for the first time." Ryan's hand slid off my shoulders, down my back, until his hand found its way into the back pocket of my jeans. "And I know Peter didn't even appreciate it."

"Well, Peter's gay, so yeah—I'd say he probably didn't care." We'd gone as friends anyway, when his crush ended up not wanting to go and Brent was out of town at a family wedding in Milwaukee.

Ryan opened his mouth to say something more, but it quickly shut when the echo of distant footsteps reached us. Both of us waited to see who might join, but no one ever did, the school guest apparently going somewhere else.

"C'mon," Ryan suggested, the reminder that we weren't actually alone seeming to get to him. He removed his hand from my back pocket and held it out to me. "I want to go see if that stain on my old locker is still there."

I unwound myself from around Ryan and accepted his offer, our fingers intertwining like they so naturally did now when our palms met, and allowed him to guide me down the hall.

"Ugh," I groaned when I pushed the door to the boys' locker room open. Ryan limped past me on his crutch. "Now I remember why I never wanted to come in here. Do these kids know what deodorant is?"

Ryan laughed. "This is decades' worth of dedication, baby."

"I'd say blood, sweat, and tears, but it seems like mostly sweat at this point."

His eyes twinkled as he looked back over his shoulder at me, shaking his head. But Ryan didn't say anything more on the matter before he made his way further into the room.

Stacked black lockers that matched those in the school hallway lined the walls, an additional set sticking out into the middle to create a sort of geometric M shape. Wood benches sat in the center of each section, both of which were currently occupied by bags and gear the boys on the current team hadn't put away before they went out to the field.

The muted cheers and chatter of the game's attendees made their way to us. The locker room connected the main school building to the athletic fields, all the sports teams sharing, depending on what was in season at the time. The whistles that blew, loud and shrill, every few minutes let me know the game had probably started.

"Think we should head out soon?" I asked. "Everyone's

probably wondering where you are."

"Nah, they don't care," Ryan countered, but I had a feeling he was just being modest. Speaking as someone whose entire family had come into town, I was pretty sure almost everyone had shown up to even just catch a glimpse of Timberland Creek's golden boy.

"I think it was this one…" he muttered. As I followed him into the room, I saw Ryan leaned in close to a locker, eyes narrowed while he surveyed it.

"Did the locker number match your football number?" I asked, pointing to the little forty-five on a silver plate at the top of the door.

"No, which is why I can't remember if it was this one or… ah-ha! Nope, it was this one." He scooched over to the right a little. When he turned to me, he wore a mischievous grin. "Wanna know how I know?"

"Because you spent four years of your life stuffing your stinky football equipment into it?" I guessed.

Ryan waved me closer before he pointed at the locker in front of him. I leaned in close like he'd just done, trying to find any sign that might make it obvious he'd used it back in the day. His initials. His number. A message that read "Ryan Caldwell was here."

I came up with nothing.

"I have no idea what I'm looking for," I admitted.

Ryan extended his index finger, and I followed its guidance.

"See that little mark?" Ryan asked. "And all these?" he added, pointing to tinier dots of the same color.

"Yeah?"

He grinned. "Remember when Wyatt Sullivan broke his nose sophomore year?"

"Yeah…" I repeated, growing more suspicious of where this was going.

"Nate Coleman did it on accident with his helmet after practice one day." Ryan tapped the biggest spot again. "That's Wyatt's blood."

"Ew, Ryan," I groaned and reared back.

"And you thought it was only sweat in here," he teased.

"Okay, I stand corrected, but that's still disgusting."

Ryan's laugh at my reaction faded into a wistful sigh as he backed away from the locker. His head turned on a swivel as he took in the room that had been so familiar to him during our four years at this school. I, of course, hadn't really ever been in it; once or twice, maybe, to chat with Coach Fitz when I knew no other guys would be here. Other than that, I steered clear.

"So much shit went down in here," Ryan said.

He shoved the stray football gear to the floor then sat on the bench and laid his crutch down. I let him have a moment before I took the open spot beside him.

"Is this where I learn all the secrets?" I whispered, nudging him in the side.

His eyes slid to me sidelong, an inquisitive brow lifted. "Whatcha wanna know?"

I shrugged. "What's one thing I would never guess? Other than Wyatt Sullivan's blood marking this room forever."

Ryan chuckled, but his smile faded as he tried to think of something to tell me.

"I guess, when I really think about it, it was just a bunch of us fucking around. Doing dumb shit." His lips pursed in thought. "Some of the guys used to stash their weed in here because all the B.O. and body sprays used to disguise the scent. Um… then there was the time Matt accidentally snapped the door off one of the lockers and blamed it on a freshman. Oh shit—then there was the time Coach caught Matt and Valerie in here."

My brows lifted. "Wait, what?"

"Guys snuck their girlfriends—or whatever they wanted to call them—in here all the time." Ryan smirked. "You didn't know that?"

I shook my head. "I never dated a football player."

"In high school," Ryan amended, his hand finding my thigh. My whole body heated when his thumb brushed up and down over my jeans. "You never dated a football player in high school."

"Semantics," I teased. Then my curiosity got the better of me. "Did you bring any of your girlfriends in here?"

"Why? Jealous?" he said, repeating the question I'd thrown

at him earlier.

"A little."

The briefest hint of surprise lit his face at my admission, but I didn't defend my answer. I *would* be jealous, even if I had no right. Even if it was a thing of the past. I'd no longer be able to feign ignorance as to where Ryan had shared moments with women before me.

He reached out, grasping my chin with his thumb and forefinger, and lifted my face just enough where he could kiss me.

"You don't have to be," he whispered against my lips. "I never brought anyone in here."

"Not once?"

He shook his head, the hand on my thigh stilling. "I never wanted to. And if I'm being really honest, by the time I was doing anything other than making out with girls, Matt had gotten his ass handed to him by Coach. I was scared shitless to get caught after that."

My snort propelled my head forward just enough that my forehead met Ryan's. He was laughing too, his hand moved to the back of my neck to keep me close.

Warm, minty breath hit my lips with each of Ryan's exhales, and when his thumb stroked behind my ear, I lifted my hand to cup his face.

"What about now?" I asked in a whisper.

"Hm?"

"Would you want to now?"

That mischievous glint returned to his ocean-blue eyes. "Harps, what are you—?"

But that small sign of his interest was all I needed. He didn't get to finish his question before I slid off the bench and onto my knees before him.

I stared up at him as I ran my hand up his length over his jeans. Just that simple movement had him hardening under my touch. Ryan gritted his teeth, but not even that stopped him from moaning.

My fingers moved up still, until I reached the button of his pants.

"I think you deserve to have a little fun in here, too—don't you?" I asked as I undid the button.

My fingers curled into the waist of his jeans, tugging them and his briefs down as far as his leg brace would allow. It was just enough to get his cock free.

My hand wrapped around him, sliding up the shaft enough to get the precum at the head, bringing it back down with me as I worked him.

Ryan moaned again, his eyes drifting shut as he relished in the pleasure I brought him.

They popped open again seconds later, right as my mouth found its way around him.

I was pulled back by fingers tangled in my hair, a gasp escaping me as he slipped from between my lips.

"Shit," he muttered. I grinned at him, innocently fluttering my eyelashes. "You know what I've said about you doing that."

I pouted, my hand stroking his shaft in slow, tantalizing pumps. "So, it's still a no?"

"Fuck, Harps, I—" Ryan huffed a laugh. "I want you to do that so fucking bad. But I…" He swallowed, his Adam's apple bobbing. "I want you to feel good, too, baby. Nothing makes me happier than knowing you're satisfied. And I can't do that for you right now. Not in the way I want."

I hummed and leaned down again, kissing the tip of his cock. "Don't worry about me." I went down further, licking from the base to the head, never taking my eyes from Ryan. "Let me do this for you."

There was nothing gentle in the way Ryan gripped my chin, preventing me from any further teasing.

"Tell me what will satisfy you, Harper," he ground out. "Tell me what you want me to do."

A sly, victorious smile made its way onto my lips. "I want you to fuck my mouth."

His cock twitched in my hold as soon as the words left me.

"And that will make *you* feel good?"

I nodded. "Please," I begged.

My panties were already soaked from the mere fantasy of finally having him in my mouth. Never in all my life had I been so eager to give a blowjob, each time I was denied just adding more fuel to the fire.

The growing ache between my thighs was making me even more impatient. "Please, Ryan," I repeated, more desperate.

For a moment, I thought he really wouldn't accept my plea. And if he didn't… that would have been fine. I would have continued to wait until he decided he was ready. I would have waited an eternity, if that's what it took.

But then his hand moved from my chin to my hair again, and he pushed me down, down, down until my mouth was around him and the tip of his cock hit the back of my throat.

He held me there until a choked noise escaped me. The pressure released, and I came up for air, finding Ryan staring down at me with pupils so dilated, his eyes had turned nearly black.

"You look so fucking good, taking my cock like that, Harps," he said.

And because I was a people pleaser, I did it once more.

Ryan groaned, fingers tightening in my hair as I worked him. He never took charge again, though. I'd given head enough in my lifetime to know what a man wanted, and Ryan—damn, did he want it.

"Fuck, baby," he moaned.

I spit on him before working him with my hand. I didn't think I'd ever felt a guy this hard before, and it made my pussy clench just thinking of how wonderfully he would fill me.

My hips naturally rolled at the thought, and that's when I decided I couldn't take it anymore.

With one of my hands still on Ryan, working in tandem with my mouth, I reached down and undid the button of my own jeans and allowed my hand to slip into my panties.

I moaned around him the moment my fingers began to circle my clit, easing some of the need.

"That's right," Ryan ground out. The palm of his free hand flattened on the bench. "Fuck yourself while you suck my cock like a good girl."

I gagged as soon as his hips pushed up, opening my throat to fit as much of him as possible. My free hand clutched his muscular thigh, needing something to brace myself on while he continued to fuck my mouth.

"God—*fuck*." Ryan's voice was tight, his thrusts becoming more frenzied. "I'm gonna come. I'm gonna come, Harps."

At this point, my eyes were watering. I was gagging with almost every thrust of his hips, but I'd never felt so good in all my fucking life. Knowing I was the one making Ryan moan the way he was. Inviting the shift from the gentle man I knew into someone so rough.

"I'm there," he said through gritted teeth. "Fuck, I'm—"

He froze, but I didn't stop my work, taking over where he left off, my head bobbing up and down, my hand wrapped around him once more.

"Harper. Shit. *Fuck*."

The salty tang of his cum filled my mouth. My lips tightened around him as his cock twitched with each new release. Only when he finally stilled did I loosen my grasp on him.

My fingers slid out of my pants as I swallowed him down. When I opened my mouth and noticed some cum still on his cock, I lapped that up too, watching him from under my lashes as I did.

"Shit," he said on a breath as he reached for my hand. "Get the fuck up here."

As soon as I was off my knees, Ryan brought my glistening fingers to his mouth where he sucked the wetness right off.

"Returning the favor," he said. He kissed the pads of each finger. "That was the hottest fucking thing—watching you swallow me."

"I didn't want to leave any evidence," I said with a grin. "Don't want Coach Fitz to yell at you."

Ryan's chuckle warmed me from the inside out, and the heat only grew when he leaned down to kiss me.

"You have no idea how badly I want to take you right here against these lockers," he practically growled.

"I'm not opposed to that." I lifted my hand up to cup his face. "But maybe we wait until you can actually stand on both legs."

This time when Ryan groaned, it was out of nothing but frustration.

"The day this brace comes off will be the best day of my life."

I chuckled. "Probably mine, too." I kissed him again. "But since that day isn't here yet, think it might be time to head back to the game?"

"I'm not gonna be able to think about anything except how hard you just made me come the whole time we're out there."

"But aren't you happy I did?"

Ryan grabbed my face in both his hands, and this time when our lips met, the same touch of roughness I'd come to love accompanied it.

"Very much," he said when he pulled back. His forehead lowered until it rested on mine. "You always make me so fucking happy, Harper."

There was no way I would have been able to stop my heart from jumping the way it did.

My hand cupped the back of his neck. "You make me happy, too, Ry," I whispered.

And as much as I wanted him to be healed—for his brace to finally come off so we could enjoy the benefits of it—I also didn't want to know what that would mean for the absolute elation I'd been enjoying.

How, inevitably, it would come crashing to an abrupt halt.

CHAPTER NINETEEN

"THERE YOU ARE. We were about to send out a search party to—"

My brothers weren't usually ones to be shut up so easily, but when Ryan and I scooted our way through the over-packed bleachers of the high school field, that's exactly what Cam did. Derek and Connor didn't say anything at all.

I normally might have guessed it was because they were starstruck. Sure, they knew Ryan, but it had probably been close to a decade since they'd actually talked to him. And he hadn't been a multi-time Pro Bowl-er back then.

But they weren't staring at Ryan.

They were staring at where my hand was joined with his—and didn't let go even after we'd successfully navigated the crowd without tripping.

All plans to keep things a secret had gone out the window.

We both figured it would have been nearly impossible to keep our hands off each other the rest of the night. Might as well bite the bullet and get the hard part out of the way.

My brothers probably appreciated catching Ryan and me holding hands to us making out under the bleachers, anyway.

"You guys remember, Ryan, right?" I asked.

Mom and Dad turned at the sound of my voice, both of them going from shocked to elated within a matter of seconds before they stood.

"Ryan, sweetie," Mom greeted, scooting past her sons and their families to give Ryan a hug. "It's so good to see you."

"You too, Mama B," Ryan said as he embraced her. I smiled at the use of the nickname he'd called her throughout middle and high school. "Mr. Bennett," he added, extending his hand when the hug was broken.

"What're you doing up here, son?" Dad asked. "Should you be climbing with that leg of yours?"

"I told him not to…" I insisted, my eyes cast sideways at Ryan. It had been a bitch and a half navigating the crowd with him on his crutch, but he'd insisted on coming up to say hi to my family.

With his arms free again, he wrapped one around my waist. Mom clocked it right away, and when our eyes met, I gave her a small smile and nod.

"I wanted to test it out," Ryan said. "And besides—I wasn't gonna go this whole game without talking to you all." He turned to my brothers. "What's up, man? Been a minute."

Cam still hadn't said anything as he and Ryan did one of those guy handshakes where they pull in and bump shoulders. Derek and Connor were equally as stunned, so thank god for my sisters-in-law being somewhat normal and introducing themselves.

"And who's this?" Ryan smiled as he booped Nora's nose. It was one of the only parts of her visible beneath the winter gear Cam and Hannah had dressed her in.

She let out a big baby squeal and clapped, legs kicking as much as they could in the thick pants.

"This is Nora," Hannah introduced.

"Hello to you, Miss Nora," Ryan said, grabbing hold of one of her chubby gloved hands and giving it a little shake.

As if my hormones weren't in a tizzy from what had just gone down in the locker room. Watching Ryan interact with my niece had them going absolutely wild.

Nora cooed again, and pulled her hands back to her mouth, half to try to eat them, but I also thought her little baby brain was trying to hide the adorable smile she was sending Ryan's way.

"Hey." Connor's hip bumping into mine knocked me out of my daze. I tilted my head up to him, and he nodded in Ryan's direction. To no one's surprise, he was charming the pants off the rest of my family. "So, you two are officially…?"

I nodded. "It's new."

Connor grinned. "No, it's not," he said matter-of-factly. Like I was the only one who'd been missing out on a long-standing secret. Then he wrapped his arms around my shoulders and pulled me into a side hug. "I'm excited for you, Harps."

"Thanks," I said, briefly leaning my head on his shoulder. "It's still kinda weird, if I'm being honest."

Connor chuckled. "At least you get to skip the awkward meet-the-family stage. I bet Ryan would *still* go right to the pantry to steal all of Dad's jalapeno kettle chips the second he stepped foot in the house."

I smiled, ready to respond when somehow over the roar of the band and cheering of the crowd, I heard, "Ryan!"

It came with such force that even people outside my family turned to look. The outburst was sharp enough to draw attention from every direction. But I didn't have to guess who it belonged to. Unfortunately, I already knew.

Dave and Gina Caldwell stood at the bottom of the bleachers, the latter casting nervous looks between her husband and son. She masked the tension well—until my whole family turned toward them.

"Hey, Diane!" she called out to Mom with a wave. "So good to see all you Bennetts together again!"

"Ryan!" Dave shouted, louder this time. "What are you doing up there? You're going to reinjure yourself!"

"I'm good," Ryan replied, his tone edged with annoyance.

But Dave didn't take the hint from his wife or his son's

reactions. Through clenched teeth, he barked again, "Get. Down. Here. *Now*."

The muscles on Ryan's neck tightened, and even though I couldn't see it, I knew he was clenching his jaw.

"You gotta go do your thing for the homecoming court or something, man?" Derek asked, trying to cut the tension.

"Yeah, don't let us hold you up if you've got other stuff to do," Cam added, clearly catching on. "I'm sure we'll see you around."

They hadn't really witnessed Dave's worst. They were older. Too far removed to remember or realize what Ryan had dealt with growing up. But Connor had been there through more of it.

So it was he who leaned toward me and whispered, "That one's still got a stick up his ass, huh?"

"Something like that," I muttered back.

Now probably wasn't the time to explain that Dave's frustration had less to do with Ryan being in the bleachers and more to do with *who* he was standing with.

In other words, me.

"Ry," I said gently. When he turned, I added, "It's all good. You should go with your parents. It's almost halftime anyway."

If Dave didn't drag him down, Principal Morales would've found him soon enough for the homecoming king and queen presentation.

Ryan didn't seem sold on the idea, but he nodded anyway.

"Hope I see you all again soon," he told my family, then limped over to me, his injured leg barely holding any weight.

Connor shifted to make room, glancing at me nervously before offering Ryan a polite, "Good to see you, man," and shuffled away.

"You need help getting down again?" I asked, lowering my voice.

The last thing we needed was more ears tuning in. Dave had already turned Ryan into the night's most unwilling spectacle.

"I'll be fine." He reached out, his fingers wrapping tenderly around my own. "It's probably better if you stay here with your family."

Translated, "It's best you stay away from my dad."

I cast a quick glance down to where the Caldwells were still waiting for their son. Gina looked ready to jet, bouncing from foot to foot and giving anyone she made eye contact with a nervous smile. Dave, on the other hand, looked three seconds away from coming up the stairs himself and dragging his son with him like a toddler, not a twenty-seven-year-old grown man.

"Yeah, okay," I agreed, eyes flicking back to Ryan. "I'll see you after the game?"

"It's more likely I'll see you tomorrow." He leaned down and kissed my cheek. "Don't forget. Six o'clock."

I gave a small nod and let him slip away, our fingers parting.

The rest of the people in the row stood as Ryan made his

exit, muttering, "Excuse me," as he passed. Knowing how stressed he was made it all that more impressive when he managed to put on a smile for anyone who complimented him or told him they were a fan on the way.

It felt like I'd just let him throw himself into the lion's den when his feet finally touched down on the turf.

Dave met him at the bottom. Ryan tightened his grip on his single crutch. I couldn't hear the words, but Dave's actions were enough. The barked reprimands. The wagging finger. The barely restrained anger. Ryan, on the other hand was stone-faced. His jaw ticked as he ground his teeth, no doubt relying on every ounce of PR training he'd ever been through to keep from fighting back.

Dave had never gone through such training. And it showed.

Right when I was beginning to think it would never end, Ryan turned just enough, his eyes finding mine in the crowd. Defeat and anger battled for the primary emotion I saw swimming in them, but neither was victorious before Dave grabbed his son's shoulder and forced Ryan to face him again.

That's when Dave followed his son's gaze. There was no question what I saw there when our eyes met, too.

Hatred.

It wasn't new. I'd known Dave blamed me for more than he should have. But this? This was the first time I realized he truly *hated* me.

Because Ryan had made his choice.

That kiss he'd given me had been as much a sign of affection as it was a declaration of war. Ryan might have listened to his dad's request to exit the bleachers, but he was done listening to whatever bullshit Dave had spewed about me being a detriment to his career.

I couldn't deny I was thrilled about that. But still, a part of me knew it didn't matter how firmly Ryan stood his ground—and I had no doubt he would. Dave Caldwell had wanted this for his son as long as I'd known him. To grow into a household name in one of the most prominent sports leagues in the world. The fame. The fortune. The notoriety.

He wouldn't let it come crashing down so easily.

CHAPTER TWENTY

I'D NEVER ONCE in all the years we'd known each other cared about what I looked like when I hung out with Ryan Caldwell.

Until tonight.

Not knowing his plans for us didn't help, so as I pulled into the Caldwells' driveway, honking twice to announce my arrival, I hoped the boot cut jeans, knit off-the-shoulder burgundy sweater, and heeled booties I'd spent approximately two hours deciding on did the trick.

I adjusted the fabric of the sweater while I waited for Ryan to come out. The damn thing wouldn't stay in place. What was the point of having a sweater that was supposed stay off my shoulders if it didn't actually stay off my—

My frustration faded as soon as I saw Ryan come out the front door, no crutches in sight.

He was… he was *walking*. Slowly and still with a brace—a

smaller one—but he had no other assistance.

"Holy shit," I said through a beaming smile after I put the car in park and stepped out.

"Surprise," Ryan replied, smiling just as hard. "One of many tonight."

"I don't know how you can top this."

Ryan stopped in front of me, his arm wrapping around my waist and settling, fingers splayed, on my lower back to pull me closer.

"I promise you haven't seen anything yet." He lowered his lips to mine. "You look beautiful, by the way," he added when he pulled back.

"So do you. I mean, handsome, that is."

And he did. In his dark wash jeans and black button up with the sleeves rolled to his elbows, Ryan could have told me he'd come from a photoshoot, and I would have believed him. Not to mention all the dark colors made his blue eyes pop even more than usual.

He chuckled at my slip-up and gave me another quick kiss. "You ready to go?"

"I'm gonna need directions."

"I can bend my knee again, remember?" Ryan demonstrated the flexibility he now had in his new brace. "I'm driving. And you are…"

My eyes followed his movements as he reached into his back pocket and pulled out a pink sleep mask, most likely stolen from Gina.

"What's that for?" I asked.

Ryan grinned. "Your blindfold."

"You're kidding."

"I told you everything's a surprise, and that's almost impossible to accomplish in this one-road town, so—" He held the makeshift blindfold out. "Put this on."

I wished I could say I was shocked by his attention to detail, but, now that the night was piecing itself together, I didn't doubt for a second he'd been going over everything since the moment we'd left that school gymnasium. And who was I to crush his spirits?

"Fine," I agreed, snatching the sleep mask from his hand. "But if we end up at a haunted house, I'll never forgive you."

WE ENDED UP at a haunted house, but Ryan promised me we wouldn't go anywhere near it.

"I couldn't find a single place in this town that didn't have some sort of haunted pop-up," he explained as we strolled hand-in-hand to the red barn that had been transformed into a winery.

Just like the rest of Timberland Creek, they'd succumbed to the fall festivities, taking advantage of the season to bring in a bit more tourism. In fairness, the name of the place was Golden

Harvest; they pretty much thrived this time of year between the apple orchards, pumpkin patches, and seasonal wine blends they offered.

We took advantage of it all. To Ryan's credit, he only asked to take a break and sit for a few minutes between the apples and pumpkin picking—which were both the precursor for Date Number Two, according to him. And by the time we made it up the stairs to my front door—yes, both of us; he'd definitely mastered them just as he'd promised—we were both full of good mulled wine and autumn delicacies.

"I think it's pretty safe to say I don't think I can eat another caramel apple for a solid year." I bent down and placed the pumpkin I'd picked in front of my door. Ryan had insisted on carrying it, but stairs and heavy objects were beyond the limit I'd allow. He'd already walked probably close to a couple miles. I wasn't about to be the *actual* reason to blame when his time on the injured reserve list was extended.

"Hate to break it to you, but you've got a week," Ryan joked. "Date Number Two is gonna be even better than this one. Assuming you had a good time tonight?"

All night, Ryan had been so confident—to the point where I wondered if he'd actually scouted the winery before taking me there. It wasn't like he'd been to it before; the last time he'd been in Timberland Creek, we'd barely been able to legally drink, let alone think wine actually tasted good.

The sudden worry that I might not have enjoyed myself made

me smile.

"I had a great time," I reassured him. "Thank you for planning everything." I lifted onto my toes so I could reach his lips, pressing my own against them in a soft, lingering kiss. "You might have managed to thaw this autumn Grinch's heart."

Ryan's arm snaked around my waist. When he pulled me closer, mine went around his neck, bringing our chests flush against each other.

"Mission accomplished, then," he said and lowered his lips back down to mine.

We'd behaved properly while at the winery. The biggest display of public affection we'd partaken in had been hand holding—and one stray kiss while in line for our mulled wine. I couldn't help myself. The way Ryan had been smiling down at me had been too perfect.

If there hadn't been so many onlookers, I might not have shown so much restraint. Most had kept their distance, but a few people had gone as far as to approach Ryan to ask for a picture, which he took then excused himself from further conversation by saying, "I'm really trying to impress this girl."

He'd done it. He'd *more* than done it. And as we stood there on my front porch, his lips moving in tandem with mine, my restraint had reached its limit.

I pulled back. "Do you maybe want to come inside?"

Ryan nodded, his eyes twinkling with mischief. There was no

way he didn't know what this invitation meant.

I reached into my bag to retrieve my keys and turned to open the door. Ryan placed his hands on my hips, his warmth still covering me as I worked on the lock. When he inched even closer, his crotch pressing against my ass—

Oh yeah. This man definitely wanted to come in.

For any other guests, I would have been a good hostess and given them a tour for their first time in my humble one-bedroom abode.

Ryan didn't give me that chance. I couldn't do much more than let out an excited squeak, my bag and keys dropping to the floor before my back was against the wall of my entryway, hands pinned above my head. He kicked the door shut, the loud *bang* coming at the same time his lips crashed onto mine.

If we'd been hungry for each other in the locker room, now we were absolutely ravenous.

I moaned against his lips when his growing erection pressed into me. My back arched off the wall, desperate for more of that delicious pressure.

Ryan dropped his hold on my hands, and I used my newfound freedom to begin undoing the buttons of his shirt. He followed my lead, grabbing the hem of my sweater and tugging it over my head.

"Fuck me," he groaned when he found me bare beneath it, nipples pebbled.

I chuckled against his lips when we resumed our kissing, our tongues tangled together as I finally finished with the buttons and slid his shirt off to reveal his gloriously muscular tattooed arms and chest.

Ryan's head dipped down, sucking at the spot where my neck and jaw met. I moaned, and it only got worse as he worked his way further down my body until, finally, he sucked one of my nipples into his mouth, his tongue flicking over the sensitive bud. My back arched, my hand flying back to press against the wall for some sort of support. It was especially needed when he pinched the other between his thumb and index finger and gave it a tug.

"I fucking love your tits," he growled. Then took my nipple between his teeth and pulled.

I bit my bottom lip, somehow managing to suppress my moan before I said, "I need you inside me. *Now.*"

Didn't need to tell him twice.

I fumbled with the button of his jeans while he undid his knee brace. He tossed it to the side just before I tugged his pants down, and as soon as his erection sprang free, I was flipped, my chest pressed against the wall. One of Ryan's hands squeezed between the structure and me, palming my breast while the other moved lower. He ran two fingers over my aching center before he somehow managed to undo my button with a single hand.

"I have condoms," he said against my ear. Ryan removed his hand from my chest to assist in tugging my jeans and panties down past where they'd gotten stuck on the curve of my ass.

I shook my head. "I have an IUD and my test came back clear at my visit to the gyno last month."

"I'm clean, too," he said as he nipped at my earlobe. One of his hands grabbed my thigh, spreading my legs wider. "I get tested every month."

"Then stop wasting time, Caldwell." I bent forward as much as I could, the tip of his cock teasing my ass in this new position. "I need you to fuck me."

We were still half dressed, neither of us managing to get our pants pulled down much further than our knees. But that was all we needed.

The moan that escaped Ryan the moment he guided his cock along my slick folds made a whole new wave of wetness release from me. I'd never wanted a man so badly in all my life.

My arousal made it easy for him to slide into me, and just when I thought he was all the way in, he kept going.

I braced my hands harder against the wall, a whimper escaping me as he finally settled. I'd never felt so gloriously full.

Ryan let out a prolonged, low groan as he pulled back out— and thrust himself right back in, testing, teasing. Letting me adjust to him, perhaps. But that wasn't what I wanted.

"Harder," I begged.

Ryan stilled within me, and I wondered if I'd said something wrong. For all his earlier talk, I'd assumed he liked it just as rough as me.

And then his hips began to move, setting a pace that proved that was *exactly* what he liked.

"Yes. Yes. Yes. *Yes*," I said with each thrust, my tits bouncing as his cock slammed into me from behind. "Just like that. Fuck—just like that, Ry."

"Look at you taking my cock." Ryan lifted one of his hands from where they grasped my waist and smacked my ass. "It feels so good. Being wrapped in your tight little cunt."

"Touch me," I pleaded through another moan. "Please. I need you to touch me."

Ryan never lost his pace as his hands moved off my waist, one going up to cup one of my breasts while the other dipped between my legs. I arched off the wall, using his hold as my new support. My head dipped back onto his shoulder, my mouth agape as his fingers circled my clit, pinched my nipple.

"Such a good girl, Harps." Ryan groaned. "So fucking good."

When he pressed down on my clit, I almost screamed.

"*Ryan*," I said on a breath. "Fuck—I'm gonna come."

"Come on my cock, baby." He pushed into me harder, faster, filling me as much as my body would allow. "Let me feel your pussy clench around my cock."

It took about two more thrusts for me to fulfill his wish. If Ryan hadn't been holding me upright, I might have collapsed to the ground as my orgasm overcame me.

I believe that's what Ryan thought was happening as his hold loosened and I sank to my knees, the final aftershocks of pleasure still wracking my body. But as soon as my hand wrapped around his shaft, still slick with my arousal, he figured out my true intentions.

He'd wrecked me, that was for sure. But not enough for me to put an end to our fun. Oh no—if anything, the pleasure he'd just given me spurred me on, more desperate than ever to keep touching him—feeling him fill me in any way possible—if only to satisfy the still-unbelievable desire burning in me.

"Fuck," Ryan groaned the moment I brought him into my mouth.

His hand fisted my hair as my head bobbed, my hand working in tandem along his shaft. When I licked up his length, watching him from under my lashes, his cock twitched.

"You don't know what you do to me, Harper," he said. He moaned when I circled my tongue around his head and brought him back between my lips. "Shit. That feels so good, baby."

I'd never been one for pet names, but the way Ryan called me *baby*—I'd never heard anything sexier in all my life.

Scratch that. The moan he didn't even bother to subdue— combined with the exasperated, *"Fuck,"* he let out—when I took him all the way in the back of my throat was definitely the sexiest thing I'd ever heard.

"That's it," he said as I gagged, opening my throat as much as I could to take him even deeper. "Choke on that fucking cock."

I was smiling when I released him with a gasp, my hand still wrapped around his impressive length. Apparently, I had a praise kink. Who knew?

Ryan tugged on my hair. "Take off your pants," he demanded. "Then stand up."

I worked my jeans the rest of the way down my legs before tossing them to the side. The second I was standing again, Ryan hooked an arm under my knee and lowered himself onto his healthy one.

My foot rested on his shoulder, and Ryan placed a hand on my thigh as his head dipped between my legs.

My fingers raked back his hair from his forehead, desperate for something to hold on to the moment his tongue flicked across my clit. Never in all my life had an orgasm started building so soon after a previous one, but that's what happened when two of Ryan's fingers slipped inside me.

"Ryan," I gasped. "Don't stop. *Please*, don't stop. I need you right there."

His fingers curled, hitting me in the most perfect place, each quick flick of his wrist bringing me closer and closer until I—

"*Shit.*"

I fell forward, bent at the waist. My hands clawed at Ryan's back as I shuddered, overcome with a second, more powerful orgasm.

He didn't stop, letting me coast through my waves of pleasure until my body finally stopped trembling.

Ryan grinned as he rose slowly back onto his feet. I matched him, a giddy giggle escaping me as I grabbed his face with both hands and brought his lips down to mine.

"You're so beautiful when you come," he whispered between kisses.

"We need to make sure you get to, too," I muttered against his lips.

"Trust me." Ryan's hand slid down to mine. He used the other to guide his pants gingerly past his knee before he shucked them and tossed them on top of mine. "I don't think that will be an issue."

Despite not getting the official tour, it seemed Ryan had figured things out on his own. He wrapped my fingers in his and pulled me with him further into my apartment. To think— I'd already finished twice, and we hadn't even left the entryway.

My attention zoned in on where Ryan stroked his cock as he lowered himself onto my couch.

"C'mere," he said, lightly tugging my arm.

I stepped forward, moving closer until I could easily climb onto his lap, straddling him.

Ryan's lips curled in when I rolled my hips, running my arousal-slick folds along his length. When I stopped with him right at my entrance, he guided himself inside me.

I rocked myself against him, putting the most amazing pressure on my clit. Ryan's hands found my hips when I adjusted my movements, bouncing on his cock slow at first, then picking up the pace.

Skin slapped against skin. I grabbed at Ryan's shoulder, trying to keep my balance so I didn't lose rhythm and found him sticky with sweat. I knew I wasn't much better at this point.

"Yes, baby," Ryan grunted. "Ride that cock. Fuck—I'm right there."

His hold on my hips tightened when he took control, pounding into me with a speed and force I'd never experienced with any other partner.

"Oh my god," I managed to say, the words coming out shaky, broken by each of Ryan's frantic thrusts.

I leaned forward, my fingernails digging into his muscular back, and kissed his neck. The salty tang of his sweat coated my tongue and only got worse when I bit down on his shoulder. It was the only way I could keep myself from crying out—screaming his name so loud the whole town might hear. Might know what he was doing to me. How absolutely incredible he was making me feel.

"I'm coming," I panted. "Ry, I'm coming. I'm—"

I was still shaking from my third orgasm when Ryan threw me off his lap. My back landed on the couch and within seconds, Ryan was above me, his cock driving into me once more. His teeth were gritted, face set in determination, as he used the waves of my pleasure to coax his own.

My entire body felt like pudding by the time Ryan finally pulled out, grunting as he worked himself to orgasm. I couldn't help but smile when he spilled himself onto my stomach.

His eyes darkened even more when I ran a finger through his cum, never taking my eyes off him as I brought it to my mouth and sucked it off—just like he'd done for me the night before.

Ryan shook his head, his body rising and falling with heavy breaths, skin glistening with sweat, and chuckled.

"I'd apologize for the mess," he said, voice low and seductive, "but it seems like you're enjoying it."

I giggled, and he brought his lips to mine for a kiss that entirely contrasted the sex we'd just had.

Some of the best sex of my life, might I add. No— undoubtedly *the* best sex of my life.

Ryan slumped back down onto the couch, looking entirely spent. I made my way onto my knees on the seat beside him. When one of my hands found his fresh-shaven cheek, pulling slightly to get him to face me, I asked, "You feeling alright?"

"I've never felt better."

"I meant your knee."

"It hurts a little," he admitted, much to my surprise. Then he leaned forward and kissed my nose. "But it was worth it."

"Maybe you can cancel your physical therapy appointment tomorrow." He chuckled again and I took my turn to kiss him. "You're sleeping over, right?"

One of his hands found my thigh, rubbing soothingly up and down. "Only if you want me to."

Oh, did I want him to. After tonight, I never wanted Ryan to leave. *I* never wanted to leave. I'd hand in my two-weeks' notice to Hemi if it meant getting to stay here like this with Ryan, enjoying orgasm marathons and tender kisses.

"I was gonna clean up a little bit. Hop in the shower," I said, rising to my feet. I grinned as I extended a hand. "Care to join me?"

That mischievous glint I'd come to know and love glistened in Ryan's eyes.

He grabbed my hand.

"Lead the way."

CHAPTER TWENTY-ONE

EVERYTHING I'D THOUGHT I'd known about sex had been wiped from my head in a matter of ten hours. Ten glorious hours where I'd learned every inch of Ryan's body. Every tattoo. Every scar. Every ticklish spot—even though that one had been an accident.

Even now, as we laid in my bed, our legs tangled together after a much-needed night's sleep, I couldn't stop thinking about the next time we'd go at it.

I was well and truly obsessed with this man. And it only took about twenty years for me to figure it out.

Ryan's thumb was tracing lazy circles on my bare arm. The only clothing we'd managed to find when we finally decided to call it a night was my underwear—and that was because I'd gotten a new pair from my dresser. The rest of our clothes and his knee brace were still scattered somewhere at the front of my apartment.

"So, I was thinking," Ryan started.

"Uh oh," I teased, earning a gentle pinch. Through a laugh, I asked, "What were you thinking about?"

"I never got your official score of last night's date."

"I assumed the sex rampage did the job."

Ryan's chuckled vibrated through his body, sending a fresh wave of want through me. I shifted, pressing my bare chest against his side.

"I had a great time," I whispered. "I don't remember the last time anyone put that much effort into making sure I enjoyed myself. On the date and otherwise."

Ryan kissed my forehead. "So, it was enough?"

I was only half paying attention when I asked, "Enough for what?" The other half of my brain was following the way Ryan's fingers trailed down my arm until they reached my hand.

He pressed our palms together. Our hands lifted before he intertwined his fingers with mine and said, "Enough for you to agree to be my girlfriend."

My head lifted off his chest. "You were serious about that?"

Ryan's eyes shifted from side to side. "Uh, yeah? Why wouldn't I be?"

"Because I'm here." I patted the bed as if that was the perfect indicator of what I meant. Then I pointed to the window. "And you're there."

His following silence worried me—until the familiar mischievous gleam shone in his eyes once more. If the sun hadn't been shining into the room, I might have missed the tiny grin that accompanied it.

"What aren't you telling me?" I asked. When he still neglected to say anything, I sat up. "Ryan Alexander Caldwell, tell me."

"Alright, alright." He curled at the waist just enough to wrap me up and pull me back down against his chest.

Ryan brushed my hair back and tucked it behind my ear. "I don't want you getting too excited, alright? I haven't gotten official confirmation yet."

"Confirmation for what?"

"You know I signed a one-year contract as a free agent this season, right?" I shook my head, my confusion evident. "My contract was the standard four seasons with the Stallions," he explained. "They offered me a pretty good renewal, but Scott told me it would be better at this time in my career to do things on a year-by-year basis. Two years, max. I've proven myself. Other teams might come in with better offers. Blah, blah, blah."

"So, at the end of the season…" I began, then my eyes popped open. "You're not retiring already, are you?"

"God, no," Ryan reassured me. "I want to play until I'm at least thirty-five, if I'm able. But that might not happen with the Stallions."

I knew he'd warned against it, but I couldn't stop my excitement from beginning to bubble. "What do you mean?"

"This isn't necessarily common knowledge, but I had Scott looking into the possibility of the Packers needing a new tight end." He gave a one-shoulder shrug. "The guy they just drafted isn't working out the way they'd hoped."

"Holy shit." I was trying *very* hard not to jump out of my skin. "You're gonna play for the Packers?"

"It's not a done deal yet," Ryan said. "But we put in a competitive offer. That's what he called me about a few days ago, remember? That other surprise I told you about? Now it's up to the Packers to—*oof!*"

Ryan's grunt of surprise turned into a rumbling laugh, his arm going around my back, when he quickly realized I wasn't trying to attack him. It was more like an awkward hug as I struggled to get my own arms around him while he laid on his back on my bed.

I lifted my head, my chin resting on his chest. "My favorite guy is gonna play for my favorite team."

"Favorite, huh?" Ryan smirked. "And I'm not talking about the team. I'm well aware you're obsessed with the Packers."

"Do you wanna know how hard it will be cheering for two teams if this deal doesn't go through?" I grabbed his face in both my hands. "*So hard.*"

I was still holding him when Ryan's arm tightened around me. I let out a girlish giggle as he flipped us. A quick glance down under where the sheet covering our lower halves had lifted showed me that he was favoring his good knee, his injured one lifted lightly to avoid having too much pressure put on it—especially with his brace off.

"Trust me, I'm praying for this just as much as you are," he said.

"What made you decide to look into the trade?" It wasn't that the Packers were a bad team; they were challengers in most every game they played, for sure. But with the success the Stallions had seen in recent years—namely due to Ryan's involvement—many people would see the move as a downgrade.

Ryan shrugged. "Oh, I don't know. Nothing really in particular…"

My legs wrapped around his, heels digging into his calves, and my hands moved from his face to hook at the back of his neck. I'd been given no choice, since he'd buried his face in the crook of my neck and started leaving a trail of kisses.

"I'd only be a few hours away," he muttered against my skin. "It wouldn't be perfect, but it would be better."

"I could move with you," I said. Ryan lifted his head. "I mean, only if you wanted me to."

And as he'd just pointed out, we wouldn't be too far away from Timberland Creek. I'd still be closer than any of my brothers, able to help Mom and Dad when they needed me. Available to visit more often so they didn't feel like all their children had decided to abandon them.

There was still the issue of Sunrise—assuming my plan to raise money for Hemi actually worked out—but maybe Hemi and I could work something out. A weekend gig situation—only during the off-season, of course. Or if Ryan had an away game.

God, I could picture it now. A private suite for every home game at Lambeau Field, decked out in green and gold Caldwell gear. I was blessed in the name of the Bart Starr, Don Hutson and Brett Favre—amen.

"Are you kidding?" Ryan's head dipped down, and he planted a huge smooch on my cheek.

I chuckled, and my fingers snuck into the hair at the back of his head. "I didn't want to impose. I'm sure you're used to having your bachelor pad."

"There is absolutely nothing I'd like more"—a kiss on my neck—"than to have you"—a kiss on my jaw—"right there in my bed"—a kiss on my cheek—"every morning when I wake up. Think about it."

I curled my lips in when Ryan shifted his hips and his half-hard penis pressed against my center.

"We'd save so much time without a commute," he whispered, his nose brushing against mine.

"What do you plan to do with so much extra time?" I taunted.

"I've got some ideas. A little of this…" Ryan's lips came

down on mine, giving me the most deliciously tender kiss. "A lot of this…"

I gasped when his hand reached down and found its way between my legs. Considering how much we'd done the night before, it was a miracle my body could still respond properly. With anyone else, I'd need a solid week-long break. But with Ryan, I was ready.

Ready for the pleasure he was already giving me as his fingers worked circles on my clit.

Ready for more time.

Ready for a second chance—at our friendship and more.

"Oh my god," I moaned when he pressed down on the sensitive bud. And I didn't know if it was the pure ecstasy of his touch or the promise of what was in store for us, but the words, "I love you," slipped out before I could stop them.

Ryan stilled, his entire body tensing where it hovered above me.

"I, um—" I cleared my throat when he lifted his head from the crook of my neck. That was definitely confusion I saw. "I just mean that—shit, I'm sorry. It's too soon. I mean, we didn't even solidly establish that I'm your girlfriend, so—"

"Harper."

Heat colored my cheeks, and it had nothing to do with his touch anymore. "Yeah?"

His hand slid back up within view all the way until my cheek was cupped in his palm.

"First, you're my girlfriend. Let's stop kidding about that, alright?" When I nodded, half in a daze, a slow smile curled Ryan's lips. "And second, if there's one thing that being back—that seeing you—has made me realize," he whispered, "it's that I love you, too. I always have."

For a moment, I was sure my heart had melted, because it couldn't possibly still be beating after hearing those words. His words. The ones I'd spent years telling myself I didn't need to hear—that the bond we'd always shared had been simply platonic. Nothing more. Nothing less.

But here they were, and here he was, looking at me like I was the only thing that mattered.

The lump in my throat made it hard to speak, but I managed to whisper, "Really?" like an absolute idiot.

"Really," he said, and then because apparently my heart hadn't been destroyed enough, Ryan pressed his forehead to mine and smiled.

All those years I'd spent convincing myself I hated him—what a sick joke. I'd told myself I'd moved on, that Ryan didn't deserve my time, my thoughts, or anything resembling forgiveness after the way he'd vanished.

Deep down, I'd known it was a lie. I'd known the moment he'd stumbled into that town hall meeting.

Because if I'd really stopped caring, seeing him wouldn't have made my stomach flip. His face wouldn't have been burned into my memory, the way he used to look at me—the same way he was looking at me now—like I was something worth keeping. Worth fighting for.

I hadn't just fallen in love with Ryan Caldwell all those years ago. I'd never stopped.

And now, with his hand on my cheek and those three incredible words hanging in the air between us, that truth was impossible to deny.

CHAPTER TWENTY-TWO

"WELL," RYAN BEGAN, sliding the final of many, *many* zip ties into place. "There she is."

He took a step back to stand beside where I was already examining the product of our hard work.

The float… well, it was something.

The Lone Star Stallions' deep teal was everywhere, splashed across the flatbed trailer in a chaotic explosion of banners, pom-poms, and props all sent to us by the team's marketing department. A slightly lopsided gold star sat in the center like a crown jewel.

As far as a Timberland Creek parades went, this thing was taking home first place. But if anyone from the Stallions saw our work of art, they might say otherwise.

But as I stood there, taking it all in, I couldn't help the laugh that bubbled up.

"It looks like a Smurf threw up on it," I said, the grin spreading across my face before I could stop it. I turned to Ryan who, at that moment, stepped forward to adjust the star for what had to be the fifth time in the last thirty minutes. "I love it."

"It could be worse," Ryan agreed. "I'd say we definitely have the Rotary Club beat. They still win the contest every year?"

"Them or the Chamber of Commerce." I stepped up to where he was standing guard of the star, waiting to see if it would lean again, and wrapped my arms around his torso. He slipped one around my shoulders in return. "They don't know what's coming."

I laughed as Ryan put on a mock sports commentator voice and said, "And Caldwell leads the Stallions to another victory."

"Modest much?"

"Stats don't lie, baby."

He chuckled and leaned down to kiss the top of my head when I scoffed.

"C'mon," I said, lifting a hand to tap his chest. "Let's get some of this mess cleaned up."

I glanced around the barn as I unraveled myself from around him. We'd keep the float tucked away until the parade out of fear of ruining the surprise. There were still plenty of people lurking to catch their glimpses of Ryan; we didn't want them seeing our masterpiece in the process.

The barn was relatively quiet aside from the soft music playing from a Bluetooth speaker Ryan had brought during an earlier construction session and the occasional rustle of boxes and supplies as we put everything away.

"The Stallions want you to ship this all back to them?" I asked, grabbing a stack of unused small foam stars. I tried to fit them into the box they'd come from, but the corners were bent, and they kept catching on the edges. "Because, uh, I'm not sure if that's gonna happen."

Ryan crouched a few feet away, utilizing his newfound bendability of his leg, rolling up a long strand of gold streamers like a hose. "You just have to outsmart the box," he said with a smirk, not looking up.

I tossed a balled-up scrap of tissue paper at him, and he batted it away with a laugh. "Okay, Mr. Perfect," I teased.

Ryan idly picked up a few more stray materials and tossed them into a box. "Could Hemi use any of it for her booth? I know it's all Stallions colors, but decorations are decorations. And, actually, the gold might work. Like a sunrise, you know?"

I paused, tying off a trash bag I'd stuffed ruined or scrapped materials into. "No," I said, keeping my voice light. "She should be good."

Ryan tilted his head, his brows knit together just slightly. "You hesitated."

"I didn't hesitate." I tossed the trash bag to the side. "She just likes fall décor is all."

"Harper," he said, his voice low and steady. "What's going on?"

I shrugged. "It's nothing. Really. Hey—have you heard from the Packers? Maybe we can just throw this all out. Replace it with green and gold."

"No, I haven't. And it also doesn't sound like nothing." Ryan stepped closer to me. He reached out and tucked a piece of hair that had come free of my ponytail behind my ear, his eyes soft. "Spill."

This time, I definitely did hesitate, biting the inside of my cheek. His tone left no room for dodging the conversation— gentle enough for me to know he was genuinely concerned, but stern enough to let me know he wasn't going to let me get away easy. In fairness, I'd gotten a lot out of him over the last few weeks. Maybe I owed him this one.

The only problem was, it wasn't my story to tell.

If Ryan hadn't been looking at me in a way that made his concern clear as day, maybe I'd have been better at keeping up the act.

"Hemi's thinking of closing Sunrise Brews," I admitted, my voice quieter than I intended. It had been the first time I'd spoken about it in a long time, and saying it outside our little employee circle made the possibility seem more real. "She hasn't decided for sure, but… things have been tight. Her mom's really sick, and she's worried she can't keep it open much longer."

Ryan's jaw tightened, his hands rubbing up and down my arms as he stared at me. "Were you going to tell me?"

"No," I said. I sighed. "I don't know. Eventually, maybe. I mean, it's *her* business, Ry. She doesn't want anyone to know, especially if it means they're going to pity her."

"It's not pity. It's support."

I rolled my eyes as I huffed a laugh. "Yeah. Tried telling her that, too. Didn't work."

My eyes strayed to the float, caught on the shimmering metallic strands that moved gently in the breeze that snuck in from outside.

I knew Ryan had figured out where my thoughts had gone when he turned back over his shoulder, following my stare, then returned his attention to me.

"This float," he said. "This whole thing we've been doing— you're worried about it because you need it to do well. For Hemi."

"Not the *whole* thing," I corrected as I reached up to grab his face in both my hands and pulled him down for a kiss. "But the part where we raise money… it would be nice if *that* did well."

"Done—and then some."

"Huh?"

"I'll donate."

"Ryan—"

"No." He held up a hand, cutting me off before I could finish. "That's your job. Your friend. I'm not just going to sit back and watch her lose her business."

I exhaled sharply, ready to argue, but stopped when I saw the look in his eyes—intense, unyielding, and so painfully earnest it made my chest tighten.

"She won't take it," I said. "She's too proud. I'm not even sure she'll take what we manage to raise organically through the fundraiser."

Ryan shook his head, his lips pressed into a determined line. "Then I'll donate to you personally, and you can give it to her. Sneak it into the register. Say someone mailed it. Leave it in the tip jar. Whatever gets her to accept it."

I couldn't stop the short laugh that escaped me. "You've met Hemi. You really think she's gonna fall for that?"

"She might," Ryan said with a shrug.

I shook my head. "Not a chance, babe." I patted his cheek twice before I dropped my hands. "You don't need to stress about it. We've done our part. Whether or not Hemi accepts help is my problem."

"Nope." Ryan's grip tightened on my arms. "That's not gonna work either."

My brow furrowed. "What's not gonna work?"

"It's not *your* problem," he said, pulling me closer. "It's our problem." Ryan's voice dipped lower, gentler, as he added, "We're a team, Harps. C'mon now."

My throat tightened at the simplicity of his answer. He said it like it was the easiest thing in the world. Like caring about what mattered to me was second nature to him.

I swallowed hard and looked away, my eyes falling on the once-again-crooked star on the float again. "You know you're gonna drive her crazy trying to help, right?"

Ryan's grin made my stomach flip. "I'll take my chances."

It still wasn't foolproof. I wasn't an idiot. Ryan could pep-talk me all he wanted, but at the end of the day, I was the one who knew Hemdeep Batra best, and Hemdeep Batra was stubborn as they came.

Maybe she would finally relent. I'd noticed the soft spot she'd developed for Ryan over the last few weeks of knowing him. Maybe he was the key to finally getting her to accept. I imagined it would be easier to accept money from someone who had millions versus someone whose paychecks she signed.

He was kind—so incredibly generous—to the point that I knew he'd do it, regardless of what Hemi or I told him. Still, I didn't want it to come down to that—for Ryan to feel like he needed to give up anything more than he already had, millionaire or not, in order to help.

My face scrunched when he leaned down to kiss the tip of my nose.

No matter what, we'd figure it out, I supposed. Just as he'd promised. Together.

CHAPTER TWENTY-THREE

PAINTING THE TOWN red took on a whole new meaning when it came to Timberland Creek's Fall Festival. Because it wasn't just limited to red. The whole town had been colored with autumnal hues of the highest saturation level.

It wasn't as if the town hadn't been decorated before. Pumpkins and garlands of leaves and scarecrows had been plastered all over town for two months now. Everything had just been heightened, catering to the aesthetic the plethora of tourists who'd flocked here expected.

"Damn," Ryan mused, his neck twisting from side to side as he took everything in. "Has this gotten more intense or is it just me?"

"No, it's crazy," I agreed. "They really stepped it up a few years ago. Catering to the social media appeal or whatever."

He hummed his understanding, but still didn't smile. I think, really, he was nervous. I couldn't say I didn't feel the same. Our float had been dropped off at the designated parade starting point the night before while everyone was asleep. Now, we were trying to make our way to it without hitting anyone who decided that crosswalks apparently didn't matter.

Some of the booths—which were just pop-up tents that the vendors within them could decorate as they pleased—had already started showcasing their offerings. A local rock band was playing a cover of *I've Put A Spell On You* from the gazebo at the center of town, a modest crowd in lawn chairs bobbing their heads in the audience.

A group of kids darted down the street, faster than I could drive with all the crowds, all of them holding some sort of seasonal treat. Who I could only assume were their guardians strolled casually behind them, each carrying a drink. Given the color, I guessed apple cider or beer.

"It's only ten in the morning," Ryan commented. "I can't believe it's already this busy."

"And it's only gonna get worse." I turned quickly to him, afraid to keep my eyes off the road for too long. "Everyone's here to see *the* Ryan Caldwell, remember?"

"And that other guy," he reminded me. "Didn't Tori say she'd managed to snag him?"

I nodded. "Sounds like it." That's what she'd told me the last time I'd asked, anyway. I'd been a bit preoccupied lately. Primarily because Ryan and I were having an *extremely* hard time getting out of bed to do anything other than work (me), go to physical therapy (him), prepare for the festival, or occasionally eat. And the eating was literally only so we had the energy to have more sex.

I lived a rough life.

Finally, we made it to the edge of town and the crowds cleared enough for me to go more than ten miles per hour. It wasn't long after that when we made it to where the parade participants were putting the finishing touches on their floats.

"About time you showed up!" Tori called when I hopped out of the truck. It was the only car that could successfully carry the trailer, so I'd abandoned my sedan for the day.

"Slow start this morning," I excused, and the smirk that grew on Tori's lips told me she saw right through it.

"Mhm," she hummed, but refrained from making any further comments as I went around the car to help Ryan down. He'd made great improvement since he'd been cleared to start walking without his crutches. Hopping down two feet from the passenger seat of the truck, however, was still not ideal.

Anything she might have teased me about was forgotten, though, when another car rolled in behind Ryan and me. I vaguely registered a door opening and shutting, but there was no way to ignore the high-pitched squeal that followed.

The attention of everyone in the general vicinity fell on Tori as she rushed over to the driver of the newly arrived Mercedes. All I could see was a brunette woman, probably in her thirties.

Otherwise, it was impossible to get any details with the way Tori and her were rocking from side to side while they bear hugged.

I did not, however, miss any details of the handsome, tan-skinned, dark-haired man who came around from the passenger side of the car.

He was older than when he'd played the role of Cain Luther in *Crimson Curse*, but there was still no mistaking Alfie Fletcher. So, that meant the girl with him must have been his girlfriend, Tori's friend Jordi.

"Hey," Ryan said, nudging me with his elbow when I let out a low whistle. "I'm right here."

"Don't worry, babe," I said with a comforting pat of his forearm. "Blonds are more my type."

Tori and Jordi broke apart just as Jackson made his way over. There was no denying the briefest bit of tension from the visitors. It made me wonder how that dynamic worked—if Jordi and Alfie knew Jackson at all. She was apparently a writer. Maybe they'd met through industry stuff.

When Jackson extended his hand to Alfie, the actor took it, a polite smile on his lips. So, they were at the very least amicable.

"Harper!" Tori called, waving me over. "C'mere! I wanna introduce you!"

"Holy shit," I muttered, and grabbed Ryan's hand. "I'm meeting a real actor."

"Yeah, sure, super cool. Especially since you don't already know *anyone* who's famous," Ryan deadpanned.

I cast him a look over my shoulder as I pulled him along.

"Harper, meet my favorite person in the whole world who isn't my husband—don't tell Rosie please," she added as an afterthought. Then she put on her best smile and wrapped her arm around the brunette woman's shoulders. "Jordi Wright. Or J.M. Wright if you're into books and shit."

Jordi chuckled. "Wow, Tor. Really great intro," she said, her words dripping with sarcasm.

"I'll say," Alfie added, placing a hand over his heart. Damn. British accents were one-hundred percent better in person. "I always thought I was your favorite, Your Majesty."

"My dearest Alfred, there is plenty of room in my heart for all of you," Tori replied. She grinned. "And it actually needs to have room for one more…"

She placed her hand on her stomach, and Jordi's jaw dropped.

"No way," she said. "No. Way."

"Mark your calendars. You don't get to miss my wedding *and* my baby shower, bitch," Tori said excitedly.

I was beginning to think squealing and hugs were the norm with these two.

"Congrats, man," Alfie said to Jackson.

"Thanks." He placed his hands on his wife's shoulders as Jordi began to assault Tori with questions about her pregnancy.

"She's been dying to tell you both."

"I'm amazed I kept it in this long," Tori admitted.

"It's been, like, five minutes," I said.

"Exactly."

Alfie chuckled, and I froze when his attention landed on me. The wide, white-toothed smile didn't help. "Harper, was it?"

"Uh huh," I managed, and accepted the hand I was offered to shake. In my state of shock, it was probably more like shaking a cooked spaghetti noodle.

"And Harper's boyfriend," Ryan quickly added, extending his hand next. "Ryan Caldwell. Nice to meet you, man."

"Oh, you must be the competition," Jordi said with a grin, her eyes sliding to her partner. "The American football player," she clarified for Alfie.

"Ah, yes. Tori warned me about you." Something told me it had nothing to do with proving a point—that Ryan had nothing to be jealous of—and all about simply wanting to touch her that had Alfie reaching down to lace his fingers with Jordi's. "May the best man raise the most money, mate," he added with a wink.

"Speaking of." Tori clapped her hands together. "We don't have a ton of time before we have to line up, so you three— come. The Turning Pages float is over here." She swooped her arm in a *follow me* motion. "I've got it all decorated: a fantasy landscape for our authors with a little vampire peeking out for Alfred. I was thinking all of you could…"

Tori spoke a million miles a minute, explaining her vision, with Jackson being the only one to initially follow. Jordi and Alfie shared a look, the former giving a little shrug as if to say *you know how she is.* Alfie chuckled and kissed the top of his partner's head before his attention settled on Ryan and me again.

"I'm sure we'll be seeing you both around," he said. "Best of luck with everything today."

"I'd love to get a picture I could send to my dad, Ryan!" Jordi called back to us over her shoulder as she and Alfie followed after their master for the day.

Ryan gave a curt nod and lifted his hand to wave. Through his teeth, he muttered, "Damn, I really wanted to hate him."

"Why?"

Ryan's face tilted down in my direction. "I wonder."

I slapped his chest with the back of my hand. "You're cute when you're jealous."

Before he could say anything to argue the point, I clapped my hands together. "Alright, let's get this show on the road. We need to latch our masterpiece to the truck. There is *no way* the Rotary Club or Chamber of Commerce are winning this year."

Ryan chuckled. "If you like Jealous Ryan, then I'm in love with Competitive Harper." He dipped his head so his lips sat a hairsbreadth from mine. "On second thought, I love any form of Harper."

Win the float contest. Raise the money. No dragging him to the back of the truck and tearing off his clothes, you horny bitch.

I did let him kiss me though, and when he pulled back, he said, "Let's go win this thing."

THE FUCKING ROTARY Club won best float *again*, and I was now fully convinced the competition was rigged. Given how many compliments Ryan and I had gotten as we'd made our way to our tent after dropping off the truck and float in the designated lot for parade participants, there was no doubt in my mind some ballots were miscounted.

But for what we'd lacked in votes, we certainly made up for in visitors to our booth.

"Great. That'll be fifty dollars," I said, taking the card from the dad of two very excited little kids to process his payment.

It had been non-stop all day. Ryan's cheeks had to be in actual pain at this point from all the smiling he'd done—both on the float as we'd ridden with the four senior football players down Main Street and for the fans who'd come to meet him. He kept at it, though. Never faltering. Always charming. And amazing to look at in his jersey and blue jeans that hugged his ass oh-so perfectly.

Sue me for objectification, your honor.

"How you doing, sweetie?" Mom asked, suddenly at my side. She'd popped up every now and then throughout the day, checking in on me. Gina, our other booth helper, did the same with her son.

"Good," I reassured her. This really wasn't all that different from a normal day at Sunrise Brews, except now I was handing out autographs and photo ops instead of coffee and baked goods.

Mom leaned down and planted a big kiss on my cheek. "You two did great. Everything turned out fantastic." In a lower voice, she added, "And I love seeing you and Ryan so happy."

I stole another sideways glance at where Ryan was saying goodbye to the family he'd been taking a picture with. We'd set up an officially licensed Stallions backdrop off to the side of the booth. He held up his hand, challenging the brother and sister duo to jump up to high-five it and laughed along with their parents when they finally managed to succeed.

Yup. The sight of him being wonderful with kids still did it.

"Your brothers are placing bets on how long it will be before he proposes."

My attention cut right back to my mom. "Oh my god. It's been, like, three seconds since we got together."

She shrugged. "You know how they are. Plus, I think they want a football player in the family."

"I'm gonna kill them…" I muttered. "If they say anything to Ryan, I swear I'll—"

"Don't you worry about them," Mom said, cutting me off. "I'm gonna go back to helping Gina. I forgot how much of a hoot that woman is." She kissed the top of my head. "Keep up the good work, princess."

She walked away, off to help Gina distribute some goodies to the family Ryan had just seen, when the next person in line stepped up.

"Welcome. What can Ryan do you for you today? Autograph? Photo? Personalization is an upcharge, but trust me—it's worth it."

The guy chuckled. "Well," he started in a normal volume, then much louder finished, "he can start by returning my phone calls every now and then."

Color me confused—and I did nothing to hide it.

I stared at the unfamiliar man for a moment before I checked to see if Ryan had heard the pointed comment. He hadn't. He was paying too much attention to the next people up for their photo op and autograph.

Over the years, I'd gone to enough Caldwell family events where I recognized most of Ryan's uncles. It wasn't like I'd held super lengthy and memorable conversations with them, but if this guy was somehow related to Ryan, I'd have thought he'd recognize me, too. *That one girl who's always at Thanksgiving brunch,* or something of the likes.

My eyes strayed across the street to where Dave had been lingering. He'd, thankfully, been smart enough to stay away for most of the day, only popping in when Gina requested he get more supplies out of the car. Otherwise, he'd been hanging out with a surprising number of friends, sipping on seasonal brews provided by the kegs Rosie had brought outside for the Ziggy's pop-up.

Stranger Guy definitely hadn't been over there before.

The mystery was finally solved when Gina appeared beside me.

"Oh, Scott!" she said, shuffling around the table to give the man a big hug. "What are you doing here?"

"Surprising my favorite client," the man—Scott, apparently—replied. The name rang a bell, but I didn't know exactly why. "He's doing terrific, it looks like. His recovery and for today's event."

Gina hit Scott's arm playfully. "Look at you being agent of the year," she said. "But yes—Ry's doing great. Physical therapy has really helped."

That was it.

This was Ryan's agent.

As if he'd known I'd connected the dots, Scott aimed what could have been an award-winning smile at me. "Looks like he found himself quite the little saleswoman here, too."

"Harper's the best," Gina complimented with a smile. "Her and Ry Guy have known each other since they were in diapers."

"Well, actually, I'd graduated to undies by the time I was six," I said, "but I can't speak for Ryan."

I made a *yikes* face, and Scott laughed. His shaking index finger was aimed my way when he said, "This one's fun."

"And she's gonna be around a lot more now."

Gina and I were completely forgotten when Ryan appeared. His agent's face lit up, and the two shared a handshake-hug over the table.

"What're you doing here, man?" Ryan asked, repeating his mother's question.

"Had to see how you were doing up here in the middle of nowhere," Scott said, clapping Ryan on the shoulder. "Look at you. Killing it. And I hear rehab's going great, too."

"It's not bad," Ryan replied. "I'm getting there. Doc says I'm ahead of schedule, but you know me—can't sit still even when I probably should."

Scott laughed, his smile wide as ever. "That's the understatement of the year. You've got no idea how much the team's missing you out there. I've gotten so many fucking—" Scott's hand flew up to his mouth, eyes darting side to side. "I mean freaking," he censored. "But regardless—McAllister is desperate to get you back out there. It's been *tight* wins this season. Real tight. You seen? Or are you avoiding watching like you're avoiding my calls?"

Ryan grinned, shaking his head. "Been a little busy."

His hand landed on my shoulder, and without thinking, I lifted my own to rest on top of it. The motion felt natural, easy, and I caught Gina out of the corner of my eye, smiling like she was watching her favorite rom-com play out in real life. Mom, too, from a little further down.

Scott's gaze darted to where our hands rested together, his brows lifting ever so slightly. "Busy, huh?" He smirked. "Well, now it's all making sense. I wouldn't want to talk to my dusty old ass if I could be talking to this beauty instead. Harper, right?"

I nodded, unsure where this was going.

"Well, Harper," Scott said, grin widening. "We're gonna have to get you a spot in the WAGs box next season. Or this season. There's still plenty of time left."

"At Summit Field?" Ryan asked, naming the Stallions' home stadium, his voice casual but laced with something I couldn't quite place.

"Obviously," Scott said, like there was no other option.

Ryan tilted his head. "What about at Lambeau?"

Scott froze, that smile he'd been wearing since he'd shown up slipping just slightly. "What?"

"Lambeau Field," Ryan repeated. "Have you heard anything from the Packers about the offer?"

The confusion on Scott's face deepened, and he straightened, his arms crossing over his chest. "Ryan… I declined their counteroffer. I thought that's what you wanted."

CHAPTER TWENTY-FOUR

MY HEART PLUMMETED, and the oxygen seemed to drain from the space around me.

I slipped my hand away from Ryan's, my stomach twisting as Scott's words hung in the air. Ryan said nothing, but I could feel the tension radiating off him.

"What do you mean you declined the counteroffer?" Ryan said, clearly trying to keep a tether on his emotions while in front of the still-waiting crowd.

Gina seemed to notice that as well and quickly stepped in.

"So sorry, folks!" she called out to the fans. "Ryan just needs to take a little break. We should be back in five minutes or so."

Those closest to the front of the line grumbled, but Mom and Gina made quick work of that, satisfying them for the time being with extra goodies while their wait time was extended.

Scott made his way behind the table, waving Ryan with him.

He placed a hand on his client's shoulder, leading them both behind the Stallions-branded backdrop—and leaving me alone at the front table, utterly flabbergasted by what had just happened.

When my senses somewhat returned, I faced the frustrated crowd, locking eyes with the first person in line: a big, burly man decked out in Stallions gear and matching face paint.

I gave him an embarrassed smile, a nervous huffed laugh escaping me. "I'll just go check on where they went," I said. "Excuse me. Thanks for your patience, everyone."

Slipping out of my plastic folding chair, I scurried back to where Ryan and Scott were talking in tense whispers.

I stopped just at the edge of the backdrop, lingering where I was still half-hidden from their view.

"…assumed that was what you wanted when I heard. I was running out of time with you not returning my calls."

"*Where* did you hear that from?" Ryan challenged. "Is it too late to go back? Let them know I'm still interested? I don't care what the terms were."

"*I* care what the terms were, and I promise you—you're better than what they wanted to pay."

"I *told you* that didn't matter. We knew it was gonna be less than what the Stallions were gonna offer." Ryan ran his hand back through his hair, his frustration written clear on his face. "Can you go back?" he asked again. "See if the offer still stands?"

"You've really been in la-la land lately, haven't you, kid?" Scott pulled out his phone. He tapped around on the screen a bit before he held it out for Ryan. Whatever he'd been presented was enough to make him groan, his eyes shut and head thrown back in defeat.

"I told you the clock was ticking. They wanted someone and they wanted them quick." Scott pocketed his phone. "If you wanted it so bad, why did your dad tell me you—"

Ryan's jaw tightened. "What do you mean *my dad?*"

Scott's confident stance faltered slightly as he held up his hands, palms out. "Look, when I couldn't get ahold of you, I called Dave. Just to check in, make sure everything was alright. I got worried when I wasn't hearing from you."

Ryan's eyes narrowed, his voice low and clipped. "And?"

"And when the Packers deal came up, I asked him if he'd heard of what you intended to do." Scott shrugged. "He told me you weren't interested. You wanted to stay with the Stallions."

The world seemed to slow for a moment as I watched Ryan process Scott's words. His lips pressed into a thin line, his shoulders, already tense, seemed to draw back even further. His hands clenched into fists at his sides, and his jaw twitched in a way that told me he was holding back from saying something he might regret later.

I didn't need to know Ryan as well as I did to recognize that look in his eyes—it was anger, quiet but intense. The kind that simmered beneath the surface before it boiled over.

The only problem was, when it came to Ryan and Dave, that anger had already been boiling for at least a month.

He didn't say anything right away, and for a second, I thought maybe he wouldn't at all. But then his gaze shifted, cutting away from Scott and landing somewhere beyond the tent.

I followed his line of sight, and my stomach twisted when I realized what—or rather, who—he was looking at.

Oh no. Now was not the time for this. Not when we had a line of people waiting to see the great golden boy of Timberland Creek.

Ryan didn't say another word to Scott. He didn't need to. Instead, he turned and stalked off, his strides purposeful and unrelenting.

"Ryan," Scott called after him, his voice tinged with confusion. But Ryan didn't stop.

I held my breath as Ryan grew closer until, finally, he spotted me frozen in place.

Just for a moment, his face softened, and I took my chance.

"Ry," I whispered, stepping away from the side of the tent.

I reached out to touch him, but hesitated. Even knowing the anger wasn't for me, I didn't want to do anything that would upset him further. Trigger him. He wouldn't do anything to me. I knew that in my heart of hearts. But still. I'd never seen him like this. Not even during the few other arguments I'd witnessed him have with Dave.

Ryan's eyes met mine, and there was something in them that made my heart ache—a mixture of frustration and hurt. Maybe even disappointment. I opened my mouth to say something, anything, but before I could, his hands came to rest on my shoulders.

The shift in him was so sudden, so startlingly gentle, that it almost stole my breath. His touch was steady, grounding, even as the tension in his body remained.

He leaned down and pressed a kiss to my forehead, his lips lingering just long enough to send warmth flooding through me.

Then he was gone, his hands slipping away as he continued his march across the street.

It didn't take a rocket scientist to figure out where he was going.

Across the way, his dad was laughing, still caught up in conversation with his group of friends, completely oblivious to the storm headed his way.

"Ryan!" someone in line called out when he passed.

"Ryan, we love you!" another shouted.

He ignored the fanfare, but knowing the crowd was watching only made my worry worsen.

"Shit," I muttered to myself, no longer able to sit back.

I jogged after Ryan. Even at a quicker speed, it still wasn't enough to catch up. Not when the Fall Fest crowds were taken into account.

"'Scuse me," I said, trying to squeeze between the people. Apparently, being a town celebrity was cause for the seas to part because Ryan was having absolutely no difficulty. "Pardon me, I just need to—"

My attention cut across the street when I heard some guy say, "Hey, there he is!"

Dave turned, smile still on his lips from whatever conversation he'd been partaking in. I wasn't even sure he'd fully registered it was his son coming up behind him before that smile was wiped right off.

A collective gasp went up among everyone within viewing distance when Ryan's fist connected firmly with Dave's nose.

Mr. Caldwell's cup dropped to the ground, his beer forming a puddle at his feet, and his hands went up to grasp the impact point.

"Oh my god."

Politeness was out the window as I shoved my way through the crowd, earning a few grumbles and frustrated looks. Nothing lasted long, though, with everyone's attention set on the scene unfolding between the two Caldwell men.

"What the fuck is wrong with you?" Dave barked, his voice sharp with pain and disbelief.

"What's wrong with *me*?" Ryan shouted, his voice booming loud enough to make even more heads turn. The chatter and laughter of the festival dulled, replaced by murmurs and gasps as they realized who, exactly, was involved in the squabble.

The whole crowd surrounding the Caldwells had gone still, a mix of festival attendees holding caramel apples, pumpkin-shaped balloons, and seasonal refreshments watching. Children clutched at their parents' hands, while other vendors leaned out from their booths to get a better view.

I dared a glance down the street and found Tori standing out front of the Turning Pages tent, her hand over her mouth. Jackson, Alfie, and Jordi stood beside her watching in just as much stunned awe, though Jackson did have a look about him that made me think he believed Dave had it coming.

I couldn't say I disagreed, but this was *not* the time for Ryan to finally react.

Ryan's face was flushed, his chest heaving like he'd just run at a full sprint across the street. "What's wrong with *you*? Why did you do it?"

Dave straightened slightly, wincing as he gingerly touched his nose. A few drops of blood landed on the sidewalk, stark against the cement. "What the hell are you talking about?"

"You know exactly what I'm talking about!" Ryan's fists curled tightly at his sides. "You told Scott I didn't want to take the deal with the Packers."

A ripple of whispers spread through the crowd, the festival's cheery atmosphere now replaced with a tense hush. Even the band playing in the Town Square gazebo had faltered, their upbeat swing tune stuttering to an awkward halt.

Dave blinked, his confusion quickly morphing into a

defensive scowl. "I did what needed to be done," he said coldly. "Your head's not in the game anymore, Ryan. Someone had to step in and stop you from making a mistake you'd regret."

Ryan's laugh came out bitter and broken. "A mistake?" he repeated. "You think my decisions about *my* career—*my* life—are mistakes? You think *you* get to decide that?"

"You've been distracted," Dave snapped, his voice rising to meet Ryan's. "And we both know why."

I froze as his gaze darted towards me, not surprised by the answer, but definitely surprised he admitted it with an audience.

Ryan took a step forward, looking every bit the menacing force he was on the football field. "Don't you dare," he growled, his voice low.

"She's part of the problem, Ryan," Dave pressed. "She always has been. Every time she's in the picture, your focus goes out the window. You're throwing away a Hall of Fame career because you're too busy fawning over some nobody girl."

Around us, the crowd shifted uncomfortably. My lower lip trembled as I tried to keep my attention on the Caldwells—not on the many, *many* people now adding me into the mix of their focus.

It wasn't like I hadn't believed Ryan when he'd told me what Dave had said to him all those years ago. But hearing it now, in person… it hit differently.

"That's bullshit," Ryan managed, the muscles of his neck

tight, his entire body trembling. "Harper has done nothing but support me my entire career. Unlike you."

Dave flinched at that, but it didn't stop Ryan. His voice cracked as he continued, the words he'd probably waited years to say spilling out.

"You've been in my way during every step, making me question every decision I've ever made. You talk about my focus—my career—like they're yours to control, but all you've ever done is hold me back. And I can't believe I let you." Ryan shook his head. "All you've ever done is place the blame somewhere else when I'm not living up to the standard *you* set, when it's always been *you* who's made me feel inadequate."

The crowd parted slightly. I glanced to where they'd created an opening and Gina walked through.

"Ryan." Her voice broke as she said her son's name. "Your father—we've both—all we've wanted to do is support you. You have to understand what he did was probably an accident. You hardly talk anymore. How was he supposed to know you—?"

"It doesn't matter if he knew or not!" Ryan shouted, making Gina flinch. He deflated slightly at her reaction. "It doesn't matter," he repeated, softer this time. "If Scott brought up something Dad wasn't aware of, Dad should have left it alone, not gone and fucked up the chance I had of moving back here and—"

"And done what?" Dave challenged. "Play for a mediocre

team? Not be utilized to your full potential? Be underpaid just to—"

"I'd be able to be with the woman I love, for fuck's sake! There wouldn't be a whole goddamn country between us anymore!" Ryan shook his head. "I wouldn't have lost her for the years that I did if you would've just stayed out of my life!"

Dave stiffened, shrugging Gina away from where she was trying to blot at his nose with a rag. "If that's how you feel," he said, tone cold, "then maybe you shouldn't come back to the house. If you want me out of your life so bad. Figure out your priorities somewhere else."

"David!" Gina's voice broke as she turned on him. "You don't mean that. He's your son."

"I do." Dave's expression didn't waver. "He needs to learn to live with his choices."

"Fine." My voice cut through the tension before I realized I was speaking. My hands were shaking, my pulse pounding in my ears, but I stepped forward anyway, putting myself between Ryan and his father. "He doesn't need to go back to your house. He can stay with me."

Ryan's head whipped toward me. "Harper—" he started, but before he could finish, another voice broke through the crowd.

"Alright, folks, that's enough."

I turned to see Sheriff Walters stepping into the circle of onlookers, his hand resting casually on his belt as his sharp gaze swept over the scene. "Let's break it up, people. Go enjoy the festival. Nothing to see here.”

There was a murmur of protest from the crowd, but one stern look from Walters had them reluctantly dispersing, albeit slower than he probably wanted.

Nosy assholes trying to get one last peek of Ryan's outburst. I wouldn't be surprised if someone had already posted a clip of him screaming. Sports commentators would be dissecting the whole thing by the morning.

Sheriff Walters's brow furrowed as his eyes landed on Dave.

“Your nose doesn't look too good,” he said evenly. “Might want to get that checked out. And I suggest keeping your arguments somewhere a little more private next time. I already have my guys camped out at your place enough. I can't sacrifice them anymore than I already am.”

Dave muttered something under his breath, but Gina tugged his arm, holding the rag to his nose again.

Walters turned to Ryan next, his tone softening just slightly. “You good, son?”

Ryan nodded, though his jaw remained tight. “Yeah,” he said shortly, glancing at me before looking away.

The sheriff's eyes lingered on him for a moment before he gave a curt nod. “If you say so.”

As he moved to corral the last of the stragglers in the crowd, I turned to Ryan, my voice low. “Ry, it's okay. You can stay with me. We'll go back to the house and pack a bag, then you can—”

I stopped short when he shook his head.

"I don't want to talk right now," he said, his voice strained. "I… I need to be alone."

"Ryan." I reached for him, but he stepped back, shaking his head.

"Harper," he said, softer this time, his gaze filled with something raw and broken that made my chest ache. "Please. I'll find you later, okay?"

He stood there waiting, his shoulders tense, his eyes searching mine for something. Permission, maybe. Or understanding.

I swallowed hard, my throat tightening. I hated that I'd once again become the reason for his stress. I hated that my name had been the one Dave had thrown like a weapon.

But more than that, I hated the fear creeping in. The fear that maybe Dave was right. That maybe, even after all we'd done to try to convince ourselves that we could make this work, it was out of our control.

Ryan shifted, growing impatient, and I forced myself to nod. "Okay," I said quietly, my voice barely above a whisper.

That was all it took. He gave me a final look then turned and walked away, his broad shoulders rigid. This time, no one dared make any comments at him as he passed them on the sidewalk. The line in front of the booth had dispersed with the rest of the nosy crowd, off to find somewhere else to spend their money.

Money I wasn't sure would be enough to save Sunrise at this point.

The festive decorations felt almost mocking as Ryan disappeared into the distance, leaving me standing there, helpless to fix any of it.

CHAPTER TWENTY-FIVE

LONG AFTER THE festivities had ended, the tourists and locals alike returning to their homes for the night, Ryan finally showed up at my door with a carry-on suitcase and a backpack.

I didn't bother yelling at him for carrying it up the stairs to my apartment with his injury. He'd had enough of that for one day.

Instead, I ushered him inside, sat him right down on the couch, and heated up some comfort food—everyone should invest in emergency frozen pizzas and ice cream—while warm apple cider boiled on the stove. It wasn't the most appetizing of combinations, but I doubted he'd eaten all day. Being picky probably wasn't a problem at the moment.

I didn't bother asking where he'd disappeared to, knowing I'd get that information if or when he wanted to tell me. He didn't seem too keen on talking as it was, opting instead to go straight to a streaming service to put on a movie. *Step Brothers*. Looked like his favorite hadn't changed since high school.

We ended up falling asleep on the couch, Ryan on his back, me squished between him and the back of the couch, my head on his chest. The first thing I saw when I opened my eyes in the morning were Will Ferrell and John C. Reilly staring at me from the movie's featured photo on the TV screen.

I grimaced when I lifted my neck just enough to check if Ryan was still asleep. Apparently twenty-six was the cut-off for sleeping comfortably on the couch without being in any pain afterwards.

My intent had been to move so little that Ryan didn't wake up, but when his arms tightened around my back, I knew I'd failed that mission.

His eyes blinked open a second later trying to adjust to the bright sunlight leaking into my living room.

"Good morning," I whispered. Ryan pressed his eyes shut, his face scrunching. "How're you feeling?"

"It hurts a little," he said, voice raw from disuse. "I don't normally sleep with the brace on."

"I wasn't talking about your knee, Ry."

His chest rose below me as he took a sharp inhale through his nose.

"I'm fine," he said on the exhale. "Or I will be. There's a lot… a lot I need to figure out right now."

I nodded slowly, my hand creeping up to rest on his chest.

"Did you find Scott again?"

"He found me. I finally answered one of his phone calls, and we met up." Ryan huffed a laugh and ran a hand down his face. "I thought they were all just check-ins. I didn't expect to hear anything about the deal for a while yet, so I didn't—I just—I didn't…"

"It's not your fault," I reassured him. "You couldn't have known your dad would have done what he did."

"That's the thing—I *should* have known." Ryan sounded so defeated as he spoke. "And it's fucking ridiculous that I'm saying that about a person who was always supposed to have my best interest at heart."

"I can't believe I'm saying this," I began, the comment piquing Ryan's interest. He lifted his head just enough to see me better, one curious brow raised. "But I think he did believe he was doing the right thing for you. Protecting you. I mean, you've worked your whole life for this career and now—"

"Hey, hey, hey." Ryan brushed my hair back from my face, jumping right into comfort mode as soon as my voice cracked. His hand cupped the side of my face, his thumb brushing across my cheek. "I've already had a great career. If you'd have asked me five years ago what I'd accomplish, I would have laughed in your face."

"I told you you could do it," I whispered.

"You did." Ryan bent at his core, lifting himself up to kiss my forehead. "Which is why I don't want to go through the next five years without you there to witness it."

"Did Scott offer any sort of solution?" I asked. "Could you, like, go back to the Packers and say there was a misunderstanding?"

Ryan shook his head. "No. The contract with the new tight end was already signed, and the deal's been made public. There're whispers that I was also in the running, but Scott's trying to squash those. Doesn't want the Stallions to think I'm not coming back after this injury and have me replaced ahead of time."

"This is such a mess."

"You're telling me."

We laid in silence for a moment, the chirping birds outside and occasional shrill coffee bean grinding of Hemi's preparations downstairs the only sounds. I should've been able to offer him something—some sort of answer that would make things seem easier, even if I knew, deep down, our situation was the exact opposite. But the most obvious solution was the one I couldn't bring myself to say.

I could move to San Antonio.

If I did, we wouldn't have to deal with the constant war of distance. We could be together—really together—in a way we hadn't been since we were kids. But even I knew it was next to impossible.

I couldn't afford to move there. Not with my current paycheck and savings. I was still paying off college loans, my car payment. Hemi gave me a pretty good deal on rent, but that would definitely change if I moved to Texas. And even if I somehow scraped together enough to make it work, I knew Ryan would still step in. He'd cover everything because that's just who he was, and I'd let him, because what choice would I have? But it wouldn't take long before that would start to weigh on me. Before I started resenting it.

Damn. Hemi's resistance to accept money was suddenly making a whole lot more sense.

At least in Green Bay, there'd been a chance. Smaller city, lower costs. I could have found a job that would help me pull my weight. We could've lived somewhere simple. Modest. Not the sprawling gated-community mansion he owned in San Antonio.

"You're quiet," Ryan said, pulling me out of my thoughts. His hand moved to rest over mine where it still lay on his chest, his thumb brushing absentmindedly across my knuckles.

I forced a small smile, though I doubted it was convincing. "Just thinking."

"About?"

"How we're gonna figure this out," I said, keeping my voice as even as I could manage. "Because we will."

Ryan held my gaze for a long moment, and I wondered if he was trying to think of what to say. Then he nodded, and his voice, when it came, was quieter than I'd hoped. "Yeah. We will."

He laid his head back down, eyes settled on the ceiling of my apartment, his thumb still moving across my knuckles. I watched him for a moment before I turned, settling the side of my head on his chest, listening to the steady beat of his heart.

He hadn't sounded convinced. Not in the slightest. And the ache that settled in my chest at hearing it told me I wasn't entirely convinced either.

ONE DOWNSIDE ABOUT working at a coffee shop in a town where you inadvertently put yourself in the middle of the biggest source of local gossip in years was that everyone knew who you were.

And not in a good way.

There wasn't a doubt in my mind that a solid ninety percent of the clientele at Sunrise Brews had witnessed the commotion at the Fall Fest. And if they hadn't, they'd definitely heard about it given the looks I was getting.

They weren't just looks. They were *looks*. The judge-y kind. The ones that told me most of these people were about three seconds away from forgoing their order in favor of getting me to spill the tea.

Too bad for them, the only tea I intended to interact with that day was the delicious seasonal chai blend Hemi had added to the menu for the month.

I'd take being on the front page of every edition of the *Timberland Creek Gazette* over this nonsense. For real.

The good news was that after this weekend was up, most of the tourists would clear out of town until the busy season returned. I wouldn't see half of these people again for another year, if at all, by which time the Fall Fest Scandal would be long forgotten. Hopefully.

The bad news, though, was that meant only locals would be around moving forward. Locals who were well aware of mine and the Caldwells' existence—and who wouldn't be as hesitant about asking what was up.

Case in point…

"Holy shit. Are you okay?" Tori asked as she rushed in through the front door, leaving Jordi in the dust. She slammed her hands down on the counter and leaned forward. "Did Hemi make you come in today? If she did, I'll yell at her. I swear I will."

"I wanted to come in," I reassured her, even though I'd thought about asking for a shift change at least three times while I was getting ready. I couldn't do that to her, though. Not when it was likely going to be our last busy day of the season.

Jordi caught up to Tori, and I mirrored her polite smile and nod.

"Where's Ryan?" Tori asked.

"Upstairs. Probably watching *Anchorman* or something."

"Has he tried *The Princess Bride*? That's also a great wallowingin-sadness-day movie."

My brow scrunched. "Not sure that's really his vibe," I told her. "Where're your men at today?"

"Bonding," Tori said proudly. "I'm determined for them to like each other, so I took this one out of the equation to force friendship upon them."

Tori linked her arm with Jordi's, earning a chuckle and shake of her friend's head.

"Sounds somewhat traumatic?"

"For Alfie, probably," Jordi agreed. She laughed again when Tori elbowed her in the side.

"I told you Jackson's better now," she defended. "I'm sure they're already deep in discussion about the benefits of vampires in fiction."

"We'll see how it goes," Jordi concluded. She leaned in towards the menu we had posted behind the counter. "In the meantime, I'm going to enjoy some Tori Time and a…" She squinted, and when her eyes opened again said, "I'll go with the maple pumpkin latte."

"So much better than the classic PSL if you ask me," I confirmed. "And decaf for you, Tor?"

"Tragically." She lifted herself onto her toes, neck craned as if searching for something. "Is Hemi even here today?"

Okay, not something. Some*one*.

"She's around here somewhere. Might have had to go down to the basement to get more syrup." I really hadn't been paying attention to my boss's whereabouts, too distracted by the steady wave of customers that morning. "Want me to go find her?"

Tori gave a dismissive wave. "Nah, just let me know if she comes back. I don't wanna interrupt anything."

It didn't seem like Tori was in the mood to wait around, either. They didn't waste any time, paying and briskly walking off to snag one of the few remaining tables in the front room, while I got to work on their drinks.

I looked up from my work only when I heard a bit of commotion behind the storage room door. Seconds later, it opened and revealed Hemi balancing a few burlap bags of coffee beans in her arms.

She set them down on the counter with a thud, brushing her hands on her apron. "We should have enough of the autumn blend to get us through to mid-November," she said, straightening. "Found these tucked away in the back."

"Do we still have the decaf variety of that blend?" I asked.

"We should."

"Perfect. Think we could get that ready for Tori?"

"Coming right up," Hemi said, dumping some of the beans in the grinder.

"She was looking for you, by the way," I mentioned as I dusted cinnamon on top of Jordi's latte.

"Tori?"

"Mhm. Said she didn't want to bother you if you're busy,

though." I snuck a peek Hemi's way when she didn't respond only to find her with a bright twinkle in her eyes. "Something I should know about?"

"Nope. I'm just excited I found more autumn blend," Hemi said, and before I could call her on the terrible lie, she pointed to the drink I was making and asked, "That her drink, too?"

"Her friend's, but yeah, it's part of her order."

"Perfect." Hemi cut the bean grinder and removed the cannister of grounds, the crisp scent of the coffee filling the air. "Why don't you go bring that to them and have Tori come over here? Her drink's gonna be a minute or two anyway while I wait for this to brew."

"This sounds suspicious."

Hemi rolled her eyes. "Just do as you're told. That's why I pay you."

I made a face, but she had a good point. And I didn't want to mess with those paychecks, especially not knowing how many more I'd get. I didn't know how well the other booths at the Fall Fest did, but Ryan's definitely hadn't ended up raising a lot.

Thanks, Dave.

"One maple pumpkin latte," I announced, setting Jordi's drink down in front of her. "Hemi's back, Tori. She's working on yours if you wanted to go talk to her. She said she's free."

"Oh, yes." Tori grinned as she pushed back her chair and stood. "Excuse me, ladies. I'll be right back."

I lingered a moment once Tori shuffled away, not quite sure if I should say anything or not. Eventually I settled on, "Well… hope you like it."

Jordi smiled. "I'm sure I will."

I fidgeted in my spot, my lips curled in as I smiled back, then saluted before I turned on my heels.

I'd made it about two steps before I doubled back. Jordi startled, her latte nearly sloshing over the side of her mug, at my sudden reappearance.

"I'm sorry," I said. "I know we just met—and literally for only three whole minutes—so this might be weird. But can I ask you something?"

Jordi cautiously set the drink down, her expression curious but kind. "Sure. What's up?"

I shifted awkwardly, feeling the weight of the question before I even spoke it. "I think Tori might have mentioned… you and Alfie. You're long-distance, aren't you?"

Her brows lifted slightly in surprise, like she hadn't expected Tori to ever talk about her to anyone. But then she nodded. "We were. Alfie moved to Chicago with me a few years ago. Right after I got my first book deal."

"And… how was it? While you were long-distance, that is."

She regarded me for a moment, probably trying to figure out why I was asking before she said, "I won't lie to you—it was tough. Long-distance isn't easy, especially since that's what we were doing in the beginning of our relationship."

I let out a deep exhale, my voice faltering as I said, "How did you make it work?"

Jordi leaned back in her seat with a sigh. "We had to make some really hard decisions, honestly," she said. "There were moments when it felt like we were on two different planets, let alone different time zones. It didn't come without fighting sometimes. I cried a lot." She shrugged. "But we talked—about *everything.* What we wanted. What we were willing to compromise. What we weren't. And it helped that I've gotten my feet off the ground a little bit with my author career. I'm not tethered to one place so much anymore. Makes it easier to travel with Alfie if he's shooting at some destination. He just wrapped on the movie based on my debut, actually."

My eyes widened. "Seriously?"

Jordi nodded. "Three months in Edinburgh. They basically forced me to be there, too, though. Wanted to have the author of the source content around or whatever." She waved her hand dismissively. "I still don't get any of that Hollywood stuff. But it was nice to be in one place with Alf for a while."

I swallowed, trying to process her words while thinking about my own situation. "Sounds like it all ended up working out pretty well for you guys, then."

Jordi let out an incredulous laugh. "Are you kidding? We still deal with stuff all the time, and we've been together almost four years," she said.

"Really?"

"Just because the long distance ended didn't mean our problems did." Jordi grinned. "But we keep at it because we both know we want to reach the same end goal: to end up together. We, by some miracle, got a second chance, and neither of us wants to waste it."

I nodded slowly, her words hitting closer to home than I wanted to admit. "Ryan and I… we haven't figured any of that out yet. And it feels like… like maybe I'm the one holding him back."

Jordi's head tilted, and in that moment—with the look she was leveling at me—I understood how she could be friends with Tori Albrecht. "You aren't letting whatever that guy at the festival said get to you, are you? Because from what Tori told me, he's a downright—"

"No, I'm not. I swear," I assured her. I sighed. "I guess it just seems like everything he's worked for seems so big. And I'm just… here. Timberland Creek is all I've ever known. I don't want him to lower his standards just to accommodate that."

Because as nice an option as Green Bay would have been, that's what he would have been doing if he'd accepted their counteroffer. They weren't a team that utilized tight ends. He would have faded into oblivion. Just another name on the fifty-two-man roster instead of shining like the star he was.

Jordi paused, her expression thoughtful. "Listen, I know we don't know each other super well," she said carefully. "But I can tell you this—you're not holding him back. If he loves you—and from what Tori's told me, it sounds like he does—you're already giving him what he needs. You."

My throat tightened. "But what if that's not enough?"

"It is," Jordi said, her voice firm but kind. "I know it doesn't feel like it right now, but love isn't about who has the bigger career or the flashier life. It's about showing up for each other, even when it's messy. *Especially* when it's messy, actually. Alfie and I have had to remind ourselves of that more times than I can count."

"And how do you know when it's worth it?"

Jordi gave me a small smile, her gaze steady. "If you're with the right person, the struggle is always worth it. Every hard conversation, every moment of doubt—it all makes you stronger in the end."

I felt my eyes burn, but I blinked back the tears. The last thing I needed was for Tori to come back and question me. Or for Hemi to do the same when I returned to my post behind the counter.

"Thank you," I said softly. "I didn't mean to… unload on you like this."

"Hey," Jordi said, her tone lightening. "We've all been there. And besides, Tori would kill me if I didn't at least try to help her friend—especially given it sounds like we've gone through some similar stuff."

"Going through, actually," I corrected. "But hopefully it'll be figured out soon. I really appreciate your help."

"Anytime," she said with a warm smile, lifting her cup in a small toast. "And if you ever need more unsolicited advice, you know where to find me. I've still got a couple days here."

I chuckled softly, as another voice said, "Girl, you're not leaving until our husbands are besties." Tori's hand landed on my shoulder. "What'd I miss?" she asked.

Jordi glanced at me, a knowing smile tugging at the corners of her lips. "Harper and I were bonding."

"Aw." Tori's hand slid to my other shoulder and all of a sudden, I was pulled against Tori's side. "I love this. All my favorite people, finally getting to know each other."

I laughed, shaking my head. "Wish I could stay longer, but I should probably get back to help Hemi." I turned to Jordi. "I hope I get to see you before you leave."

"Wait." Tori pulled away, staring up at me with a confused expression. "Aren't you and Ryan coming to dinner?"

"What dinner?"

"I texted you this morning. Seven o'clock? Bella Luna?"

I wracked my brain, trying to remember if I'd seen that particular text. I'd mostly been focused on ones from my mom and dad, the former particularly worried after witnessing what had gone down between Ryan and Dave. She'd already offered to cook us a casserole.

But other than that, I didn't remember anything about a dinner.

"Must've missed it," I admitted. "It's been a little crazy."

Tori's face went from excited to sympathetic in the blink of an eye. She pulled me in for another side hug.

"I totally get it if you two want to lie low for a bit," she said. "But if you decide you want a distraction—that isn't a slap-stick comedy from the early two-thousands—I made the reservation for six people. We'd love it if you two came."

My eyes slid to Jordi who, as soon as she realized my attention was on her, nodded reassuringly.

"I'll check with Ryan," I said, offering them both a small smile. "I'll letcha know what he says."

"Of course," Tori said, her tone not quite back to its normal cheery tone, but close as she gave me a smile in return.

I offered them one final goodbye with the promise to keep them updated before I headed back to the front counter. As I slid behind the register, I glanced over at the duo, their heads already bent close together, chatting like no time had passed.

Maybe Tori was right. Maybe spending time with friends tonight wouldn't be the worst idea—even if Tori and Jackson were really the only friends I'd have at the table. Ryan... he hardly knew any of them.

Even as I thought it, my mind drifted upstairs to where he was probably watching his movies.

I'd leave it up to him.

CHAPTER TWENTY-SIX

"LET'S DO IT."

The words surprised me enough that I couldn't stop my eyes from widening. "Really?"

Ryan nodded. He reached for the remote and hit pause on the mafia TV show he was watching before standing up. "Seven you said?"

"I, uh—yeah. But, Ry…" My brow furrowed. "Are you sure? We really don't have to if you don't wanna go."

"Nope." He propelled himself off the couch much quicker than someone with a mostly recovered knee injury should. "If I keep sitting here, I think I'm gonna melt into the cushions. And you said it's an Italian place, right?" I nodded. "Perfect. It'll be dark. No one will notice me."

He seemed so hopeful that I didn't bother arguing it wouldn't just be him that was in attendance; Alfie Fletcher might draw a few eyes as well. But I wasn't going to be the one to crush his first sign of high-spirits.

So that's how I ended up in my bedroom, most of my closet on the floor because what the hell did you wear to what was technically only your second night out with your boyfriend while three other well-known names would be sharing the table with you?

I sighed, my lips trilling, as I tossed yet another sweater on the bed. The whole thing was covered at this point. I couldn't even see my comforter.

It was official. I didn't go out nearly enough. If I did, I would have definitely been able to find something decent by now. Instead, all I'd found were old pairs of jeans, a few halfway-decent sweaters—one of which I'd worn on Ryan's and my first date, so I definitely couldn't wear it again—and a dress I'd bought for my great-aunt's funeral three years ago.

I knew better than to ask Tori what she was wearing. The question massively stressed her out. I'd learned that even before we became close friends.

So that left me to my own opinion, since Ryan would tell me I looked good in anything I put on.

Holy shit.

That was it.

I shuffled through a few articles of clothing before I managed to find my phone. Even better, the woman I wanted to text— and needed an answer from pretty rapidly—had just sent me a message two minutes ago.

Unfortunately, Mom was going to be left in suspense. It wasn't like my childhood home was far away, but we were cutting it close on time as it was, seeing as I hadn't even gotten off my shift at Sunrise until five.

I rushed out of my room and knocked on the bathroom door, behind which I could hear the steady flow of water from the shower.

"Ry?" I called, unsure if he could even hear me. "I'm heading out. I'll be right back."

I didn't give him a chance to reply before I hurried to the door, snatched my keys, and left.

I RAN MY hands down the front of the dress, the satin cool beneath my fingers. Part of me was trying to smooth out invisible wrinkles, but mostly, I was marveling at the fact that it still fit after over a decade.

The deep green fabric hugged my body, the delicate rouching down the sides creating subtle curves in all the right places, while also hiding any potential bloating in my front. Sure, the style was outdated—the spaghetti straps and a bodycon silhouette didn't exactly scream modern chic—but it didn't matter. The dress did its job.

And I couldn't deny it: the scoop neckline was working some serious magic for my cleavage.

To bring it into the modern fashion era, I'd added a pair of sheer black tights and knee-high boots. It wasn't much, but it was enough to breathe some life into a look that had spent the better part of ten years buried in the back of the storage closet in my parents' basement.

Thank god I'd never been a sequins girl. The plain, shimmering satin was more than enough.

I sighed as one of the spaghetti straps slipped down my shoulder yet again. I tugged it back into place and glanced at my reflection in the full-body mirror.

This was as good as it was going to get.

My heels clicked softly on the wood floor as I made my way to the living room. Ryan was already there, scrolling on his phone, long legs stretched out on the couch like he didn't have a care in the world.

He'd dressed up a little nicer than for our first date, trading the jeans for black slacks, the brace around his knee making the fabric synch there. He still wore a button-up, though. This time it was white, and I couldn't help but notice how perfectly it stretched across his broad shoulders. His sleeves were once again rolled up to his elbows, showcasing his forearms, and the top two buttons were undone, giving him an effortlessly polished look that made my pulse quicken.

As soon as Ryan heard me, his head lifted, and then his phone was forgotten. His mouth fell open, his eyes wide as they swept over me from head to toe.

Oh yeah. He definitely recognized the dress.

Ryan didn't say a word at first. Instead, he pushed himself off the couch slowly, like he was afraid moving too quickly might break the spell. His gaze never wavered, never once left me as he crossed the room.

My heart thudded in my chest as he stopped in front of me, close enough that I could smell the faint trace of his cologne—warm, woodsy, familiar. He didn't speak right away, and I didn't either. I stayed quiet, letting him drink me in, the weight of his stare making my skin tingle.

Finally, his hands slid to my hips, and I wondered, with the way he was looking at me, if we'd make it to dinner at all.

When his eyes met mine, my breath caught.

"You look just as beautiful in this dress now," he said, his voice low, "as you did at homecoming."

Even though I'd hoped for that reaction when I'd selected my outfit for the night, it still made my cheeks warm.

Ryan smiled, a slow, teasing curve of his lips that told me he wasn't done yet. His hold tightened on my hips. "Brent Taylor really fucked up not taking better care of you."

I batted my eyelashes up at him. "I didn't want Brent Taylor anyway."

"Good." His hands slipped down over my ass, squeezing. "Because Brent Taylor wouldn't have had a clue what to do with a woman like you."

Ryan's hold forced me closer until our bodies were pressed together.

I tilted my chin up, giving him better access to my mouth as he lowered his head. But he paused, his warm breath caressing my lips, just before they met his.

"You know if I kiss you now, I won't be able to stop," he warned. "Not when you look like this."

"That's too bad," I mock pouted. "We have a reservation we're about to be late for."

"Think they'll notice if we don't show?"

I chuckled. "Definitely."

Ryan groaned, and I reached behind my back to grab his hands.

"C'mon," I said, lacing our fingers together. "We need to be there in ten minutes."

"Fine." His reluctance made me smile. "But I'm warning you—the second we come back through your front door tonight, I'm ripping your panties off and fucking you in this dress."

I tried to ignore my sudden urge to ditch the dinner as well as I lifted onto my toes and kissed his cheek. My mouth lingered near his ear, and I whispered, "Who says I'm wearing any panties?"

My head fell back as I laughed at Ryan's whining, tugging him out of the apartment.

FOR A GROUP of strangers, the conversation flowed pretty well during dinner. The glasses of wine probably helped—for everyone except Tori, that was. She knew everyone anyway, so she was in need of the least social buffers.

The soft hum of conversation and the clinking of glasses filled the warm, intimate Italian restaurant. The small, candlelit table was crowded with the proof of our wine consumption and plates of fresh bread.

Alfie's charming British accent pulled everyone in to any story he told. I hadn't been sure what to expect of him from the little we'd spoken, but he was exactly as Tori had described—effortlessly likeable, the kind of guy who made you feel like you'd known him for years, rather than a guy who flaunted the fact that he was probably one of the most popular actors of the early turn of the century. And Jordi proved even further that she was equally as wonderful. Grounded and sharp, with a quiet confidence that balanced Alfie's charisma. It was easy to see why they worked so well together.

Jackson, on the other hand, had seemed a little out of his element. I could tell he was trying, though, leaning forward when Alfie spoke, laughing at the right moments, and making an effort to ease whatever tension I'd noticed the day before.

Seemed like Tori's plan to make them best friends was off to a start. A slow start, but a start nonetheless.

By the time the dinner was over, Jordi had gotten her selfie with Ryan for her dad, and the rest of us were stuffed with carbs. I'd been more than ready to return home. Ryan was too, if the sigh he'd let out as soon as he closed the door behind us was any indication.

"Well," I said, tossing my bag and keys on the entryway table. "You survived."

He huffed a laugh, emptying his pockets of their contents and placing everything right next to my stuff. "They're good people."

I hummed my agreement, bent over to undo the zippers on my boots before I kicked them off. Ryan was already behind me, his hands on my waist when I stood back up.

"Making good on your promise?" I asked, feeling the way the fabric of my already-short dress rose even higher under his hold.

"I will," Ryan said, voice low. "First, I just want to…"

His hands moved off my hips, his arms wrapping around the front of my body, pulling my back tighter against his front. Then his chin was on my shoulder, his face buried in my neck, not to kiss me as I'd expected. Instead, Ryan took in a deep inhale through his nose before he nuzzled closer.

One of my hands found its way over his on my stomach, the other reached up, wrapping around the back of his neck, my fingers playing with his hair. Any tension in his body eased, and he went loose around me.

"I just want this," he whispered against my skin.

A moment of peace. Of quiet. Where it was only the two of us, not saying anything or doing anything other than simply being. After all the chaos of—well, of since he'd come back to Timberland Creek, I hadn't realized how necessary this had been.

"I love you, Harper," Ryan whispered again, after I-don't-even-know how long passed with us standing in the entry of my apartment in silence. "I love you so much."

"I love you, too," I replied. I twisted myself in his hold, both my arms wrapping around his neck while his settled on the small of my back.

I stared up at him as I said, "They all went through it, too. Every single person at that table with us tonight."

"Through what?"

"The distance," I clarified. "The challenges. And look where they are now."

"But we're not them," Ryan argued. "What if we—what if *I*—"

The tension returned. I could feel it in his hold on me, see it on his face as he closed his eyes, refusing to say what I already knew he'd been thinking.

He only allowed me to see the shining blue of his eyes again when my hand cupped his face, my thumb running over his stubble-covered cheek.

"You're right. We're not them." A small smile curled the corners of my lips. "We're *better*. We've been through years of challenges already, Ry. If that couldn't stop this from happening between us, what's one more obstacle? And this time your dad won't even be involved. It's gonna be a cakewalk in comparison."

A strangled laugh escaped him, making my smile grow as he lowered his forehead to mine.

"I know you're scared," I continued, my voice soft. "I am, too. But I *really* think we can do this."

"As long as I'm not a dumbass again."

"You were never a dumbass." I stroked his cheek one more time. "Just a… a half-dumbass. It's not nearly as bad. Much more easily forgiven."

"Jesus, Harps," he said through another laugh. But my reassurances, no matter how unserious, did the trick.

Ryan's arms tightened around me, forcing my back to arch, my chin to tilt up in order to meet his eyes.

He smiled down at me. "How did I ever think I could go the rest of my life without hearing you say shit like that?"

"Half. Dumbass," I repeated, patting his cheek with each word. "But I'm glad to hear it sounds like you've realized you won't have to go without it again."

"Ideally, no." He bent down the few inches required to place a tender kiss on my lips. "As long as you're in it for the long-haul, too."

"Are you kidding? I'm about to make sure we're the Relationship Super Bowl Champs. Those couples tonight? They're gonna be *crying* over how easy we make long distance look."

I squealed when Ryan's hands found my ass, using the hold to lift me up, so easily it was like I weighed nothing more than a football. My legs wrapped naturally around his hips, my dress now bunched around my own.

He planted another kiss on my forehead, my nose, finally my lips, before he said, "We still have a bit of time before that happens."

I smiled. "What do you plan to do with that time?" I teased.

"I think you know I'm a man of my word," Ryan said.

And that time when he kissed me, we didn't stop, my fingers tangled in his hair, as he carried me into my bedroom.

CHAPTER TWENTY-SEVEN

I'D ALWAYS FOUND that time moved the fastest when you wanted it to move slow. Which was exactly what happened over the final week of Ryan's stay in Timberland Creek.

Thank god the bulk of the tourists for the season had cleared out shortly after the Fall Fest because the shiny black Cadillac SUV idling in the Sunrise Brews parking lot would have drawn a lot of attention otherwise. Even now, the locals who were well aware—and probably tired of—Ryan's presence stole curious glances as they walked in and out of the café.

I sighed, checking my phone again for the umpteenth time. Maybe Ryan was purposely taking an extra-long time in my apartment as he did his final checks, making sure he'd packed everything. Gina stood beside me, appearing just as impatient over her son's tardiness. She'd brought over whatever he'd neglected to transfer from his parents' house the night of the

Festival.

Dave hadn't come with her.

Couldn't say I was surprised. For someone who was entirely at fault for disrupting his son's life plans, he was acting mighty bitter. We'd only seen him once, on accident, since the public argument had broken out. He and his nose bandages had high-tailed it out of Ziggy's quicker than a wide receiver on a breakaway as soon as Ry and I stepped in the door.

Coward.

"Ope, there he is."

I looked up from my phone as Ryan came down the stairs that led up to my apartment, his backpack slung over one shoulder, a duffle on the other.

His physical therapy had worked wonders. No longer did he limp down the stairs, though I could tell he was still careful to take them one at a time. If not for his knee brace, no one would have known he'd been injured.

Even more reason for him to get back to his team, I supposed.

"That should be everything," he announced. The driver of the car stepped around to take the bags and put them in the trunk with the rest of Ryan's belongings. To Gina, he said, "If you find anything else at the house, can you ship it to me?"

Gina smiled softly as she stepped forward, arms already outstretched. "Oh, honey," she murmured, wrapping Ryan in a tight hug. "I'm going to miss you so much. It's been so nice having you around again."

Ryan hugged her back, his chin dipping down to rest on the top of her head. "I'll miss you too, Mom," he said, his voice a little thicker than usual.

I stood a few steps back, my hands in my pockets, watching them. Gina's words hit me harder than I expected. She was trying to keep it light and cheery as she so often did, but the emotion in her voice was unmistakable. And all I could think about was how much more complicated this goodbye was now, with everything so strained between Ryan and Dave.

Ryan's lack of promise to visit soon had been missing, and for good reason. I doubted there'd be any cozy Caldwell family holidays in the near future. He'd avoided them before. Now, I couldn't even imagine what it might take to get Ryan to visit.

Visit *them*, anyway. He'd already made a promise to come see me as soon as he was able to.

I'd make sure Gina got the memo when that happened.

When Gina finally let go, she dabbed at her eyes and laughed softly, almost self-conscious. Ryan offered her a small smile before he turned toward me, his gaze softening.

"Harper—" he began, but before he could finish, the bell above the café door jingled, the door itself opening so wide it whacked into the side of the building behind it.

"Goodness," Gina gasped, her hand going up over her heart as I turned to see Hemi bounding down the steps, her grin wide and a to-go cup in her hand.

"Good, you're still here. I thought I'd miss you," she said as she came to a stop in front of us. She held out the cup to Ryan. "Don't think I'd let you leave without one last drink. Your usual. Americano. One pump of no-sugar vanilla. Splash of cream. Extra hot. On the house, of course."

Ryan chuckled, taking the cup with a nod of appreciation. "Thanks, Hemi—for everything. You've been amazing. I seriously hope everything works out for you."

I tensed at the little something that accompanied his words. A hopefulness that made them sound more loaded than anyone else might pick up on. Namely people who weren't aware of the situation with Sunrise.

My eyes darted nervously to Hemi, hoping she hadn't picked up on it. She still wasn't exactly aware I'd told Ryan about the café's probable closure.

Luckily, she just grinned. "Anytime." Hemi turned toward Gina. "I heard you wanted to learn how to make a pumpkin spice latte."

Gina blinked, then nodded, her smile growing. "I do! Oh, Harper—we never got the chance, did we?"

I was about to respond as politely as possible that there was a reason why I'd hardly visited the Caldwell house, let alone spent extended amounts of time within it, when Hemi cut in. "You're in luck. It's not too busy right now, so I've got time to teach you if you want."

Gina lit up, glancing at Ryan for approval to leave him. He

nodded encouragingly. "Go for it, Mom."

Before heading inside, Hemi glanced over her shoulder at me and winked—a quick, mischievous gesture that said her invitation to play teacher wasn't entirely out of the kindness of her heart. She knew exactly what she was doing.

Giving Ryan and me space.

The door closed behind them, and suddenly it was just the two of us—and the driver. But he was much more interested in some game on his phone at the moment. The little chime noises that indicated he'd won sometimes managed to reach my ears.

The quiet between us wasn't uncomfortable, but it was heavy. The way Ryan pursed his lips told me he was struggling just as much as I was to figure out all the things he wanted to say. Each time I thought I might finally be able to fill the silence with something worth-while, I chickened out. No matter how many times I worked and re-worked the sentences in my head, they all felt inadequate.

"So," I said finally—because *that* was so much better than anything else.

I fought the urge to bring my palm to my forehead.

"So," Ryan repeated.

At least the struggle was real for the both of us.

"I'll, uh, try to find some time to come down for one of your last games, maybe?" I tried. "I've made pretty good tips this season, so I should have enough saved. And that means it won't be *too* long before we see each other again."

Ryan's lips curved into a small smile. "I'd like that," he said, his voice soft. "I can get you some tickets. Maybe one of your brothers or your dad could come with you, too."

I nodded. "Yeah. We'll see. They're kinda all over the place."

"Right. Yeah."

The silence stretched again, and my throat tightened. The fresh sting of tears threatening to spill over filled my eyes. I'd gone all week without crying, no matter how hard I'd sometimes wanted to—as Ryan and I enjoyed breakfast together or as he held me close to him while we watched a movie or as we slowed down in bed, forgoing the rough sex we'd become so used to in favor of savoring every moment of pleasure.

Now, here I was. Finally breaking.

I ducked my head, pretending to brush a strand of hair out of my face. But it didn't work. I could feel the warmth of his gaze, the way it seemed to cut right through me.

"Hey," Ryan said softly. His fingers brushed under my chin, tilting my face up so I had no choice but to meet his eyes.

"We're not them," he said, his voice steady.

I nodded, barely able to speak past the lump in my throat, as I said, "We're better."

Ryan leaned in, his hand slipping behind my neck as his lips met mine. The kiss was slow, deliberate, filled with all the things neither of us had managed to say. It felt like a promise and a goodbye all at once, and I wanted to cling to it—to him—for just a moment longer.

A muttered curse and blaring phone alarm ruined that possibility.

"Almost broke the high score," the hired driver hissed under his breath. The alarm cut off, and he dipped around to the front of the car. "Mr. Caldwell, I'm afraid we're going to need to get going if we want to make it to Milwaukee for your flight."

I bit the inside of my cheek, holding back the fresh set of tears that threatened to escape. Ryan pulled back, his forehead resting against mine for a brief moment before he straightened. His arms wrapped around me, enveloping me in what could have possibly been the best hug of my entire life, before he kissed me once more. When he took a step back, his hand lingered on mine until the last possible second.

"I'll call you as soon as I land," he said softly.

I nodded again, forcing a small smile. "Safe travels."

He climbed into the SUV, the door closing behind him with a soft click. The engine rumbled back to life, and I stood frozen as the car pulled out of the lot, watching until it disappeared down the main road of Timberland Creek and out of sight.

CHAPTER TWENTY-EIGHT

"AND MOVING ONTO the AFC South. The Texans are gonna need to put in the work if they want to see a much-needed victory over the dominant 49ers."

"I couldn't agree more, Malik—especially with the Titans knocking on their door to claim that number one spot in the division."

"I will say, I think I'm even more excited to see what the Stallions have to offer. They've been a bit of a wild card in recent weeks, but today's a big day for them."

"You're right about that. It'll be interesting to see how the team responds to Ryan Caldwell's return to the game after being out for nearly all of the season."

"Ten weeks is a long time."

"Damn right it is. And it's plenty of time for a team to lose its momentum. Chase Porter has been relying heavily on Jamal

Harris in Caldwell's absence, so it will be interesting to see how he transitions back to utilizing his best weapon."

"Well, best *before* the injury."

"Right again. And not to mention—"

I hit the power button on the TV remote, and the early-morning sportscasters on ESPN were replaced with a silence only interrupted by the sounds downstairs.

Unlike usual, I'd been up well before Hemi had started her daily prep. Today was game day. And not just any game day. As the gentlemen on my TV had so kindly reminded me—as if I could forget—it was a *big* game day. Huge. Massive.

Ryan's grand return to the field.

And I had a shift at Sunrise.

I wished more than anything that I could have been there, but even my savings couldn't have afforded to take the dent necessary to purchase a last-minute plane ticket to San Antonio. I hadn't bothered telling Ryan I'd even considered coming down, partially because I hadn't wanted to get his hopes up right before such a big day, but also because I knew he would have paid for it himself.

I definitely wanted to try to keep my promise to visit before the end of the season, although there weren't many weeks left now—unless the Stallions made the playoffs. The way things were looking right now, however, they were on the brink of elimination. *Maybe* they could squeak by with a wild card. That would give me until at least mid-January to figure something out. Plenty of time to buy a flight without the time-crunch price gouging getting in my way. A solid two months.

For now, though, I'd have to settle for streaming the game on my phone when it started in a few hours.

I pushed off the couch and went into my room to take one last look at myself in my brand-new Stallions hoodie with CALDWELL stitched on the back.

This shit was nice. Easily one of the comfiest sweatshirts I owned. Probably helped that the player whose name was on the back had sent it to me—with a note that told me he expected me to wear it every game day from now on, of course.

I prayed the ghosts of Packers past didn't look down too hard on me for the sacrilege.

"Nice gear," Hemi complimented as I rushed down the stairs into the café, my hair halfway in the ponytail I was trying to create. "Big day today, huh?"

I nodded as I got straight to work on my usual routine. I'd gotten back in the flow a little bit, now that Ryan was gone and wasn't distracting me in the mornings. Not that Hemi had ever said anything when I came downstairs a little bit later than usual during his stay. "Do you mind if I watch the game on my phone? I'd just have it propped up by the register or something."

"Not at all. Actually, I was thinking we could close early today. Head over to Ziggy's to watch?"

"It's gonna be packed," I said. Ryan Caldwell's first game

back after a visit to Timberland Creek meant the hometown bar wouldn't have a single empty seat. Tourists would come in for the day just to say they sat on the same stool Ryan might have sat on at some point over his eight-week stay.

Hemi shrugged. "Then we cut out at ten? Right after the rush."

My eyes slid sideways to my boss as I poured more beans into the grinder, prepping them for later if we needed them. "You an American football fan now or something?"

"I've had a soft spot for that kid whose name is on your back ever since he slept on my beanbag," she said, earning a small smile from me. "Besides, I'm sure you want to watch on an actual TV?"

"If anything, I'd just go back upstairs to my apartment," I admitted. It was now *very* public knowledge that Ryan and I were an item. If I went to Ziggy's I'd spend more time answering questions than I would actually watching the game.

Why aren't you there? would likely be the most popular, and also the one I'd be least eager to answer.

"It's fine," I continued. "We should stay open, anyway. There might be a bigger rush than we expect today because of the game. Wouldn't want you to miss out on that revenue."

Now that we were mid-way through November, a lot of the businesses around here had closed for the season, many of whom had been recipients of the Fall Fest funds. From what I'd heard, enough money had been raised to help most of them, or at the very least give them a nest egg to hold them over, help fund renovations, provide enough for increased marketing—all those fun things involved in running a small shop in the middle of Wisconsin.

Hemi hadn't said a peep about receiving anything, which made me wonder if Mayor Turner had ignored my request to have a portion of Ryan's earnings transferred to her. Not that there would have been too much to be distributed after the early closure of his booth. Still, it would have been something.

Come to think of it, Hemi wasn't saying a peep now either. No argument about how I needed to stop worrying and mind my own business. No snarky remark about how she was doing just fine.

I narrowed my eyes as I set the burlap sack of beans back on the counter. "Hemdeep."

"Hm?"

"Why are you being quiet?" I asked, suspicious. "You're never quiet."

"I don't have anything to say."

"Liar. You *always* have something to say."

Hemi slapped her cleaning rag down on the counter and turned to face me. I mirrored her position, one hand on my hip, the other on the countertop, as we stared each other down.

When I narrowed my eyes further, she sighed.

"I wasn't going to tell you yet," she said.

My heart dropped into my stomach. "Tell me what?"

This was it. I was going to lose my job. Sunrise was closing. Everything that Hemi had worked for would be coming to an end, a staple of Timberland Creek closing its doors forever.

My anxiety was still climbing as Hemi walked over to one of the cabinets behind the counter—the one with the lock where I knew she stored extra cash and rolls of coins in case we needed to provide change for any customers.

I watched as she used one of the keys on the ring attached at her hip, unlocking the unofficial safe. She retrieved a white envelope stored next to the old toolbox where she kept the money protected.

"Here," Hemi said, holding it out when she stood in front of me again.

I reached for it gingerly, as if the envelope would jump out of her hand and bite me. My eyes darted between it and the woman holding it, but Hemi never flinched, remaining steadfast in making sure I took the offering.

So, that's what I did, and as soon as I tore the seal open, my eyes widened at the absolutely astronomical number on the check inside.

"Holy…" I said on a breath. I lifted my gaze to Hemi. "What is this?"

"Your Christmas present," she said, a touch of bitterness in her tone. "Or it was supposed to be."

"No." I stuffed the check back in the envelope and shoved it towards Hemi. She moved her hands away just in time, which resulted in me pressing it against her chest. "Hemi, take it. I can't accept this."

"You can, and you will."

"I'll accept the fifty-cent raise I get every year, but this is too much." I pressed the envelope harder against her chest. "Where did this even come from?"

"Turns out there were a couple of very substantial donations added to the Fall Fest Fundraiser earnings, one for Turning Pages and one for Sunrise Brews." She leveled a stare at me. "Know anything about that second one?"

I shook my head, mouth gaping.

It was the truth. I had no idea that anyone had made any donations. As far as I knew, the activities at the Fall Fest had been an honest fundraiser—whatever we earned at the booths was what would be given to the struggling businesses.

Turning Pages hadn't even been in consideration for any extra funds. Tori was absolutely killing the game as the only bookstore in town. So, why would anyone—?

Oh.

Alfie. He'd probably given the donation—a "little" gift to an old friend—if it was as substantial as the one in my hand. But he didn't know diddly squat about Hemi's problems.

Another celebrity present at the Fall Fest had, though.

Oh, Ryan…

Tears started to well in my eyes. I didn't know when he could have managed it, but somehow he had. He'd snuck behind my back and given Hemi the surprise of a lifetime.

And now she was trying to give it to me.

"I didn't know he did this," I said, not feeling the need to clarify. There was only one person we both knew who had enough money to provide such a generous donation. "I swear, Hemi, I—"

"But you told him? About the café closing?"

I nodded slowly, embarrassed. "I only did because I planned on giving the money we raised directly to you and wanted to make sure he was on board. I... I swear, that was the only reason."

And when the booth had failed, he'd gone and provided the funds on his own.

God, if he wasn't going to be playing in potentially the biggest game of his life in a few hours, I would have killed him.

"I wanted to help you," I said through the tightening of my throat. "That's all I wanted to do. You mean so much to me— Sunrise means so much to me—and I didn't want to see anything happen to it."

Hemi's stern expression softened at my confession. When I blinked, a tear spilled over and slid down my cheek.

"Harper," Hemi said, her voice soft. She reached out a hand and latched onto my free one. The one not holding the life-changing check. "I appreciate you more than you will ever know," she continued. "But things are still going to happen to this café."

I sniffled as the reality of her words set in. Maybe the money had come in too late. Maybe she'd already figured she wouldn't make enough this year to keep the doors open. The decision had been finalized.

"Can… can you at least give me a recommendation?" I asked. "I think Elise mentioned she saw some openings at the home décor store when I ran into her last week."

Hemi shook her head. "I'm not giving you a recommendation," she said. "I'm giving you that money, and, if I have to, a termination notice because you're going to San Antonio come hell or high water."

My whole body froze. "W-what?"

The envelope was pushed back in my direction, Hemi's hands folded over mine until it settled on my chest, right over where my heart thundered.

"Harper," she said firmly. "You deserve to get out of Timberland Creek. You've spent your whole life here, working, helping everyone else. You're young. You should be out there enjoying life—taking risks, exploring, falling in love. Or building love, I suppose. I think you've already done the falling thing." A strangled laugh escaped me, and Hemi's gaze softened. "You're never going to be able to do that if you stay tied here."

I stared at her, the words echoing in my head.

You deserve to get out.

The statement was equally freeing and terrifying. I didn't

even know how to respond because of course part of me agreed with her. I'd spent so much time trying to be dependable for everyone—my family, this shop, even Ryan when he'd been here. The idea of leaving had always felt impossible.

"Hemi, no," I finally said, shaking my head. "You'll need this. With everything going on—your mom, the shop—"

"I'm downsizing," Hemi said, cutting me off sharply. Tired of my arguing, most likely. "I've already made the decision. I'm putting this space up for rent—hopefully at a price one of the other struggling businesses might be able to better afford—and moving Sunrise into Turning Pages."

I blinked, the words taking a moment to set in. "You're what?"

"It's the right move," she continued. "It might piss off a few people who like to sit and chat, but overall, most people are in and out with their coffee as it is. Tori's open to adding in a few spaces where people can relax, though. Cozy up with a coffee and a new book."

"But… but what about staffing?" I asked. "Don't you need me to help?"

Hemi gave me a soft smile. "I've loved having you on this staff. But Tori will be there. She's been pretty thrilled about the whole idea, actually. Calls it repayment for when I helped her get off the ground. I'm gonna train her up so when I need to travel to take care of my mom, she can step in. And when the baby comes…"

"You'll be available to help run the bookstore." Hemi nodded as I placed the final piece of the puzzle. "That's what you two were talking about that day after the Fall Fest, wasn't it?" I asked, the realization dawning.

Hemi nodded, her smile widening. "It was. Tori and I have it all worked out."

I should have known. Hemi didn't do anything without a plan, and she clearly had one now. A really good one, at that.

"I don't know what to say," I whispered.

"There's nothing you need to say," Hemi replied. Her voice had grown soft again, but the determination in her eyes hadn't faded. "What you need to do is take this money and use it for something good. For *your* good."

"But—" My voice cracked, and I tried again. "You've done so much for me. I don't deserve—"

"Stop." Hemi's take-no-shit voice had officially returned. "You *do* deserve this. It's time you stopped thinking of everyone else for a change and started thinking about yourself."

I bit my lip, my grip tightening on the envelope. The thought of leaving Timberland Creek—leaving everything I'd ever known for the last twenty-six years—was overwhelming.

The envelope crinkled slightly under my hand as Hemi pulled away. Her smile softened, the edges of her tough love warming.

"Now," she said, gently. "Go work on your plan, Harper. Because I've got mine all figured out."

SIX YEARS LATER

"THEY SAY THERE'S no event in all of sports like the Super Bowl, and that's proving correct as we hit the two-minute warning."

"The Stallions are going to need a massive play here if they want to take home the victory."

"That loss of Rafael Navarro in the third quarter really turned the tides."

"I mean they *did* say it's a questionable return."

"There's two minutes left, Mike. I doubt the Stallions are gonna be bringing him back. Especially when so much is on the line. They want all their healthiest players in right now."

"It's been an interesting season for the Stallions, that's for sure. Not many people thought they'd make it to the playoffs, let alone the Super Bowl, and it seems like they'll end up having to rely on another superstar to pull off the W."

"I've never seen Ryan Caldwell play the way he has in this game. He's been absolutely on-fire, and I'm sure the Stallions can only hope he keeps it up for what will be their final few plays."

"Can you imagine? Your last game after a Hall of Fame-worthy NFL career and it's the Super Bowl."

"A nail-biter Super Bowl at that. But I don't think he's the only one worrying right now."

"No, I don't think so either, Mike. Caldwell's fiancée looks nervous as can be there in those stands. She must know McAllister is relying on her man now more than ever. The whole Stallions fanbase is, really."

"How long have they been together now? Three years?"

"Five years, at least. Ever since he came back from that MCL injury."

"She's made just as big a name for herself in the football community since she showed up. Girl knows her stuff."

"That she does. I'd be very interested to hear what she's thinking right now as the Stallions line up for this next play..."

I WAS GOING to shit myself right here at the Super Bowl. That's how I'd forever be known: Ryan Caldwell's fiancée who shit herself at the Super Bowl. All the progress I'd made as a self-appointed social media commentator for the league—offering weekly insights I knew men would like to hear, but also delivering the reports in ways that women could appreciate and understand without any prior knowledge—would go to waste.

No one would listen to a woman who'd shit her pants at the Super Bowl.

The crowd was absolutely buzzing in the neutral-territory Las Vegas stadium as the Stallions lined up. Over the crazy thundering of my heart in my chest, though, I could barely hear it. I only knew it was happening because I'd been in the midst of it for the last three hours.

I glanced up at the clock. Twenty-four seconds left. No timeouts. Third down. Ball on the opposing team's forty-seven-yard line. The Stallions were down by five after being held to a field goal on their last drive. That meant another one wouldn't do it.

We *needed* the touchdown.

I bit down on the side of my index finger. Bite marks would be the least of my worries, though. I probably had a minimum of three fractured fingers from the way Gina held my other hand in an absolute death grip.

At least she didn't have a wedding ring anymore. I didn't want to think about the damage that would have done.

My eyes found Ryan—number eighty-seven—lining up near the right tackle. Even in a sea of jerseys, he was impossible to miss. His size, his presence, the sheer command he had on the field—it drew my focus like a magnet.

"C'mon, babe…" I muttered around my finger.

The play clock wound down. Five… four… three… two—

The center snapped the ball right into Porter's hands and the play was set in motion.

The offensive line surged forward, locking into battle with the defenders. Ryan feigned a block, his arms coming up to shove at a linebacker in front of him. The defender bit the fake, stepping forward and Ryan broke free, charging up-field through the gap in the defense.

Twenty seconds left.

"C'mon, c'mon, c'mon," I muttered, the intensity growing with each iteration. Beside me, Gina was bouncing, her grip somehow growing tighter.

He was running a seam route. The wide receivers on either side pulled the safeties with them, leaving Ryan wide open.

Porter saw it had worked, too. He dropped back, his arm cocking, and launched the ball.

Every head in the stadium turned to watch the football as it spiraled perfectly through the air.

Fifteen seconds left.

I covered my mouth, watching as the ball sailed toward Ryan. He never hesitated, his strides long and confident as he tracked it. When it reached him, he leaped, arms outstretched, and pulled the football in with both hands.

The defenders reacted instantly, charging toward him. But Ryan wasn't done. He turned up-field, dodging the first tackle with a quick step to the side. The second defender lunged at him, but Ryan lowered his shoulder and plowed through the hit, keeping his legs pumping.

My heart pounded so loud in my chest that I couldn't hear anything else. He was twenty yards out. Ten.

Ten seconds left.

Five more yards!

The defenders were closing in, but he dove, stretching his arm out as the ball crossed the goal line—just as the clock ran down to zero.

Touchdown!

The roar of the stadium was deafening, but it couldn't drown out the sound of my own voice as I screamed, leaping up and down in pure exhilaration. Gina's arms wrapped around me as confetti in the Stallions' dark teal and gold rained down over the field. The jumbotron showcased the vibrant logo of that year's Super Bowl, now accompanied by "Champions: Lone Star Stallions."

Ryan pushed himself off the ground, holding the ball high, and his smile lit up the illuminated field even more. His teammates swarmed him, slapping his helmet as they all screamed in celebration, but amid the chaos, all I could see was him.

My Ryan.

"I need to get down there," I shouted to Gina, not bothering to wait for her answer before I started to push through the crowd.

I made my way down the aisle, muttering apologies to the fans celebrating around me. My heart was racing, the same way it had when Ryan had been running for the end zone.

I reached the stairs and darted down, the security guard near the field entrance already looking at me with a raised brow.

"Family pass," I said breathlessly, fumbling with the lanyard around my neck. I held it up, the bright lettering confirming my access to the field.

The guard nodded and opened the gate, letting me through before quickly shutting it to prevent a rush of fans from joining behind me.

I stepped onto the turf, my feet unsteady as the noise of the stadium seemed to magnify. The field felt so much bigger up close, the players towering as they made their way through the swarm of media, desperate to get the first interview, the best shot.

That's where Ryan was, his helmet off, hair darkened with sweat.

Still, I didn't hesitate. I walked toward him, weaving through the chaos, the lanyard around my neck keeping the sideline staff from stopping me.

Ryan turned slightly, the grin on his face bright enough to outshine the blaring stadium lights. His gaze swept over the crowd then froze when it landed on me.

For a moment, everything seemed to stop. The noise, the

crowd, the fluttering confetti—it all fell away as his eyes locked with mine.

Ryan's smile widened, his face lighting up in a way that made my chest ache. He didn't wait for the interview to finish or for the cameras to move. He handed the ball to a nearby staffer and jogged toward me.

I barely had time to react before he reached me, scooping me up into his arms. I laughed as my feet left the ground, his strength and warmth—and absolutely rank body odor—enveloping me as he spun us around.

Ryan set me down gently, his hands still on my waist as he leaned in, his sweat-slick forehead resting against mine. "You're here," he said softly, his voice a mix of disbelief and joy.

"Of course I'm here," I replied. "Where else would I be?"

His lips found mine then for one of the most electrifying kisses we'd ever shared. I wrapped my arms around his neck, holding him as tightly as I could, not caring who was watching or how many cameras were pointed at us.

When we finally pulled apart, his hands stayed on my face, his thumbs brushing away tears I hadn't even realized had fallen. "We did it," he murmured, his voice thick with emotion. I couldn't imagine how he was feeling, knowing that this, of all possible outcomes, was how his career would end.

We'd talked about it a lot—that inevitable conclusion to what would, at some point, be named a Hall of Fame-level career. His dad had been right about that, I supposed. But anyone could have told you Ryan Caldwell was destined for nothing but greatness from the moment he stepped onto the field. Both before and after the injury many thought would put a premature end to his time in the league.

He'd proved them wrong, of course, breaking record after record. Earning accolade after accolade.

Until the day finally came where he sat down at the kitchen table of our house—okay, *his* house that I'd moved into—in San Antonio and told me, "I think this is it, Harps."

We'd put a lot on hold to accommodate his career, neither one of us feeling like we could give things like a healthy marriage or children our full attention while he was on the road so much.

So, here he was. A few years sooner than he'd hoped to retire, but with a whole lot to look forward to now that he'd made the decision to call it quits on this part of his life.

Even though that wasn't even necessarily one-hundred-percent true.

He'd only be away from football until our co-hosted talk show—based in part on the online career I'd started for myself—began. One where we could plant ourselves wherever we wanted, film in a home studio, and take all the time we wanted for ourselves and our future family in between.

"*You* did it," I corrected, my voice trembling as I, too, realized this was the last time I'd watch him on the field. "I just got to play cheerleader."

His smile softened, and he kissed my forehead before pulling me back into his arms. "No," he said. "*We* did it. You've always been a part of this, Harper. Always."

For a moment I couldn't speak. I could only stare at him, this man who'd been my friend, my rival, my everything. We'd come so far together, between the fights, distance, injuries, and fears that had nearly torn us apart. And yet, here we were—stronger than ever, standing on the field where he'd just made history.

There was so much behind us to be proud of. But I knew there was just as much that lay ahead.

He'd made it. We'd made it.

And somehow, I knew, no matter where life took us next—in this world after football—we always would.

ACKNOWLEDGEMENTS

Well, that's it. From the dazzling city of London to the small-town world of Timberland Creek, I can't believe the Written in the Stars Series has reached its end.

As always, thank you to my mom, dad, and brother for their unending support in what has become a very busy "author life." Thank you all for showing up for me in any way possible. I will never take it for granted and appreciate it so much.

Thank you, Jessica, for helping me put the finishing touches on yet another one of my books. It's truly an honor to keep working with you, and I can't wait for the next one!

Thank you, Nicole, for helping me create the character artwork for all three Written in the Stars books. I'm so grateful that you agreed to help me… three years ago? when I randomly brought the idea up during one of our email design brainstorming meetings at work.

Thank you to my friends, family, and work colleagues who continue to show more support than I could ever imagine, even after so many books!

Thank you to the town of Fish Creek, WI for continuing to serve as my inspiration for Timberland Creek. My home away from home, always!

Thank you to Blue Horse Beach Café for being the inspiration for Sunrise Brews, as well as the location where I finished writing the prologue of this book *and* implemented the final proofreading edits. My favorite coffee shop forever!

Thank you to my real-life "Hemdeep"—Yogi. Thank you for being so supportive of my author career from the first day I stepped foot in your café. You are a true gem to our community!

Thank you to the Green Bay Packers. Being able to cheer for this team—from my couch, a bar, or at the legendary Lambeau Field—instilled my love of football. Whether you win or lose, I'm proud to call myself a life-long fan.

Thank you to the online writing and bookish communities for your support through the years. Whether you joined recently or before I'd even started publishing, you all continue to give me the courage I need to put my stories out in the world. (You also give me a place to vent with others who "get it", and for that I'm so thankful!)

And last, but certainly not least, thank you, dear reader, for picking up this novel and giving it a chance. By doing so, you are helping me achieve my dream, and I am forever grateful for that!

ABOUT THE AUTHOR

MCKENZIE BURNS is a multi-genre author from Chicago with a passion for writing stories that involve different cultures, witty banter, and women who don't take 'no' for an answer. Her spare time is spent drinking copious amounts of coffee and searching for obscure music.

STAY CONNECTED

Want to be the first to hear about new releases from McKenzie Burns? Visit her website or follow her on social media!

www.authormckenzieburns.wixsite.com/home

@author_mckenzieburns